'Hunter, an old hand at storytelling, comes up with an especially good one in *Far From the Sea* . . . a book that is impossible to put down; clearly bestselling material'

Publishers Weekly

From his first highly acclaimed and explosive novel, *The Blackboard Jungle*, to this, his seventeenth Evan Hunter novel, he has proven himself time and time again a masterful storyteller.

As Ed McBain he is the author of the immensely successful 87th Precinct police novels and his screenplays include the film versions of his own novel *Fuzz* and of Daphne du Maurier's *The Birds*.

Far From the Sea

EVAN HUNTER

SPHERE BOOKS LIMITED
30-32 Gray's Inn Road, London WC1X 8JL

First published in Great Britain by
Hamish Hamilton Ltd 1983
Copyright © 1983 by Hui Corporation
Published by Sphere Books Ltd 1984

Phototypeset in Bembo

Printed and bound in Great Britain by
Collins, Glasgow

This is for my wife –
MARY VANN

Hence in a season of calm weather
Though inland far we be,
Our souls have sight of that immortal sea
Which brought us hither,
And see the children sport upon the shore,
And hear the mighty waters rolling evermore.

— WILLIAM WORDSWORTH

Monday

From his hotel room he could see the ocean on the east and the bay on the west. The hospital was on the bay side, not very far from the sea. He stayed in the room only long enough to unzip his bag and lay it flat on the bed.

It was stiflingly hot in the street outside.

The cab driver who responded to his hand signal wheeled the taxi up onto the hotel ramp and asked where he was going.

'St. Mary's Hospital', he said.

The light on the corner took an eternity to change. He looked at his watch. It was ten minutes to three. Visiting hours were at eleven, two, four, and seven – for ten minutes each time. On the telephone last night, the doctor had told him he would leave word to admit him whenever he arrived.

'You got somebody in the hospital?' the driver asked.

'My father.'

'What's the matter with him?'

'He's sick.'

'Well, sure, a hospital,' the driver said, and fell silent for the remainder of the trip.

The receptionist in the main entrance lobby told him what floor Intensive Care was on and then said he could visit at 4:00 P.M. He thanked her and took the elevator up to the third floor. He walked past the nurses' station opposite the elevators and then followed the signs directing him to Intensive Care. He passed a small waiting room, walked to the end of the corridor, and opened a door. There were overflow beds in the unit's hallways. A thin, balding man with a mustache was sitting up in one of the beds. Smiling, he began walking towards the man, and suddenly realized it was not his father.

A nurse in green tunic and pants approached him.

'Can I help you?' she asked.

'I'm Morris Weber's son,' he said. 'I just got here from New York. Dr. Kaplan said he would leave word . . .'

'He's in five.'

'How is he?'

'His condition is stable.'

He moved down the hall and stepped into the room he thought she'd indicated. A doctor was examining a woman on the bed. He saw her pale white breasts, her pale white belly, and backed

2

away in embarrassment, out into the corridor again.

'I'm sorry,' he said, 'what room did you . . .?'

'Number five,' the nurse said. 'On your left.'

'Thank you.'

His father's eyes were closed. There was a tube in his nose. There were tubes taped to his arms. There were tubes running under the sheets. There were plastic bags with yellow fluids in them hanging on metal stands beside the bed. A brownish liquid bubbled and seeped along one of the tubes and drained into a soiled plastic bag hanging on a machine. Another machine on a higher stand alongside the bed beeped and flashed with orange digital numbers, glowed with the cool blue electronic peaks and valleys of his father's heartbeat.

'Pop?' he whispered.

His father's eyes fluttered open and then widened in surprise. 'David?'

'Yes, Pop.'

Disoriented for a moment, his father blinked into the room. The last time David had seen him – on his eighty-second birthday, three months ago – his hair and his mustache had been tinted black. Tufts of white now stood out on either side of his otherwise bald head. What had once been a neatly groomed line of black hair on his upper lip was shaggy and white. The upper lip seemed caved in. It took David a moment to realize they'd removed his father's dentures.

'How are you?' he asked.

'What are you doing here?' his father said.

'Dr. Kaplan phoned me.'

'Dr. Kaplan,' his father said, and pulled a face. 'I went to him for two weeks, telling him I had pains. He said they were gas. Some gas. He probably *still* thinks it was gas.'

'He knows it wasn't gas, Pop,' David said, and smiled and took his father's right hand between his own. There were puncture marks all over his father's arm, dark angry bruises.

'So what was it?' his father asked.

'You know what it was.'

'Blockage.'

'It was a tumor, Pop. Dr. Kaplan told you that.'

'Malignant.'

3

'Yes, Pop.'

'But he got it.'

'Yes, Pop. No spread. He got it all.'

'So why am I still in the hospital? I came in three weeks ago, it's three weeks already. What's the *matter* with me?'

He did not know what to say. Now that he was here, he did not know what to say. The silence lengthened.

'They still have to do another one, don't they?' his father asked.

'Another what?'

'Operation.'

'Well, that won't be for a while yet. When they . . . they have to close up the intestines. So you won't need the bag anymore.'

'Maybe *this* time I'll get rid of the *gas*, too.'

David smiled again. His father seemed to be his same alert, cantankerous, sarcastically humorous self, and he was wondering whether Dr. Kaplan's call last night hadn't been somewhat premature. But all these tubes –

'You're not in any pain, are you?'

'No.'

'You're sure?'

His father nodded.

'I sent a check for your rent,' David said, 'so you don't have to worry about that anymore. Bessie called and said you were . . .'

'My mail must be piled up to the ceiling there.'

'Don't worry about your mail.'

'I told Bessie not to bother you. I knew you had that big case.'

'Well, I thought I'd better come down.'

'How's the case doing?'

'The trial ended last Friday.'

'Did you win?'

'We lost.'

'Terrific,' his father said, and shook his head.

'I've been talking to the doctor almost every day,' David said. 'He tells me you're coming along fine.'

'Then what are you doing down here?'

He hesitated.

'Well, you're running a slight fever, Pop.'

'You'd run a fever here, too,' his father said. 'They're in here

4

day and night, poking needles in my arm. How slight?'

'I don't know exactly. Nothing to worry about.'

'When will they do the next operation?' his father asked.

'Well, as soon as you start getting better. You've got to help them beat this fever, Pop. Dr. Kaplan said you've been very depressed these past few . . .'

'There's a hole in my belly,' his father said.

'I know that, Pop, but that's because you've got the bag, you're draining into a bag. Once they close up the intestines again . . .'

'Sure,' his father said. 'Another operation.'

'Yes, but that'll be the end of it. And then you'll be able to go back to your normal life again.'

'Hello, swee'heart,' a woman's voice said from the door.

'Here's the bane of my existence,' his father said. 'What is it this time?'

'I wann to check your dressin', darlin'.'

She was wearing a green tunic and pants, like the other nurse. Her hair was black, pulled to the back of her head in a ponytail. Her eyes were a dark brown. She was quite pretty, no older than twenty-four or twenty-five, David guessed.

'Won't leave me alone,' his father said. 'Can't keep her hands off me.'

'That's ri', darlin'.'

'Used to run a butcher shop in Cuba.'

'Tha's ri',' she said, and lifted his gown.

'Who gave you permission to look at my belly?' he said, and winked at David.

'I don' *nee'* permission,' she said, smiling. 'I'm dee *boss* here.'

'Some boss. If you're such a boss, tell them to feed me. I haven't had anything to eat in three weeks.'

'You're gettin' t'ree t'ousan' calories a day, darlin'.'

'Through a *tube*.'

'There's some nice Jell-O on the windowsill, you wann it.'

'I don't want Jell-O. I want a cigar. A good Havana cigar. Tell your cousins down there to send me one.'

'My cousins are all here,' she said, and smiled. 'You have any pain here?' she asked, her hands moving over his belly.

'No. Listen, you don't expect me to take this lying down, do you?' he said, and again winked at David.

The nurse pulled the sheet up over him. 'Are you Mr. Weber's son?' she asked.

'Yes,' David said.

She turned to the bed again. 'Aren't you happy your son's here?' she asked.

'I'd be happier if he could speak Spanish. They jabber in Spanish day and night out there. At the nurses' station. They have wild parties in Spanish.'

'Champagne parties,' she said.

'You think I don't know it? Six years of French, what good will it do him down here?'

'Four years, Pop,' he said, smiling.

'What good will it do you? They only speak Spanish at the nurses' station. Are you happy with your station in life?' he asked the nurse. 'Are you finished here?'

'For now, swee'heart. We goin' to nee' some blood from you later.'

'It's a wonder I've got any left. They've got Dracula here, in the basement, in a coffin. They keep sending my blood down to him.'

'I'll be back in a li'l while, okay, darlin'?'

'No, *not* okay,' he said.

'Nice to mee' you,' she said to David, and went out.

'In and out all day long,' his father said, shaking his head. 'Won't give me any peace.'

'They're trying to help you, Pop.'

'Sure.'

'She seems very nice.'

'Bane of my existence. Anyway, *what* help? I'm already over the fence.'

'Come on, what does that mean?'

His father shook his head.

'Come on, Pop.'

'Another operation,' his father said, and closed his eyes.

The doctor came into the waiting room at a little past three-thirty. There were several other people there by then, waiting for the four o'clock visit.

'Mr. Weber?' he asked.

'Yes,' David said, and immediately got to his feet.

'I'm Dr. Kaplan,' he said, and extended his hand.

He was a short, dark man with thick eyeglasses, thirty-five or thirty-six years old, David guessed. There was a somewhat rueful expression on his face. He was wearing a brown tropical suit with a yellow shirt and a riotously patterned silk tie.

'Could you step out into the hall, please?'

They stood beside a window streaming bright sunlight.

'I'm glad you could come down,' Kaplan said. 'Have you seen him yet?'

'Yes,' David said, and hesitated. 'He seems all right.'

'Well, yes, he's a bit more alert today. But he still has serious problems.

'What *are* the problems, exactly?'

'As I told you on the phone last night, he simply isn't healing. We know there's an infection someplace, but we –'

'How do you know there's an infection?'

'Well, the fever for one thing. And the white-blood-cell count. We've tried a wide variety of antibiotics on him, but the count keeps going up. We've run all the pertinent tests – cultures of the wound, liver and blood cultures, urine counts, X rays and so on. It's truly baffling, Mr. Weber, a very difficult case.'

'How high is his fever?'

'This morning? A hundred point four.'

'Is that very high?'

'Only in that it indicates infection. I've got him scheduled for a gallium scan this afternoon, perhaps the pictures will show something in his belly that will –'

'Like what?'

'Who knows? That's the problem.'

'But you think that's where the infection might be? In the belly someplace?'

'Possibly. We simply don't know.'

'From the surgery, do you mean?'

'No, no.'

'Then what?'

'Well, that's why we're running the scan, Mr. Weber.'

'What do you *hope* to find?'

7

'Anything positive. An abscess we can drain. Or maybe a small piece of fecal matter that's become opportunistic in there. Once we can find the source of infection . . .'

Kaplan paused.

'Yes?' David said.

'Well, let's see what the scan shows, shall we?'

'When will you have the results?'

'It'll be a *series* of pictures, we won't know anything definite till sometime tomorrow.'

'Will you keep in touch, please?' David said. 'I'm at the De Rochemont.'

'Yes, of course.'

'And I have your number.'

'Call me anytime,' Kaplan said.

Bessie arrived at the hospital at a quarter to four.

'You must be his son,' she said. 'I would know you in a minute.'

She was in her late seventies, he guessed, a thin birdlike woman with beautiful blue eyes. His mother's eyes had been blue, too. It was Bessie who'd accompanied his father to the hospital three weeks ago. It was Bessie who'd called New York two days after the trial started, to tell David his father would be undergoing surgery. David couldn't get away just then, even though he'd wanted to. Besides, Kaplan had assured him on the phone that his father's heart and lungs were very strong, and whereas no major surgery could be considered 'routine,' the tumor was in an easily accessible spot, and he foresaw no complications. Before Bessie's call three weeks ago, David had not even known she existed.

'Did you see him yet?' she asked.

'Yes. He looks okay.'

'Not yesterday,' she said. 'Yesterday, he looked like I never seen him since he came here. I'll tell you the truth, I almost called you, but I was afraid to.'

'Dr. Kaplan called last night.'

'So it's bad, huh?'

'Well . . . he's not healing properly.'

They had been talking in whispers. There were perhaps ɔ

dozen people in the waiting room now. The clock on the wall read five minutes to four. A television set high on the wall, angled into a corner, was tuned to a soap opera. The people waiting kept looking from the clock to the television set. The volunteer worker behind the desk, an old woman in a pink uniform, kept watching the clock.

'We usually go in a few minutes early,' Bessie whispered. 'They don't say nothing.'

'I appreciate your coming here every day,' David said.

'Well, I do the best what I can,' Bessie said. 'He should have been out of here by now. They should already be taking away the bag, closing up the intestines. Instead . . .' She shook her head. 'What does it mean, he's not healing properly?'

'There's an infection someplace.'

'From what?'

'They don't know.'

'Some doctors, they don't know,' Bessie said.

'Well, there are still some things even doctors don't know.'

'There are *plenty* things they don't know,' Bessie said.

The clock on the wall read two minutes to four. Several of the people in the waiting room were already standing.

'We can go in now,' Bessie said, loud enough for the volunteer worker to hear her.

'Yes, go ahead,' the woman said.

They went into his father's room.

He watched as Bessie leaned over the bed and kissed his father on the cheek.

'Hello, kiddo,' his father said softly.

In the next ten minutes, his eyes never left Bessie's face.

They talked quietly together, in a sort of hush, almost as if David were not in the room.

He realized all at once that he didn't even know Bessie's last name.

He got back to the hotel at four-thirty.

When he'd told the cab driver where to take him, his pronunciation was corrected with a curt, 'You mean the Rocky Mount, don't you?' Four years of French, he'd thought. What good will it do me down here, where the Hotel De Rochemont

9

becomes the Rocky Mount and the Fontainebleau is the Fountain Blow?

The room was suffocatingly hot.

He jiggled the ON–OFF switch under the thermostat and then reached up to the vent to see if he'd had any effect. Nothing. Not a ripple. He went to the window and opened it. A blast of hot, moist air rushed into the room. Fifteen stories below, the pool was empty. Miami Beach in the off-season. He looked out over the sea. Cool, and vast, and eternal. A lone swimmer paddled toward the shore. David turned from the window, picked up the phone, and dialed twenty-two for the front desk.

'Is there something wrong with the air conditioning?' he asked an assistant manager.

'Yes, sir, they're working on it now.'

'When will it be fixed?'

'I don't know, sir. They're working on it now.'

'Thank you,' he said.

Nobody knew when anything would be fixed. His father was in the hospital and nobody knew when *he* would be fixed, either, or even what was wrong with him. All those tubes, he thought. He picked up the phone again and dialed twenty-one for room service.

'This is Mr. Weber in fifteen twenty-nine,' he said. 'I'd like a Canadian Club and soda, please. In fact, make it two.'

'Two Canada Dry club soda, yes, sir,' a man with a Spanish accent said.

'No, two Canadian *Club* and soda,' David said.

'Two Canadian club soda, right,' the man said.

'Are you sure you've got that?' David said. 'I'm talking about *whiskey* and soda.'

'What kind of whiskey?'

'Canadian Club.'

'Yes, sir, Canadian club soda, right.'

'Is there someone there who speaks English?' David said.

'I speak English.'

'Do you know what Canadian Club whiskey is?'

'Sure.'

'That's the name of the whiskey. Canadian Club.'

'Sure.'

'Look, never mind. Make it *scotch* and soda, okay? Scotch whiskey and soda. Two of them.'

'Two scotch whiskey and Canadian club soda, yes, sir,' the man said, and hung up.

David sighed and replaced the receiver on its cradle. He was still wearing his tie and jacket. He carried the jacket to the closet. Hangers attached to metal loops on the rod, insurance against theft. Class. But it was only four blocks from the hospital. He hung up his jacket, loosened his tie, pulled it free from under his collar, and then unbuttoned the top button of his shirt. He would have to call home. Molly would be waiting for his call. He would do that after the drinks arrived. If they arrived.

He began unpacking.

'Molly?'

'David, hi, how is he?'

'Not so good.'

'What is it?'

He told her everything the doctor had told him, trying to repeat the conversation word for word. Molly said nothing during the recitation. When at last he finished, she said, 'Shall I come down there?'

'No, no, what for?'

'You're alone.'

'I'll be okay.'

'If you want me to come down . . .'

'No.'

'. . . just say so.'

'I'm all right, really.'

'Did you have lunch?'

'On the plane.'

'When will they have the results? Of the scan?'

'Tomorrow sometime.'

'When will you be going back to the hospital?'

'At seven.'

'How's the weather down there?'

'Hot,' he said. 'Very hot.'

He remembered them as stained-glass summers. The summers

11

of his boyhood. Warm yellow sunshine and vibrant green leaves, the deeper green of the sea. The flawless blue of summer skies. A silvery breeze blowing in off the ocean.

His grandmother lived in Bensonhurst, and every summer Sunday they would make the long subway journey from the Bronx to Brooklyn, where the family would congregate for the outing to the beach. There were three brothers: Morris, Max, and Martin. 'The Three Stooges,' Uncle Max called them. He was the youngest and the handsomest. He wore his hair parted in the middle, thick black hair, though both his brothers were already going bald. Uncle Max drove a brand-new Studebaker, all shining chrome and gleaming paint. Uncle Max had a black mustache under his nose – 'The famous Weber nose,' he called it, 'hooked like Julius Caesar's, the Roman greaser's.' David's father kept his own mustache trimmed to a neat narrow line, but Uncle Max's was thick and full, and he had a little silver mustache comb for it. David loved to watch the little comb flash out of his uncle's pocket, silver glinting in the sunshine, his uncle's swift slender hands stroking at the mustache, the silver comb disappearing like magic into his pocket again. Uncle Max dressed like a movie star. Uncle Max was what David wanted to be when he grew up.

Uncle Martin was the oldest of the brothers, lean and thin, somewhat gaunt-looking, with sorrowful brown eyes. 'I'm the only Jewish house painter in the city of New York,' he said. He was also the only one of the brothers who didn't have a mustache. There was always the smell of turpentine around him. David could smell his Uncle Martin clear across a room. He loved the smell of him, and he loved his soft, gentle voice. But he loved his Uncle Max best of all. The three brothers all wore gold signet rings with tiny diamond stones. Grandma had given them the rings for their separate bar mitzvahs, two years apart, first Martin, then his father, and then Max. Their initials were woven into the thick gold like trailing snakes, the identical initials on each ring, M.W., M.W., M.W. The brothers always wore the rings. He had never seen any of them without those rings on the pinky fingers of their right hands. They even wore the rings when they went into the ocean, although Grandma warned they would attract sharks, all that gold, the diamonds, the diamonds.

Every summer Sunday, if the weather was good, they rode out

to the beach in two cars, Uncle Max's great big Studebaker leading the caravan and Uncle Martin's rumbleseat Ford behind it. David rode in the rumble seat with his fat cousin Rebecca on one side of him and his skinny cousin Shirley on the other. They were Uncle Martin's daughters; his Uncle Max wasn't married, his Uncle Max was a handsome man-about-town who always showed up on Sundays with a new and beautiful dark-haired, dark-eyed girl on the front seat of the Studebaker – 'I like my coffee light and my women dark,' he said, and winked at David. His fat cousin Rebecca had blond hair that Uncle Martin said came from his wife's side of the family. His wife's name was Anna, thin, pale-haired, pale-eyed Aunt Anna. David didn't like her because she was always pinching his cheeks and saying, 'How's my dumpling?' when David wasn't fat at all, not like her own daughter Rebecca, anyway. But his mother said Aunt Anna's heart was in the right place.

David hated sitting in the rumble seat with Rebecca because she was so fat and because she squirmed a lot. Shirley was much, much thinner, with the dark eyes and hair all the Weber side of the family shared. There was always a flushed, excited look on Shirley's narrow face, as if she had just come from running somewhere and was out of breath. He liked Shirley a lot. She was the one who told him she had seen two dogs doing it behind Grandma's house, and one of them was turned backwards and couldn't get out. 'Couldn't get out of where?' David asked, and Shirley just turned away with that flushed, excited look on her face.

It was always very breezy in the rumble seat of Uncle Martin's Ford.

'Cool enough for you back there?' Uncle Martin shouted.

The trees flashed overhead, sunlight glanced.

In the front seat were Uncle Martin and his pale wife Anna, with Grandma squeezed between them and telling Uncle Martin to slow down, did he think he was going to a fire? In the car ahead was Uncle Max with his latest dark-eyed, dark-haired beauty, and on the back seat were David's father and David's mother (who always complained about getting carsick) and also a friend of the family who everyone said was Grandma's boyfriend, which was okay since Grandpa had died years ago. The man's

13

name was Louis Klein, and he ran a dry-goods store on Thirty-fourth Street, where David had never been in his life. Mr. Klein was always criticizing everything. 'Tessa,' he would say to Grandma, 'is this really and truly supposed to be borscht?' Grandma would smile. 'Tessa,' he would say, 'these *kreplachs* are like stones, actual *stones*.' Grandma would smile. Grandma had very big bosoms. Whenever she hugged David to her, he thought he would smother. 'I'll bet she has the biggest minnies in the entire world,' skinny cousin Shirley said one day, her face flushed and excited. It took a moment for David to realize she was talking about Grandma's bosoms.

The beach was on Long Island someplace.

That was all David knew. Long Island someplace.

It always took them what seemed like *hours* to get there. There were picnic tables under the trees near the beach, and the whole family helped carry out all the food the women had prepared, and then spread a tablecloth on one of the big picnic tables, and then went to Uncle Max's Studebaker and hung big towels inside all the windows all around, and changed into their bathing suits. David and the girls changed into their bathing suits together. Cousin Rebecca was even fatter without any clothes on.

They all went into the sea.

Uncle Max warned him to watch out for horseshoe crabs.

Grandma told her sons to take off their rings, but they never did.

David's father held his hand, and they waded out to where it was a little deeper, and he swam in the circle of his father's strong arms till his father got tired; then his father blew up a red inner tube for him and let him float and swim free under the wide blue sky.

It was so much fun at the seashore.

There was a coffee machine in the waiting room, but no coffee.

'They lock everything up after the four o'clock visit,' a woman explained to him. She was very thin, with pale hair and pale eyes. She was in her sixties, David guessed, and wearing a dark brown pants suit and wedgies. 'You'll learn,' she said. 'We've been coming here for two months straight now.'

The woman sitting beside her was in her late forties, David

14

guessed. Very fat, with hair bleached platinum, false eyelashes, scarlet slash of lipstick on her mouth, big gold rings on three of her fingers. He thought suddenly of fat Rebecca on his left in Uncle Martin's rumble seat, squirming while the trees flashed broken sunlight overhead.

'Who's your patient?' she asked.

'Mr. Weber. Morris Weber.'

'What's wrong with him?' the thin, pale woman asked.

'He had a colostomy,' David said. 'He's not healing.'

'Well, give him time,' the fat woman said.

'My husband's had open-heart surgery twice,' the other woman said.

'My father,' the fat woman said.

'This is his second time. He won't eat anything. Been here three weeks this time, suddenly stopped eating. He threw himself out of bed this afternoon. Yanked out his IV, threw himself right on the floor. They're restraining him now. They've got this strap across his shoulders so he can't throw himself out of bed again.'

'We'll have to come feed him,' her daughter said.

'Why? Will he eat if it's us?'

'Do you live here in Miami?' the daughter asked David.

'No. New York.'

'So you came down here to see him.'

'Yes.'

'Who's that woman who's here all the time? Is she your mother?'

David hesitated. 'A friend,' he said.

'She's very loyal.'

'Yes.'

A man sitting under the television set suddenly said, 'I'm here on vacation, *supposed* to be on vacation. My wife fell the other day, near the pool, slipped on the tile. She's in coma. I don't know what to do. Should I take her back to Toronto or leave her here, stay here with her?'

He was a tall, gaunt-looking man with sorrowful brown eyes and a soft, gentle voice. He was wearing a colorful Hawaiian-print, short-sleeved sports shirt and dark blue slacks. David could smell his aftershave clear across the room.

15

'What does the doctor say?' the fat woman asked.

'He doesn't know how long she'll be in coma.'

'They *never* know,' her mother said.

'How would you get her back home?' the daughter asked.

'I'd have to charter a plane, I guess.'

'They have these planes with oxygen equipment and everything, you know.'

'Yes, but they cost a fortune. Six thousand dollars, they told me.'

'Would it be safe to move her?'

'Oh, yes.'

'I'd move her then. You can't stay here *forever*, you know. She might be in coma for a long time.'

'I just don't know.'

'I'd move her.'

'I just don't know.'

'My mother's been here for two weeks now,' a skinny woman across the room said. She was sitting on one of the green leatherette couches, smoking a cigarette. She had dark hair and dark eyes, and there was a flushed, excited look on her narrow face, as though she had just come from running somewhere and was out of breath. 'Came in for a hernia operation. That's a simple thing, am I right? Doctors. She's still in Intensive Care. I hate doctors. Now she's hallucinating. She told me they're beating her. Is it possible they're beating her? She wants me to call the police. She says if I don't take her home, she'll throw herself out the window.'

'Well, how can you take her home?' the pale woman said.

'I can't! How can I take her home?'

'So tell her.'

'I *told* her, do you think she listens?'

'They'll hallucinate,' the fat daughter said, and nodded.

'It's all the drugs they give them,' the gaunt man said.

'Doctors and lawyers,' the excited woman said. 'I hate them both.'

David said nothing.

The clock on the wall read three minutes to seven.

'You can go in now,' the pink lady said.

16

'What were those X rays this afternoon?' his father asked.

'They're trying to find the cause of infection,' David said.

'What infection?'

'You've got an infection. That's why you're running a fever.'

'I'm running a fever because they're driving me crazy here.'

'Well, the sooner you get rid of the fever, the sooner you'll get out of here.'

'I'll *never* get out of here,' his father said.

'Of course you will,' David said.

'Never. I keep getting worse every day.'

'Everything's fine except for the fever.'

'Sure, everything's fine. I've got a hole in my belly and tubes sticking out all over me, everything's just fine and dandy.'

'You'll get better, Pop, don't worry. You'll be out of here in no time at all.'

'And *then* what? Then another operation.'

'Not till you're ready for it.'

'I'll *never* be ready for it.'

'Well . . .'

'Back in again for another operation.'

'A very simple one.'

'Oh, yes, very simple. They'll just cut me open again. Very simple.'

'To connect . . .'

'Sure, connect. Two *weeks* I went to him. He tells me it's gas pains, the *pisher*. What kind of gas? It was *blockage*, is what it was.'

'Yes, Pop.'

'So why did he tell me it was gas?'

'I guess he didn't know at first.'

'He's *supposed* to know, he's a doctor, isn't he, the *pisher*? I had to check *myself* in here, you think *he'd* have checked me in here? Had to get here on my own steam. Thank God Bessie was here to help me. She wanted to call you, I told her no, you had the trial. You lost it, huh?'

'Yes, Pop.'

'A big one, huh?'

'Well, yes.'

'What was it, a contingency case?'

'Yes, Pop.'

17

'How much?'

'Our fee, do you mean?'

'Yes, your fee.'

'Well, a few hundred thousand.'

'And you lost it. So what good did it do, after all? I should have told her to call you. You could have kept an eye on that *pisher* with his *gas*.'

'Well, he seems like a good doctor, Pop.'

'What's his name again?'

'The doctor, do you mean?'

'Yeah.'

'Kaplan. You know what his name is, Pop.'

'Yeah, right, Kaplan. I thought it was Wolfe.'

'No.'

'There must be another doctor named Wolfe here. They're in here all the time, you'd think there was a convention in my room. They have more doctors in this place . . .' His voice trailed. He shook his head. 'So how's The Shiksa?' he asked.

'Fine, Pop.'

'I want her to have my ring.'

'What do you mean?'

'When I die.'

'Pop . . .'

'It's the same initials. M.W. I want her to have it.'

'Well, we don't have to think about that just now.'

'I want Molly to have it, do you hear me?'

'Yes, Pop.'

'How's little Stevie?'

He looked at his father.

'Pop . . .' he said. 'Stephen's dead. You know that, Pop.'

'Come on,' his father said.

'He died five years ago, Pop.'

'Come on, don't kid a kidder,' his father said. 'I can remember when Bessie used to change his diapers.'

'Bessie?'

'What?'

'You said . . .'

'Your mother, I meant. When she changed his diapers. Does he know his grandpa's in the hospital?'

18

'Pop, please, he's . . .'

'Does he know I have to have another operation?'

'Well, not for a while yet,' David said, and sighed.

'You don't know how I suffered after the first one,' his father said, and closed his eyes.

The bar in the main lobby was closed. The clerk at the front desk told him it would be open next week, when a large party from South America would be arriving.

'Things should pick up next week,' he said. 'Meanwhile, the disco bar is open.'

The empty lobby was vast, its vaulted ceiling supported by marble columns. His footfalls echoed on the polished marble floors, grew hushed when he crossed the Oriental throw rugs, clicked noisily again as he went down the wide curving stairway to the disco on the lower level at the far end of the hotel. There was no music playing at eight o'clock; a sign on the door advised him that the hours were from 9:00 P.M. to 3:00 A.M. But lights were rotating over the small dance floor, blinking, flashing. They reminded David of the lights on the machines all around his father's bed. He sat at the bar and ordered a Beefeater martini, on the rocks, two olives, please. Aside from the bartender, he was alone in the place. The bartender told him they were expecting a large party of South Americans next week. He drank the martini and then went upstairs to the hotel restaurant. It was done entirely in red. Red crushed-velvet wallpaper, tablecloths and napkins the color of blood, waiters in red jackets. It was completely empty of diners.

He sat alone in a room he guessed could comfortably seat at least a hundred people, and he ordered clams on the half-shell and a New York strip, medium rare. As an afterthought, he ordered a Heineken beer. The waiter told him it might take a few minutes because he had to go all the way to the disco bar for it; the bar right next door wouldn't be open till next week when they were expecting a big party from South America. David assured him he wouldn't mind waiting, so long as the beer was very cold.

He was eating the clams when the girl walked in.

She was very tall, five-eight or five-nine, David guessed, with masses of blond hair piled on top of her head. She was wearing a

19

pastel blue suit and matching patent leather pumps. David guessed she was in her late twenties. She hesitated just inside the doorway, her eyes opening in mild surprise as she surveyed the empty room. The headwaiter rushed over.

'Are you still serving dinner?' the girl asked.

British, David thought.

'Yes, Miss.'

'I don't suppose you could *possibly* find me a table,' she said.

David smiled.

'Yes, Miss, of *course*,' the waiter said, '*please*,' and bowed from the waist and escorted her to a table on the far side of the empty room. She sat, crossed her long legs, and accepted the menu he handed her.

'One Heineken beer, very cold,' David's waiter said at his elbow. 'Your steak'll be along in a minute, sir.'

'Thank you,' David said.

The tall girl with the blond hair was still sitting alone at her table when David signed for his check and went upstairs to his room.

Ah, God he thought, ah, Molly, he thought, how the hell did we get so old so young? You appeared – long blond hair blowing in the wind, the flutter of a summer dress, a hint of petticoat below – you appeared. And started to turn from the boardwalk railing, from the sea, green eyes flashing in the sunlight, golden sunlight splashing wanton freckles onto an Irish button nose (a shiksa, no less), recklessly tossing freckles onto a perfect Irish phizz. You laughed to a girl friend, the laughter was carried by the wind far out over the sea. And you turned. You turned in slow motion, perky Dublin breasts in a flimsy summer bodice, cotton print flapping, ocean breeze lifting the skirt over long legs, your hand reached down to flatten it. All in slow motion.

You stepped out of sunlight, Molly.

And my heart raced like the swift click of your sandals on that splintered Rockaway boardwalk. I stood transfixed and watched you moving away, chattering with your girl friend, drifting off into a crowded distance of hot-dog stands and cotton-candy carts. And I thought, oh, my God, I thought, *Move*! Follow her! Don't let her get away! And I . . .

20

I don't remember, he thought.

Flotsam and jetsam. Fragments of memory adrift. There was a storm, wasn't there? One of those sudden summer things that rolled in off the sea and inundated the boardwalk and sent everyone scurrying for cover. The smell of kosher franks sizzling on a grill, delicatessen mustard, sauerkraut boiling in a big aluminium pot. A fringed awning dripped water. Water and wind lashed the steaming boardwalk. Beyond, the sea was gray and roiling. And beside me, under the melting awning, alone now, her girl friend magically whisked away by wind or water – Molly.

There was a flash of lightning, wasn't there?

Drenched now, the long blond hair hanging limp, green eyes running mascara, summer cotton print clinging to breasts and legs and belly and thighs – I almost reached out to *touch* her! 'It's scary,' she said, or words to that effect, I forget, 'Lightning always scares me,' something like that, and another ozone-stinking flash in that moment, a boom of thunder, she covered her face with her hands, I longed to see her face again.

Ah, Molly, Jesus, what a face!

In close-up now (you were standing no more than a foot or two from me, your hands unmasking your face as the thunder receded), the eyes seemed greener, the freckles more pronounced, a riotous bloom of pointillist dots. You took a tissue from your bag, and wiped smudged mascara from your eyes and your cheeks, and said – I don't remember now. Do I look all right? Am I all right now? Something like that. And I said, I must have said, Yes, you look fine. The storm faded and was gone. There was sunlight again. We walked together, out from under the awning, onto the puddled boardwalk. I said (did I?), I said, 'You've lost your girl friend,' and you said, 'I seem to have, yes.' *That* I remember. The odd construction. *I seem to have, yes.* There was another flash of lightning, far out over the water. You didn't flinch this time.

I was David Weber, twenty-six years old in that August of 1957, about to enter my second year of law at N.Y.U., my education interrupted by the Korean War. And you were Molly Regan – of course, what *else* could you be, the map of County Cork all over your face, eyes like shamrocks, hair like lager,

21

those runaway freckles, what *else*, an Arab? A nurse, you told me. (Of *course*, a nurse.) At New York Hospital. Almost twenty-two years old, as fresh as the wind that blew in off the sea.

Were we ever that young?

But there were still surprises then. Back then, there were still surprises.

He fell asleep listening to the sound of the ocean.

He had left the window and the drapes open, and a faint breeze was blowing in off the sea. He imagined teeming life under the water.

In the middle of the night, he dreamed that someone was complaining about the plumbing in their New York apartment. Someone leaned over the bed and shouted, 'You don't know how to *fix* anything!' The white lampshade on the bedside lamp became a person's face. The person shouting was a woman wearing dead white powder on her face. The woman shouting was Molly.

He screamed himself awake.

Tuesday

Sunlight was streaming through the window.

He looked at his digital watch. It was a little past 6:00 A.M. The room was still hot. He didn't know whether he should close the drapes, blotting out the sunlight but also the air, or simply get up to face the day. It was almost five hours before he could see his father again.

He got out of bed.

He was naked, he always slept naked. Molly went to bed wearing a T-shirt and panties. Never just the T-shirt alone. He kept asking her if she was expecting a rapist in the middle of the night. She always answered, 'Well, what business is that of yours?' That first time on the phone in Rockaway, she told him she was wearing a white T-shirt and blue bikini panties, WQXR lettered across the front of the shirt. She still listened to classical music a lot. He had never developed a taste for it.

He went into the bathroom and sat on the bowl to urinate. Whenever Molly asked him why he *sat* to pee, like a woman, he told her he was resting. More and more, over the past few years, he had felt the need to rest. He thought about the case he had just lost. The plaintiff rests, Your Honor.

He flushed the toilet and then looked at himself in the mirror. He rarely studied his face in the mirror, except when he was drunk. When he was drunk, he looked at himself long and hard and said aloud, 'You're a damn fool, Counselor.' He thought it sad that the times he could remember most vividly were the times he'd made a fool of himself. Molly kept telling him he was guilt-ridden. All Jews are guilt-ridden, she said; that's why so many Jews become lawyers. He honestly could not see the connection.

He looked at himself in the mirror now.

He studied himself for a long time.

Then he went into the shower.

He was waiting for room service to bring his orange juice and coffee when he saw the girl crossing the tiled area around the pool, fifteen stories below. The pool was empty, the entire area was empty, this was still only seven in the morning. The girl was surely the same one he'd seen in the restaurant last night, tall and slender, her blond hair loosened now to fall below her shoulders.

24

She was wearing a scanty black bikini. Her skin was very white. She strode across the tile in high-heeled sandals. At the steps leading to the beach, she took off the sandals. With the sandals dangling in one hand, she stepped down onto the sand. He watched her as she crossed the beach to the edge of the sea. Sandals still in her hand, she began walking along the shore. He watched her for a long while, until she was very small in the distance.

He had smoked almost a full pack of cigarettes by a quarter to nine. He had watched a morning talk show on television. He had finished his coffee and ordered another potful. He looked at his watch again. He did not want to call Kaplan until after nine. The digital seconds ticked away, the minute indicator changed. The room-service waiter brought the second potful of coffee.

'Another scorcher,' he told David.

'Have they fixed the air conditioning yet?'

'Still working on it. Place feels like a tomb here, don't it? Six hundred rooms, we only got sixty booked. Mostly English people. But we got a big party of South Americans coming in next week. Should be a lot livelier then. You here on vacation?'

'No,' David said.

The waiter offered him the check and he signed it.

'Have a nice day, anyway,' the waiter said, and went out.

David poured himself a cup of coffee and dialed Kaplan's number. The answering service told him she would make sure the doctor got his message. On the television screen across the room, a talk-show host was leading a group of fat women through an exercise class. Legs moving like scissors. Thick thighs. Leotards. David sipped at his coffee. He looked at the phone. Across the room, the women on television were doing pushups now.

He went to the window and looked down at the pool. A handful of people were in the water. Mostly English, the waiter had said. He remembered a conversation he'd had with a London barrister (or solicitor, he never *could* get them straight) when he and Molly were planning a side-excursion to Clovelly. 'You won't like Clovelly,' the man had said. 'All you'll find there are a great many lower-class Englishmen sitting on jackasses to have their photos taken.' He wondered now what kind of Englishmen came to Miami in the month of June.

They were younger then, he and Molly, much younger.

Time weighed heavily in this room.

He debated going down to sit by the pool before it was time to go to the hospital. Or perhaps a walk along the beach. The sea was calm today, it was a season of calm weather. But what if Kaplan called? He supposed he could leave word that he was at the pool. He decided against it. He lit another cigarette. He smoked too much, he knew he did. Molly was always nagging him about how much he smoked. Molly nagged him about his drinking, too. His father drank only in moderation. His father rarely smoked more than three cigars a day, one after each meal. His father watched his diet. His father was careful to get enough exercise. But his father was lying in a hospital, unable to heal properly.

He poured another cup of coffee.

He sat watching the television screen.

They were all laughing on the television screen.

He looked at his watch.

Kaplan did not call until a quarter past ten.

'Mr. Weber?' he said. 'Dr. Kaplan.'

His voice was soft and tired, somewhat sad. For a frightening moment, David thought the doctor was calling to tell him his father was dead.

'How is he?' he asked at once.

'The same,' Kaplain said in his soft, tired, sad voice. 'No change at all.'

'Have you seen the X rays yet?'

'They're not X rays exactly. The scan works somewhat like a Geiger counter.'

'But there *are* pictures?'

'Yes, and I've seen the first of them. I didn't want to call until I'd had an opportunity to discuss them with the radiologist.'

'What did they show?'

'Nothing. Well, that isn't precisely accurate. There *was* a tiny dot that might or might not indicate something. We'll know better when we complete the series.'

'What might it indicate? The dot?'

'A possible area of infection. But, really, it's too early to tell yet. When the dye's been more fully assimilated, we'll have a better idea of what's there.'

'What will that be?' David asked.

'Sometime this afternoon.'

'May I call you then?'

'Yes, of course.'

'What would be a good time?'

'Five? A little after five.'

'I'll call you. Thank you, Dr. Kaplan.'

'Mr. Weber,' he said, and hung up.

His cousin Sidney came into the waiting room at a quarter to eleven. Sidney was a distant cousin, so damn distant that David hadn't even known him till after his father moved down to Florida. Sidney was related on his mother's side of the family, the Katz side. His mother's uncle's son's son, which made Sidney a second cousin to his mother, a second cousin to his father by marriage only, and a total stranger to David.

Sidney lived in Fort Lauderdale. He came to Miami every Tuesday for rehabilitation therapy at the Veteran's Hospital. Sidney had served with the U.S. Army during World War II. In the mechanized cavalry. A mine had exploded under his tank. He was a little older than David, fifty-three or -four David guessed, and he looked reasonably whole and healthy. But he collected his pension nonetheless, and he went every week for rehabilitation therapy. Sidney was a stream-of-consciousness talker who said everything that came into his mind. He did not need a conversational partner; Sidney was a one-man soft-shoe duet.

'So when did you get down here, Davey?' he said. 'I came to see him right after the operation, you know, he looked fine then, the doctor told me there were no complications, it was cancer, huh, was that what it was, malignant, huh? I've been having trouble with the car, what kind of a car do you drive up there, had to get a new muffler, two hundred bucks it cost me, well, you have to have a car that runs, am I right? He didn't know you were coming down, he said he didn't want to bother you when you had that big case, how'd it turn out, did you win it or lose it?

What's happening with him, anyway, he's still in Intensive Care? I call the hospital, they tell me his condition is critical, that's what they tell anybody who calls about a patient in Intensive Care, his condition is critical. That doesn't mean he's dying, it only means he's in Intensive Care. So how'd the big trial go? Where's your office now, still in Manhattan? I don't miss New York at all, you can shove New York. My mother's still up there in the Bronx, neighborhood all full of spics and niggers, I can't get her to budge. Says she was born there, and that's where she'll stay till she dies. I got this great house in Lauderdale ask your dad, he'll tell you. Swimming pool and everything, have you got a pool up there? Do you live right in the city, or outside someplace? You got a pool? I keep telling your dad he should move to Lauderdale, all these Cubans here now, it's worth your life to walk up Collins Avenue. He tells me he *likes* it here, worth his life. Listen, I do my best for him. I take him anywhere he wants to go, he's eighty-two years old, never did like to drive even when he was younger. I take him anywhere he wants to go, it isn't cheap to run a car these days, gas is expensive, I had to put in a new muffler, cost me two hundred bucks. I've got close to sixty thousand miles on that little buggy, keep it in top-notch shape, where are you staying down here, at the old man's apartment? You should be staying at the apartment, save a few bucks, what are you doing, staying at a hotel? It's like a ghost town right now, all those reports about crime in Miami, there's crime *everywhere*, am I right? Not only in Florida. They make such a big deal about it on television, it scares everybody off, it'll kill this town, what they're saying on television. I was telling your dad last week, he should be careful walking late at night, these Cubans. Still, there's crime everywhere, am I right, look at Atlanta. What are you doing about his bills, are you paying his bills? I'd pay them myself, I told him I'd lay out the money, but I'm short of cash just now, I had to get that new muffler, you know, and Lillian, your cousin Lillian, had a big dental bill, it's murder trying to keep up these days. But you should pay his bills or they'll cut off his electricity, everything in the refrigerator'll spoil, the apartment'll stink like a city dump. The phone, too, you don't want them to cut off his phone, you should be paying his bills, Davey, I'd pay them myself if I wasn't so short of cash. How'd you come down here, did you drive down? What kind of car do you drive up there? When did you get here?'

'It's eleven o'clock,' the pink lady said. 'You can go in now.'

He had the feeling, as he passed the open doors to the rooms in the unit, as he passed the overflow beds in the corridor, that all of the people here looked alike. They were all old, they were all very sick, and they all resembled his father. Even the old women resembled his father. He could understand now the mistake he'd made yesterday, when he'd thought the man in the corridor bed was his father. They all looked alike in their misery and their sickness. They all looked as if they were dying.

'Hey, Morrie, how you doing?' his cousin boomed. 'Look who's here, *Davey's* here! Do you know Davey? Can you recognize Davey? Can you recognise *me*, Morrie?'

'Hello, Sid,' his father said wearily.

'See,' Sidney said, 'he recognizes me. Good, Morrie, that's very good. I was just telling Davey he ought to pay your bills. I'd pay them myself, but I'm a little short of cash just now. You don't want your electricity cut off, do you, Morrie? They cut it off in a minute nowadays, you miss a single bill you're in the dark for the rest of your life. I was telling Davey . . .'

'Don't bother him about bills,' David said. 'How are you feeling, Pop?'

'Just wonderful,' his father said.

'You're looking better.'

'I must look *terrific*,' his father said, 'the way they're taking pictures of me day and night.'

'Pictures?' Sidney said. 'What pictures? X-ray pictures?'

'No, technicolor pictures of my *putz*,' his father said.

'That's very funny,' Sidney said. 'He's still got his sense of humor, you see that? Keep your sense of humor, Morrie, that's the main thing. Did you hear the one about the three old guys sitting around talking about their health? The first one says he's in perfect health, these are three old *cockers*, you understand, Morrie?'

'Like me,' his father said.

'No, not like you,' David said quickly.

'So the first one says he's in perfect health, except that he's

29

constipated, he can't move his bowels. The second one, another old *cocker*, says he has no trouble at all with his bowels, but he can't urinate, he has trouble urinating. The third old *cocker*, he says, "I have no trouble with my bowels. Every morning, as soon as I wake up, I move my bowels like clockwork. Then I urinate every morning like clockwork. And then I get out of bed." '

Without blinking an eye, deadpan, David's father said, 'That joke'll be the urination of me.'

'It's a killer, ain't it?' Sidney said, laughing. 'I told it to Lillian yesterday, she said. "Sid, you're disgusting," but she was laughing to beat the band. You got to keep your sense of humor in this world, otherwise what's it all about? What's it all about, Alfie, that was *some* song, that was a song that told people what it was all . . .'

'Sidney,' David said, 'I'd like to talk to my father privately.'

'What?'

'I said I'd like . . .'

'Sure, hey, you want to be alone with him, sure, I know we only got just a few minutes in here, sure. I'll try to come back on Thursday, Morrie, OK? It's a long drive from Lauderdale, but that don't matter. I had to get the buggy fixed, you know, I was having trouble with the muffler. Cost me two hundred bucks, just what I needed like a *loch in kop*. That's why I can't pay your bills just now, I'm a little short of cash, otherwise I'd lay it out for you. Get him to pay your bills, Morrie, you hear? Pay your dad's bills, Davey. Otherwise you'll go home, the apartment'll stink. I'll see you outside. So long, Morrie,' he said, 'keep your sense of humor,' and walked out.

'I'm paying your bills,' David said.

'I know you are.'

'Pop, I talked to Dr. Kaplan a little while ago, he won't really know what the pictures show until sometime later today. If they find something, and they can clear it up, you'll be out of here in no time.'

'Sure, no time at all.'

'That's the truth, Pop.'

'Sure. I'm in Intensive Care; it's been three weeks already, who are they trying to kid?'

'Your heartbeat looks good and strong . . .'

'When did you become a doctor all of a sudden?'

'Well, I can see your heartbeat up there . . .'

'I never had any trouble with my heart. That's not the trouble. The trouble is I have a hole in my belly.'

'Only temporarily.'

'Only till I die.'

'You're not going to die, Pop.'

'Who says? My son the doctor?'

'Well, I'm . . .'

'My son the lawyer who can't win a case?'

The room went silent.

'You see that wall?' his father said.

'Which wall?'

'The wall there. Can't you see the wall?'

'What about it?'

'It's a fake wall.'

'What do you mean?'

'There's nothing behind it.'

'There's another room behind it, Pop. The room next door.'

'No, there's no room next door.'

'Sure, there is. I saw it myself. There's another patient in the room next door.'

His father shook his head. 'There's no room there, David, are you telling me? There's only *shelves* behind that wall.'

'Shelves?'

'With goods for sale. The stuff they steal from the patients. Their suits and rings and watches and robes and slippers, all the stuff the people come in with. When they die, they put all that stuff on the shelves there, and they have a sale. They mark it up, of course, they have to make a profit on it. There's nothing behind that door there. Just a big hole in the wall. People go through that hole day and night, to look over the goods on the shelves, pick out what they want. There's a sale day and night.'

'Your robe is behind the door there, Pop. Just your robe and the wall. There's no hole behind the door.'

'There's a *hole* there, David. Bigger than the one in my belly. It *has* to be bigger, all those people marching through to look at the goods.'

'I'll close the door if you like, so you can see there's no hole behind it.'

'You don't have to close the door.'

'Pop . . .'

'I can *see* there's a hole, am I blind?'

'No, Pop.'

'So don't tell me there's no hole there.'

'Okay, Pop.'

'Did you meet Alvin?'

'Who's Alvin?'

'Allan, I mean. One of the nurses. He used to lift weights. He picks me up like I'm a baby, lifts me right off the bed. They want me to sit up a little each day. I don't *want* to sit up. All I want to do is get *out* of here.'

'You'll get out of here. Soon, Pop.'

'Where's Bessie? She didn't come this morning?'

'She'll be here for the two o'clock visit.'

'How do you know? Did she tell you that?'

'She had to do her marketing.'

'She told you that?'

'Yes, Pop.'

'That's more important than coming here? Her marketing?'

'She'll be here at two.'

'Her marketing is more important than I am. *I'm* going to die, and *she's* out buying oranges.'

'She'll be here later.'

'Who needs her? What are those things they brought in? Those cartons?'

'Where?' David said.

'Over there. On the sink.'

He went to the sink. There were two white cardboard cartons like the ones Chinese takeout food came in. One of them was marked in pencil with the words 'Strawberry Jell-O.' The other one was marked 'Cherry Jell-O.'

'It's Jell-O,' he said. 'Would you like some Jell-O?'

'No, I wouldn't like some Jell-O. I hate Jell-O. I always hated Jell-O. Even when Jack Benny was doing Jell-O, I hated Jell-O.'

'Is there anything you *would* like?'

'No.'

'Are you hungry?'

'No.'

'The doctor is hoping you'll start feeling hungry again.'

'Is that all the doctor is doing? Hoping? I can hope, too, and I'm not a doctor.'

'I'll be talking to him again later today, after they take the other pictures. He'll . . .'

'You try to get him on the phone, it's like trying to reach the President.'

'He'll tell me then what the pictures showed.'

'They took twelve pictures already.'

'But who's counting?' David said, and smiled.

His father reacted with a weak smile of his own.

'Don't let them put my stuff on the shelves behind that wall,' he said suddenly.

They talked in whispers in the corridor outside the waiting room.

'So what's it all about?' Sidney said.

'It's about him being a very sick man who doesn't need bowel-movement jokes,' David said.

'What?' Sidney said.

'He had a goddamn *colostomy*,' David whispered, 'he doesn't need you making jokes about . . .'

'I beg your pardon, sue me,' Sidney said. 'I was only trying to cheer him up.'

'And he's got *enough* damn worries without you mentioning his *bills*!'

'Why? Is it wrong to suggest his bills should be paid? I'd lay the money out myself if I wasn't . . .'

'You'd lay *shit* out,' David whispered.

'What? What?'

'He loaned your goddamn son five hundred dollars to put down on an automobile. Did he ever get it back? Did your son ever repay the loan?

'My son is out of work,' Sidney said.

'My father's not a bank,' David said. 'Your son should have gone to a bank.'

'Why? Is it a sin for a family . . .'

'Don't give me any "family" bullshit,' David said.

'You're in a riot, you know that?' Sidney whispered. 'Where the hell have *you* been these past three weeks, when I've been shlepping to the hospital every Tuesday? Where've you been the past three *months*, the past three *years*, Davey? Who's the one drives him wherever he wants to go, you think I'm a taxi service? I got headaches of my own, I don't have to take care of *your* father because *you* put him out to pasture down here in Miami!'

'He moved to Miami because he *wanted* to,' David said.

'Sure, because his big-shot lawyer son had no time for him up in New York. You think I don't know? I'm wise to you, Davey. You send the old man a box of cigars on his birthday, and you think that's enough. Well, it ain't. I'm the one who's been wiping his ass ever since he moved down here. So now you tell me my son should've paid back the money, you think he doesn't *plan* to pay back the money, these are rough times, we're not all of us big-shot lawyers with fancy offices in New York, driving Cadillacs. You think I don't know you drive a Cadillac? You think your father didn't tell me? I'm driving a Chevy with the fenders falling off, I had to spend two hundred bucks for a new muffler, and you're driving a Cadillac and complaining my son should pay back a lousy five hundred bucks when I'm shlepping your father all over the countryside! That's what I call chutzpah, Davey, that's what I really call chutzpah.'

'And don't call me Davey.'

'What?'

'I said don't call me Davey! Nobody calls me Davey! Not in my entire life has anybody called me Davey!'

'Calm down, willya? You don't want to be called Davey, I won't call you Davey. But don't call me *pisher*, either, not when I've been busting my ass for the old man, doing what *you* should be doing for him. Look, he'll get the money back, you think he won't get the money back? What do I look like, what does my son look like, some kind of *gonif*? He's out of work just now, all I got is the pension, your father keeps buying stamps and plates and first-day covers, I had to spend two hundred bucks for a new muffler, he's got more than he knows what to do with, your father, you think I don't know? Who do you think drives him to the bank where he socks away the social security checks? He's got *four* banks, your father! *Four* of them! He doesn't *need* those checks, he just socks them away, you think I don't know he's clipping coupons and spending the money on all those stamps and plates? He's got them stacked to the ceiling in his apartment, three locks on the door, it's like Fort *Knox*, that apartment! You ever been in that apartment? Or are you too busy chasing ambulances in New York? Why don't you move down here, you want to take care of him so bad? Why don't you do *that*, Davey – I beg your pardon, sue me, I'm not supposed to call you Davey. Why don't you move down here and drive him wherever he wants to go, and invite him to parties in Lauderdale where I have to come down and pick him up and take him back home again? *You're* his son, why don't *you* do that, huh? I tell a joke to cheer him up, next thing you know I'm getting mugged in a dark alley. Listen, who needs gratitude, who needs thanks? Take of your own father, do me a favor, okay? Pay his bills, don't pay them, who gives a shit? He's *your* father, not mine!'

'Where do we send the Oscar?' David said.

'Sure, make smart-ass wisecracks,' Sidney said.

'Maybe you'd better go now, okay?'

'I'm going, don't worry. Be sure to tell your dad you chased me out. He'll be tickled to death to hear that. Tell him you chased his cousin out of the hospital. Is that what you want, Davey? You want me never to come back here again? How long you think he's going to be in here? How long are *you* going to be here? What happens when you go back to New York? Who comes to see him *then* every Tuesday? Chase me out, go ahead.'

David sighed.

'I'm not chasing you out,' he said.

'You sound like it.'

'I'm sorry.'

'I know you're upset just now, don't you think I know? We're all upset. But that's no reason to turn on your own family. No reason at all.'

'Okay, Sidney, I said I was sorry.'

'Forget it,' Sidney said. 'I'll come back Thursday night, the seven o'clock visit. I got things to do during the day, I got a life of my own, too, you know. It's a long drive from Lauderdale, but the old man may need me.'

35

David watched him walking heavily down the corridor. For the first time, he noticed that Sidney walked with a limp. His anger was gone now. He stood watching his distant cousin as he turned out of sight around the bend in the hall, and he wondered why he'd been so angry.

And suddenly he was confused.

What of this man is me? he wondered.

The looks, he supposed. The Weber looks. He was taller, of course; his father was only five-eight, and David was five-eleven, the generational advantage. His own son had been almost – he closed his mind to the thought. But the dark hair and brown eyes, the 'famous Weber nose,' as his Uncle Max called it, refined a bit in David, the Semitic curve smoothed out somewhat, but distinctive nonetheless. And the mouth perhaps, with its pouting lower lip, especially when his father was in a self-pitying funk about all the taxes he had to pay each year, the big entrepreneur whose successive businesses had collapsed even in the best of years, living solely on the money David – but that was another story. *Clipping coupons*, cousin Sidney had said. Clipping coupons from the investments in the irrevocable trust David had established for him fifteen years ago. 'I worked hard for my money,' his father was fond of saying, but he'd been virtually penniless back then when David established the trust. 'I worked hard for every nickel I've got.'

Perhaps.

Worked hard, and went under, each and every time.

David to the rescue – listen, what difference did it make? He'd have had to give half of it to Uncle Sam, anyway, so what difference did it make, really? The crochet-beading business, back in the twenties, before David was born, going very strong for a while, until the fashion changed and women wouldn't be caught dead in beaded gowns. The pool hall on Fordham Road in 1936, when David was five and they were living on Jerome Avenue, in the shadow of the elevated structure. ('The wops there love to shoot pool,' his father said.) He took the train to work every day, banker's hours even then; wouldn't open the pool hall till noon and then left it in the hands of a 'trusted employee' at five sharp. The trusted employee was stealing him

36

blind; the pool hall went under in less than a year. And the parade of businesses after that, the shoe stores, first in Harlem ('The niggers love fancy shoes') and then on Fourteenth Street ('Lots of spics moving in, they love fancy shoes') and then in New Rochelle ('Lots of rich kikes there') – his father's prejudices were all-encompassing. 'I'm a merchant,' he said about himself. 'What else can a poor Jew do?' the appraisal punctuated with the self-pitying pout.

He formed the Weber Bureau of Clipping in 1938, when David was seven years old. This enabled him to work out of the new apartment they were renting on Mosholu Parkway. In those days, they changed apartments frequently. David later learned that this was his father's way of beating the landlord. The Depression was still exacting its toll; the war in Europe – America's economic salvation – hadn't yet erupted. Most landlords offered a month's free rent as an inducement to lease. They threw in all sorts of perks like a new refrigerator, a fresh paint job, sometimes even free gas and electricity for a month when you rented one of their empty apartments. The Webers moved every month. David had trouble remembering what his address was.

His father sat in the living room of the Mosholu Avenue apartment, scanning copies of all the city's daily newspapers, searching for items about ordinary citizens. There were always items of local interest. He clipped out all the engagement notices, wedding announcements, obituaries, human interest stories, anything that mentioned the name of someone who lived in New York. He consulted the telephone directories for all five boroughs and then either wrote or phoned the persons the news items were about, asking if they'd like a clipping of what had appeared on them in the newspaper. The people would come to the house for the clippings, paying cash on the barrelhead. There was a steady stream of people to the front door of their apartment. ('Our neighbors'll think I'm a *courva*,' his mother said; back then David didn't know the word meant hooker.) His father charged twenty-five cents for each clipping. He was forced to end the business when a six-foot two-inch, two-hundred-pound *shvartzer* appeared at the front door one day while his mother was alone, frightening her half to death. 'I could've made a fortune with that business once the war started,' his father said. 'All those kids being drafted, stories about them in the papers, I could've made a fortune.'

He could have made a fortune, too, David supposed, with the men's clothing store he started in the latter part of 1940 (*was*, in fact, making money enough to afford a permanent address for a while) if only half the young men in America hadn't been drafted in 1942, thereby drastically reducing the demand for civilian attire. ('How can you operate a business when your only customers are twelve-year-olds and *cockers*?') The business went under in the fall of 1943, just after David's twelfth birthday. When the war ended, David's father opened a new store grandly called Weber's Army & Navy Surplus Supply Outlet, a good idea in that many such stores were doing good business. Maybe that was the trouble. Maybe there were *too* many of them, or maybe he'd opened in a bad location, or maybe – who the hell knew? He finally sold his entire stock to a chain store at an 80 percent discount. 'It was all a matter of timing,' he said later. 'If I just could've waited till the hippies started . . .'

By the time 'the hippies started' – David set the date as approximately the same time the Beatles achieved recognition and prominence, sometime in 1964 – his father had been through at least another dozen failed businesses, and David had been through the Korean War, four years of college, three years of law school, a wedding, an apprenticeship with Dolger, Pierce and Parsons, the birth of his son, and the formation of his own law firm. Two years after that, David established the trust for his father, the man who'd 'worked hard' for every nickel he had. However many nickels he now possessed, David knew, had been generated by the trust. Whatever David inherited from his father would really be David's own, anyway. He was his father's sole beneficiary; he knew because he had drawn the will himself – well, wait, that wasn't quite true. He had drawn the will ten years ago. Stephen had been alive then; his father had willed him his stamp and plate collection.

The stamps and plates were no surprise. His father had been an inveterate collector for as long as David could remember. He collected everything. When David was growing up, his father was always counting coins (he stopped collecting those when things got really bad), or pasting stamps into albums, or sorting through first-day covers, or cutting out articles from newspapers (a residual habit from the days of his clipping bureau). He sent away for anything that captured his limitless fancy. David caught the bug – well, there, he thought, *that* of him is in me, or at least was. He sent away for a Tom Mix Six-Shooter, and a Little Orphan Annie Shaker, and a ring The Shadow sent you that glowed in the dark like Blue Coal, and another ring that you could look into and see whoever was behind you. He sent away for Omar the Mystic code books and Dick Tracy badges. He waited for the mail to come each day, just the way his father waited for the mail to come. He constantly searched the newspapers and magazines for new opportunities to send away for something exciting, just the way his father did.

'A chip off the old block,' his father said. 'Ike and Mike, we look alike.'

'A lot of *junk*,' his mother said.

She was always telling him to get rid of it.

'Clear out all this junk, and I could make a nice room for my sewing machine,' she said.

'Esther, it's my *hobby*!' David's father protested.

'Your whole *life* is a hobby,' his mother said.

Maybe it was.

The way he would throw himself into any of David's school projects, as if they were challenges to his own ingenuity and imagination. David could remember once – this was when he was in the third grade, he guessed, and there was a class contest for the best scrapbook on transportation. David's father dug into his cartons of newspaper and magazine clippings (God, why had he *saved* all this stuff?) and came up with hundreds of pictures relating to transportation: ox carts and camels; horses and rickshaws; coaches and wagons; Chinese junks and sampans; steamships and steam locomotives; automobiles from the first Model-T right through the rumble-seat Ford his Uncle Martin had owned and including the streamlined prewar models (this was 1941 or thereabouts, David guessed); dirigibles and airplanes; and even some science-fiction drawings of what transportation in the future might look like, spaceships and Buck Rogers rocket packs – had his father *known* somehow that one

39

day David would be in a scrapbook contest on transportation? David arranged all the pictures by topic (Land, Sea, Water, Air), in chronological order, and then painstakingly lettered onto each page a description of the pictures he pasted into the book. He won first prize. His father was thrilled. 'We won it, David!' he said. David always felt his *father* had won it.

And the puppet show.

Not really a full-scale puppet show in that there was only a single hand puppet in it, which David's father had helped him to make out of papier-mâché. The sole puppet was the master of ceremonies, who introduced each act from a small curtained arch cut into the proscenium David's father had built from a cardboard grocery-store display for a beer – David forgot the brand –two giant golden lions on a blue field, flanking the opening that was the stage for the show. Rheingold, was it? David manipulated the hand puppet from behind the curtained arch (the curtain was operative; David's father had made it with pulleys and strings), announcing each act in a falsetto voice. The other actors in the show were David's toy soldiers, either arranged in tableaux or else mounted on orange-crate slats that could be moved back and forth from either side of the stage. There was a Western scene with David's *cowboy*-soldiers sitting around a fire (David's father rigged a flashlight with a red piece of cellophane over it), and Hymie the Mutt, so-called because he was a Western Union delivery boy, singing 'Home on the Range.' And there was a World War I scene with David's *soldier*-soldiers mounted on the orange-crate slats and being moved back and forth in counterpoint to simulate them marching off to battle while Hymie sang 'Over There' in his high, sweet soprano voice. Then there was a battle scene with his father banging pots and pans behind the stage in imitation of an artillery attack, and David and Hymie yelling 'Gas! Gas!' and his father running from one side of the stage to the other to blow cigar smoke in from the wings. It really looked like a gas attack; everyone in the audience was amazed. All the kids in the building came to see that puppet show. They charged ten cents' admission for each kid. 'We should've charged a quarter,' his father said, 'we'd have made a fortune.'

And the newspaper David started when he was eleven, and

they were living in a better apartment on Mosholu Parkway, bigger than the first one up the street. His father did all the hand-lettering for the four-page newspaper, on the stencils you had to make for the Hectograph. The Hectograph was a tray of yellow Jell-O, it looked like, and first you rubbed the stencil with its lettering over the stuff in the tray, and then you put the blank sheets of paper in the tray and you rubbed those, and what was on the stencil appeared on the blank paper, in purple ink. The lead story was about a two-headed cat. David's father copied it word for word from a clipping he'd cut out of the *Bronx Home News*, and then he made up a new headline for it: DOUBLEHEADER FOR KATZ FAMILY! The puns, ah, yes ('That joke'll be the urination of me'), the puns were something else David had inherited, he supposed.

They were his father's revenge upon the English language, perhaps, his way of coming to terms with the fact that he'd never got beyond the first year of high school because his *own* father (the grandfather David had never met) died when he was just a boy and he and his brother Martin had been forced to find jobs to help out their widowed mother. That was when Uncle Martin became the only Jewish apprentice house painter in the city of New York. It was also when his father became the only Jewish kid on the Lower East Side who was rushing the growler for an Irish bar on Canal Street, a job that was short-lived because the owner of the place learned first that he was only fourteen and not sixteen (as he'd claimed) and next that his name wasn't Webb (as he'd further claimed) but was instead Weber. 'He took me for a Sweeney,' his father later told David, 'but I was only a sheeny.'

Whatever the psychological roots of his word games, they never ceased. When he caught David smoking for the first time, he said, 'Put out that cigarette before you make an ash of yourself.' He described an inept tailor on Fordham Road as a man 'panting for customers,' and then compounded the felony by adding, 'ill-suited to his trade.' Of an uppity barber, he said, 'He thinks he's hair to the throne,' which was better, but only somewhat, than his constant remark about his own baldness, 'Oh, well, hair today, gone tomorrow.' He punned interminably and often outrageously. When his brother Max caught a trout he claimed was two feet long, David's father said, 'You don't expect

41

me to swallow that, do you?' and then immediately added, 'Well, maybe I will, just for the halibut.' When his cousin Bernice began cheating on her violinist husband, David's father said, 'He's fiddling while Bernice roams.' The first time he met Molly (but that was another story) and learned she was a nurse, he said, 'I've always wanted a panhandler in the family.'

During the trial David had just lost, opposing counsel was a man who prefaced each of his harangues by first removing his eyeglasses and then jabbing them in a witness's face whenever he posed a question. In objecting to one such verbal and physical attack, David said, 'Your Honor, my brother is harassing the witness,' and then could not resist adding, 'and he's also making a spectacle of himself,' which the judge did not find amusing. ('Chip off the old block. Ike and Mike, we look alike.') But back in 1943, when his father came up with the 'MRS. KATZ' headline and despite the fact that his mother's maiden name had been Katz – was there more to the headline than David guessed? – he'd thought it was the cat's meow. ('What has four legs and follows cats?' his father asked that very same day. 'What?' David said. 'Mrs. Katz and her lawyer!' his father bellowed in triumph. Jesus!) In fact, David believed that the headline, together with a gossip column about all the kids in the neighborhood, was what sold out the first issue. They made fourteen dollars on that first issue because there were ads in it from all the neighborhood merchants, including one for David's father's clothing store that was about to fold in the fall, a full-page ad that had cost a dollar. The newspaper suspended publication after its second issue, but only because David dropped the Hectograph tray one afternoon and the now thoroughly purple jelly spilled out all over the floor. 'That jelly's gonna get you in a jam,' his father said, smiling, even though he'd already hand-lettered his way through half of the third issue.

His father had good penmanship ('I like to keep my hand in,' he said), and he was a good letterer as well ('A man of letters,' he said), a skill he had acquired when making signs for the front windows of all his failed businesses. David's mother yelled that he'd ruined the rug on the floor of the room where his father kept all his collected junk and which had been the newspaper office.

David said he would give her all the paper's profits to have the rug cleaned. His mother graciously declined the offer, but she never stopped telling everyone how David had spilled all that purple *shmutz* on the heirloom rug her grandmother had carried on her back all the way from Russia – 'See the stain? You can still see it. This is *exactly* where he dropped the tray.'

His father said, 'That stain has real stayin' power,' which was reaching, even for him.

His father used to cheat at poker.

His poker game was on Wednesday nights, a floating game that met at their house every seventh Wednesday. If David had finished his homework, his father would let him pull up a chair beside him, and he would explain all the poker hands to him. The men played for pennies; none of them could afford higher stakes. But every now and then, David noticed his father shortchanging the pot when he put his 'lights' in. Each time, his father gave him a little wink that meant he was just kidding around, there wasn't any *real* theft involved here, he was just putting one over on these wisenheimers. 'A penny saved is a penny urned', he said, whenever he dropped a coin into David's piggy bank. It took David years and years to realize he was making another pun, a rather literary one at that since its appreciation depended on visual input. His father's cheating delighted him. He kept fearfully waiting for the other men in the game to catch his father at it, but they never did. His father invariably won. Years later, when David was on the troopship heading for Inchon and monumental poker games were being played on blankets all over the deck, David wished his father were with him. His father would have cleaned out all those fancy gamblers in a minute.

Everything about his father had delighted David when he was a boy.

He wondered when it all had changed.

He wondered when his father had become a pain in the ass.

The waiting room, and his father's room, and his own room at the hotel were beginning to blend into a single unit. The only reason David went back to the hotel between visiting hours was to get away from the hospital, but the hotel room was becoming an extension of the hospital. He had been here only since yesterday afternoon, and already his life was ordered by the sign on the waiting room door:

VISITING HOURS
11:00 A.M., 2:00 P.M.,
4:00 P.M., and 7:00 P.M.
PLEASE LIMIT VISITS
TO TEN MINUTES

The other people in the waiting room seemed to spend their entire day there, watching television, talking to each other or to whichever pink lady was at the desk, going down for lunch in the hospital coffee shop, returning to wait for two o'clock and then the four o'clock, and only then leaving the hospital to return later for the seven o'clock. Their patience was infinite; they all had people who were maybe dying in there.

He sat beside Bessie on one of the leatherette couches and listened to the voices all around him.

'My mother hit me this morning,' the thin woman with the flushed, excited face said. This was shortly before the two o'clock visit. Or perhaps the four o'clock. It was all becoming a blur for him. 'She wants to go home, she hit me. I don't know if I'll come to see her again. She gets upset whenever I come. Maybe it's better if I stay home.'

'No,' the pale woman in the wedgies said. Her daughter was not here today. Neither was the man from Toronto: David assumed he had already flown his comatose wife back to Canada. 'You have to keep coming. They can carry on all they want, but they like to see you.'

'I don't think she likes to see me,' the other woman said, and lit a cigarette. 'I really don't think so. If she likes me so much, why does she take a fit every time I come?'

'Because you're the only one she can take it out on.'

He was beginning to learn their names. The pale woman in the wedgies, the one whose husband had had open-heart surgery twice, was Mrs. Daniels. Her fat daughter, who was not here this afternoon because her little girl had a ballet recital, was named Louise. David did not yet know her last name. The woman with

44

the flushed face, the one whose mother had come in for a simple hernia operation and who was now violently insisting that she be taken home, was Mrs. Horowitz. She smoked even more than David did. There were other people in the waiting room now, strangers, the way Mrs. Daniels and her daughter and Mrs. Horowitz had been strangers to him yesterday. On the television screen, a man wearing a tuxedo was talking to a woman in a slinky evening gown. They were both sipping brandy from large snifters.

'That guy's been wearing a tuxedo for the past two weeks,' a swarthy man across the room said.

'Things go slow on soap operas,' Mrs. Daniels said.

'Things go slow right here,' the man said.

He was growing a mustache; it sat like a smudge on his upper lip. He kept touching it constantly, checking on its progress. He had black hair and very dark eyes. He introduced himself as Albert Di Salvo. He told the others that his mother had suffered a stroke two weeks ago. He came to visit her whenever he could. He was worried that she was still in Intensive Care. He was an only child; he wanted to visit her more often, but he had to go to work, didn't he? As it was, he was losing a lot of work hours. Mrs. Daniels comforted him. She told him he was of *course* doing the best he could; he couldn't come here every *minute*, could he, and maybe lose his job?

'Same tuxedo for the past two weeks,' Di Salvo said. 'I'm forty-three years old, I don't have a tuxedo. That kid there on television is what, twenty-four, twenty-five, he's got his own tuxedo.'

'It really belongs to the show,' Mrs. Horowitz said, puffing on her cigarette.

'Yeah, but it's *supposed* to be his,' Di Salvo said. 'He's supposed to be rich.'

'He probably is rich,' Mrs. Daniels said. 'I mean, in real life. Those TV actors make a lot of money.'

'Sure, they do,' Di Salvo said.

David lit another cigarette. Mrs. Daniels turned to him and gently said, 'You shouldn't smoke so much, Mr. Weber. I know this is a difficult time for you, but you have to watch your own health, too.'

45

'Let him smoke if he wants to,' Mrs. Horowitz said. 'My mother never smoked a day in her life, she's here in Intensive Care hitting her own daughter. Let him smoke.'

'You should eat, too,' Mrs. Daniels said. 'To keep your strength up. There's a coffee shop downstairs, they serve a nice lunch. Did you have lunch today, Mr. Weber?'

'Yes, thank you.'

'Keep your strength up,' Mrs. Daniels said.

'When he finally takes off that tuxedo,' Di Salvo said, 'it'll walk across the room all by itself.'

Bessie, silent until now, suddenly said, 'It always seems like forever. Waiting.'

It must have been during the four o'clock visit that David met the psychiatrist. The man walked into the room unannounced, the way they all did. He was holding a clipboard; David figured at once he was a doctor.

'Hello, Weber,' he said, 'how are you feeling today?'

'Great,' his father said.

'Better than yesterday?'

'Better than yesterday, worse than today,' his father said.

The man looked at him shrewdly.

'What do you mean by that, Weber?'

'You're the psychiatrist, you figure it out.' He looked at David. 'They're sending me a psychiatrist, they think I'm nuts.'

'That's not true, Weber.'

'I'm his son,' David said, and extended his hand.

'Dr. Wolfe,' the psychiatrist said. He did not take David's hand. 'He's been very depressed,' he said as if David's father were not in the room with them. 'We thought he'd be happy when they took the tube out of his nose, but he's still depressed. Why are you so depressed, Weber?'

'Some psychiatrist,' David's father said, and shook his head.

'Why are you depressed, can you tell me?'

'No reason at all,' David's father said. 'I've got a hole in my belly, they're taking pictures to see if I've got more blockage, why should I be depressed? I should be dancing in the streets instead.'

'They're trying to help you,' Wolfe said. 'We're all trying to help you.'

'You can help me by leaving me alone. I never had such a crowd of people around me in my life. It's like the New York subway system in this room.'

'*Have* they . . .?'

'During rush hour.'

'*Have* they been taking more pictures?' Wolfe asked. Whenever he talked directly to David's father, he raised his voice a decibel or two, as if he were talking to a dull child or a deaf person.

'No, I made that up so your day'll be interesting,' David's father said.

'Have you been making anything else up?'

'I've been making up all the beds on the floor.'

'When do you do that, Weber?'

'After I get through making the nurses. They're very hot numbers, these Cuban nurses.'

'How about the shelves behind the wall, Weber? Have you been seeing those again?' He turned to David and lowered his voice. 'He's been hallucinating,' he said.

'By the way,' David's father said, 'I may have a hole in my belly, but my hearing's fine.'

'I didn't say anything to your son that I wouldn't say to you,' Wolfe said, raising his voice again.

'Why do you sound like you're calling long distance when you talk to me?'

'What?'

'You yell like you're on long distance. I'm not in Philadelphia.'

'Have you been seeing those shelves again, Weber?'

'I don't know what shelves you're talking about.'

'The ones you told me were behind the wall.'

'That isn't a wall, it's a *fake* wall.'

'It's a real wall. With a room behind it,' Wolfe said. He was writing on the clipboard pad. 'When you get up and can walk around, you can see for yourself there's a room there. No shelves.'

'I'll give you a full report when I can get up and walk around,'

David's father said. 'Don't hold your breath, though, it may be a while.'

'How's your memory? He's been forgetting things,' Wolfe said to David, lowering his voice. 'Can you remember things a little better now, Weber?' he asked, raising his voice again.

'What was your question?' David's father said. 'I forget your question.'

'Can you remember things a little better now? Do you remember when you came into the hospital?'

'The first Thursday in May,' David's father said.

'That's close, it was May twenty-sixth.'

'But a Thursday.'

'No, a Tuesday.'

'Close, but no guitar,' his father said. 'All these Cubans,' he said to David, explaining the pun.

'If I gave you a hundred dollars . . .' Wolfe started.

'I wish you would.'

'If I gave you a hundred dollars, and you gave seven back to me, how much would you have left?'

'You give me a hundred . . .'

'Yes. I give you a hundred, and you give me seven back. How much is left?'

'Seven from a hundred,' David's father said. 'That's . . .'

It was painful to see him struggling with the arithmetic. He had always prided himself on his meticulous bookkeeping. His checkbooks were as balanced as a high-wire act. His brow furrowed now in concentration. He wet his lips. 'That would be . . . well, sure, that . . .'

'Pop, what he wants to know . . .'

'Let him do it himself, please,' Wolfe said, even though David hadn't been about to prompt his father.

'It's ninety-seven,' his father said.

'No, it's ninety-three,' Wolfe said.

'Somebody must be hitting the cash register,' his father said. 'That *gonif* who worked for me in the pool hall.'

'If you had three wishes, Weber, what would they be?' Wolfe asked.

'I wish you'd go away, that's my first wish.'

'And the other two?' He was writing on the pad again.

'That's all three. I wish you'd go back to Vienna.'

'Why Vienna?' Wolfe asked, still writing.

'Why not Vienna?'

'He's making a reference to Freud,' David said.

'Let him answer himself, please,' Wolfe said. 'Why Vienna, Weber?'

'Go away, will you, please?'

'Tell me your three wishes, seriously.'

'Serially?' David's father said. He was looking up at the ceiling. 'I wish I could get out of this place, that's my first wish.'

'And your second wish?'

'I wish I could go someplace and sleep in peace, without people coming in all the time and bothering me.'

'Yes?'

'Yes what?'

'Your third wish?'

'I wish I could go to temple again soon and thank God for relieving me of the pain of this suffering.'

'Those are all really the same wish, aren't they?' Wolfe said.

'Are they?' David's father said, and turned his head into the pillow.

He called Kaplan from the hotel room at ten minutes past five. The answering service told him the doctor would get back to him. Kaplan called fifteen minutes later. The same soft, tired, sad voice.

'Mr. Weber?' he said. 'Dr. Kaplan.'

'Hello,' David said, 'how are you?'

'Fine, thanks.'

'Have you seen the new pictures yet?'

'Yes, I have.'

'And?'

'Well, there's a slightly larger area that may be an abscess, but we can't be certain.'

'By larger . . .?'

'The size of a dime.'

'Why can't you be certain whether . . .?'

'It may simply be a scar. From the operation.'

'Can't you *tell* whether it's a scar?'

49

'No, I'm sorry, we can't.'

'I mean, don't you *know* where the scars are supposed to be?'

'Yes, but . . . Mr. Weber, I wish I could be more definite, it would make life easier for all of us. This may or may not be something, we simply can't tell.'

'Let me understand this,' David said. 'If there *is* something in there, an infection, an abscess, whatever, wouldn't it *have* to show on the pictures?'

'Not necessarily. There are yards and yards of intestines in the abdominal cavity, all of them in loops. There may be something hidden between the loops, inaccessible to the scan.' He paused. 'Mr. Weber,' he said, 'I feel I ought to be perfectly frank with you.'

'Please,' David said.

'We're doing everything possible for your father, but if he keeps deteriorating at his present rate . . . Mr. Weber, it would have been very nice if we'd found something positive on those pictures, something we could really have gone after. But lacking such evidence – and I've asked for other opinions on this, believe me – lacking such positive evidence, I feel obliged to do exploratory surgery, anyway.'

'He's eighty-two years old,' David said.

'I realize that. And we're all well aware of the risk . . .'

'How great a . . .?'

'. . . but if we go in and find something that isn't showing on the pictures . . .'

'How do you know you'll find it?'

'If it's there, we'll find it.'

'And if it isn't?'

'We'll keep trying to isolate the source of the infection.'

'How great a risk is involved?'

'An estimate? Fifty–fifty.'

'I see,' David said.

'That's an estimate.'

'And if you *don't* do the operation, the exploratory surgery?'

'Well . . . unless something unforeseen happens in the next few days . . .'

'Like what?'

'A marked and dramatic improvement. Normally, we

shouldn't be having this problem at all. Your father should have healed by now.'

'But he hasn't.'

'No, he hasn't,' Kaplan said, and sighed. 'Sometimes a patient loses his will to live, Mr. Weber. He simply gives up. I hope that isn't happening here.'

'What do *you* feel his chances of improvement are?'

'I don't know how to answer that. That may be up to him, you see.'

'Up to *him*?'

'His will to stay alive, yes.'

'But do *you* think there might be a marked and dramatic improvement?'

'No, I do not.'

'Then what you're saying is if you *do* the operation he's got a fifty-fifty chance of survival, and if you *don't* do it, he'll die.'

'In effect, that's what I'm saying.'

'In effect? Well, that *is* what you're saying, isn't it?'

'Your father tells me you're a lawyer,' Kaplan said.

David visualized the man smiling and for the first time felt some sort of kinship with him. 'I'm sorry,' he said. 'I'm simply trying to get this straight.'

'I'm giving it to you as straight as I know how,' Kaplan said. 'If he continues on his present downward course, I think he'll die, yes. And his chances of surviving surgery in his present condition are fifty-fifty. That's all I can tell you, Mr. Weber.'

'He's very fearful of another operation, you know,' David said.

'Well, of course,' Kaplan said.

'Apparently the first one was very painful.'

'Not the operation itself. There's always some pain *following* surgery, of course. But we try to moderate that with drugs.'

'He told me he was suffering.'

'Not now? You don't mean now?'

'No, not now. After the first operation.'

'Well, yes.'

'Are you *sure* you have to operate again?'

'I would not take the risk unless I were positive.'

'When would you do it?'

51

'Tomorrow. First thing in the morning. He should be back down by the time you get there.'

'At eleven, do you mean?'

'Yes.'

'Back down where? The Recovery Room?'

'Intensive Care.'

'Will he recognize me?'

'Not until the anesthesia wears off.'

'But I can see him.'

'Yes, of course.'

'Will you be the only surgeon?'

'I plan to ask the chief surgeon to attend.'

'What about my father? Will *you* tell him, or shall I?'

'I've already told him,' Kaplan said. 'He had to sign an authorization form. I think we'll need your signature as well. His hand was a bit shaky.'

His father's signature on the hospital form almost moved David to tears. The fine curlicues and loops of the *Morris L. Weber* had deteriorated to a scrawl that meandered across the page. He looked at his father's signature for a long time, remembering the signs he had meticulously hand-lettered for the puppet show and posted all over the building, the signs he had made announcing the first issue of the short-lived newspaper. He read the consent form while the Cuban nurse waited. He signed his name in the space provided for next-of-kin and hoped he was not signing his father's death warrant.

He went into his father's room. The machines blinked and beeped beside his bed, electronic sentinels. His father's eyes were closed. It occurred to David that he had never seen him asleep before. He kept looking at his face. They had not shaved him today; a gray beard stubble covered his chin and his jowls. Asleep, he did not look sick. Three thousand calories a day, the Cuban nurse had said. He hadn't lost a pound of weight. But he was dying. He would die unless they found whatever they were looking for and cut it from his body, or drained it, did whatever they had to do to it.

His father's eyes popped open.

He let out a startled little gasp.

52

'Oh,' he said.

'Hello, Pop.'

'Another operation, right?' his father said, instantly awake.

'Yes, Pop.'

'When?'

'First thing tomorrow morning.'

'Terrific. Just what I need, first thing in the morning.'

'It *is* what you need, Pop.'

'What'd they find? All those pictures.'

'Something that may be an area of infection.'

'How'd I get so infected all of a sudden? I've never been sick a day in my life.'

'Well,' David said.

'I forgot to dot the i,' his father said.

'What?'

'On that thing they gave me to sign. I forgot to dot the i in Morris.'

'That's okay, Pop, don't worry about it.'

'They'll think somebody forged my signature.'

'No, they won't think that.'

'Maybe you ought to get it back, so I can dot the i.'

'I don't think that's necessary.'

'The ayes have it,' his father said, and suddenly twisted his head on the pillow. 'Where's my jaw?' he asked.

'Your jaw? Right there, Pop, where it's supposed to be.'

'My jaw, my *jaw*.'

'What do you mean?'

'Half of my jaw is gone.'

'No, Pop, all you . . .'

'How am I supposed to chew, if I ever get anything to eat here?'

'Your teeth, do you mean? Your dentures?'

'My jaw,' his father said, and nodded.

'They're right over there in the tray. On the sink there. Do you want to see them?'

His father nodded.

David went to the sink. He picked up the pink plastic tray in which his father's dentures rested. He carried the tray to the bed.

'Okay?' he said.

53

His father nodded. He kept nodding. He seemed very tired all at once. 'They steal things, you know,' he said. 'To put on the shelves.'

'Well, I don't think they'll steal your teeth,' David said, carrying the tray back to the sink.

'They'll steal *anything*,' his father said.

'They'd get about thirty cents for them,' David said, smiling.

'More than that,' his father said. 'For the jawbone of an ass? At least a buck and a quarter.'

He took his father's hand between his own.

'Pop,' he said, 'you're going to get better after this operation, you'll see. They're going to fix you up this time.'

'They fixed me up *last* time,' his father said. 'They fixed me up just fine.'

'I mean it,' David said.

His father nodded.

'I have to go,' David said, looking up at the wall clock opposite the bed. 'I want you to get a good night's . . .'

'That thing keeps going around,' his father said.

'What thing?'

'On the wall.'

'The clock, do you mean? The sweep hand on the clock?'

'No, no.'

'What then?'

His father pointed to the wall. His finger rotated in a small circle.

'The wallpaper? The design in the wallpaper?'

'No, no. The thing they have. The shelves with all the stuff on them. It goes around and around, so the people can see the goods.'

'Pop, don't worry about all that, okay? You get a good night's sleep.'

'Fat chance of that.'

'Well, you *try* to sleep, okay? And tomorrow, once they finish the operation, you're going to feel much better. I promise you.'

'Who are you to promise me?' his father asked, and then abruptly said, 'Did I give you Josie's address?'

'Josie? Who's Josie?'

'A friend of the family,' his father said, and David remembered

54

when they used to call his grandmother's boyfriend 'a friend of the family.'

'I don't know her,' David said.

'I know it by heart. Her address. Write it down.'

'Josie who?'

'Write it down,' his father said.

The Cuban nurse appeared in the doorway. 'I'm sorry, swee'heart,' she said, 'your son has to go now.'

'I'll see you in the morning,' David said. 'Right after the operation. I'll be here at eleven, waiting for you to come down. You get a good night's sleep, okay?'

'You can write it down tomorrow,' his father said.

'I will.'

'Bring a pencil and paper. They don't have any paper in this cheap hotel. Why don't you get some paper in here?' he asked the nurse.

'We ha' paper, darlin'.'

'Bring a mirror, too. I want to see what I look like.'

'You look beautiful, swee'heart.'

'I'll bet. Mirror, mirror, on the wall . . .' his father said, and then his voice drifted.

David leaned over the bed. He kissed his father on the forehead. His flesh was hot and damp.

'Good night, Pop,' he said. 'I'll see you in the morning. Sleep well, okay?'

His father nodded and closed his eyes.

It suddenly occurred to David that he might never see him alive again.

He called home at seven-thirty and got the answering machine. Molly's cool voice: *I'm sorry, we can't come to the phone just now. Will you leave a message when you hear the beep?* He left word that he was going down to dinner and asked that she call him later tonight. He debated whether or not he would need a jacket for dinner, decided against it, and left the room. The fifteenth-floor corridor was empty. He rang for the elevator and waited. He could hear it whining down the shaft. The doors opened.

The British girl was standing against the far wall. Tonight, she was wearing white slacks, high-heeled sandals, and a shrieking-red blouse. Her blonde hair was loose. He stepped into the elevator.

'Good evening,' he said.

'Good evening,' she answered.

The elevator doors closed.

They rode in silence for a moment.

Then, suddenly and unexpectedly, she said, 'Wasn't that comical last night?'

'The empty dining room, do you mean?'

'Last Year at Marienbad,' she said, nodding.

Her voice was soft, well modulated, very English. She was wearing an Elsa Peretti heart on a gold chain around her neck. *I almost bought you a heart at Tiffany's*, he thought. There were freckles across the bridge of her nose. She had taken a bit too much sun today. Her cheeks and the tip of her nose were almost as bright as the blouse she wore. Her eyes, he noticed, were intensely green.

'I felt as if the Russians had dropped The Bomb,' she said, smiling, 'and no one had bothered to tell us. We were the last two people on earth, but we hadn't been informed.'

The elevator doors opened.

'Is this the lobby already?' she asked, surprised.

'Yes,' he said, and held his hand over the electric eye while she walked past him. He detected the faintest scent of mimosa.

'Well, good night,' she called over her shoulder.

'Good night,' he said.

At the front desk, he handed the clerk his key and then asked if there was a good restaurant close by. He did not want to eat in the hotel dining room again. The clerk told him there was a French restaurant on Collins Avenue, just a few blocks north, but he had never eaten there.

'Have you tried *our* restaurant, sir? They serve a nice veal parmesan.'

David thanked him and went out into the street.

The air was hot and humid; it smelled of fetid things rotting in the sun. The stretch of Collins Avenue along which he walked was lined with souvenir shops, lingerie shops, stores selling bathing suits and inflatable rubber rafts. He remembered floating inside his inner tube, the vast blue sky overhead. 'Watch out for

56

horseshoe crabs,' his Uncle Max used to say. He would have to call his Uncle Max. After the operation tomorrow, he thought. An Englishman wearing a white T-shirt and wrinkled blue shorts, brown walking shoes and white socks, strolled past, savoring Miami Beach. David *guessed* he was an Englishman. His wife wore wrinkled yellow shorts and a purple tube top. Their pudding-faced children were eating chocolate ice cream cones. He caught a cockney accent. *Lower-class Englishmen sitting on jackasses to have their photos taken*. He wondered how accurate the description of Clovelly had been. He and Molly had never made it to Clovelly, only one of the many places they never seemed to have made it to. How does it go by so fast? he wondered.

The restaurant was small and empty.

He took a table near a fish tank with three tropical fish in it. He watched the fish. In the kitchen, a radio was going. Frank Sinatra. He did not recognize the tune. A waiter came to the table.

'Would you care to see a menu, sir?' he asked.

'Yes, but first I'd like a drink. Canadian and soda, please,' he said.

'I'm sorry, sir, we don't have a liquor license,' the waiter said.

'Oh,' David said.

'Only wine and beer, sir.'

He debated leaving. He wanted a drink very badly. He had been wanting a drink ever since Kaplan told him they would be doing the operation tomorrow morning.

'Well, let me have a . . . do you have any Beaujolais?'

'Yes, sir.'

'A bottle of Beaujolais then. A half-bottle, if you have it.'

'I'm sorry, sir, we don't have Beaujolais in the half-bottle.'

'What *do* you have in the half-bottle?'

'Nothing, sir. We have only the full bottles, or you can order by the glass.'

'Let me have a full bottle then.'

'Yes, sir, a bottle of Beaujolais.'

'And I'll look at the menu, please.'

'Yes, sir.'

The waiter came back a few moments later. David was watching the fish in the tank.

'Shall I open it now, sir? Let it breathe a little?'

'Please,' David said. He didn't know you had to let Beaujolais breathe.

The waiter showed David the label on the bottle. David nodded. The waiter uncorked the bottle and poured wine into David's glass. He handed David a menu.

'The special tonight is seafood *marinîere*,' he said. 'That's catch of the day with shrimp and lobster, sautéed in a tomato sauce with garlic and shallots.'

'What's the catch of the day?' David asked.

'Red snapper.'

'Well, give me a minute to look this over.'

'Take all the time you need, sir,' the waiter said, and walked off.

David lifted the wineglass to his lips. He sipped at the wine. He raised his eyebrows. Nice, he thought. Not much body, but amusing nonetheless. And a trifle foxy. He smiled. They used to make a game of imitating wine mavens, he and Molly.

They walked, he and Molly, off the boardwalk and out into the side street where her hotel nested in a warren of similarly gray-shingled buildings. The storm clouds had blown far out to sea. The leaves were wet and brilliantly green after the storm. The streets were wet, too; they glistened and steamed in the sunshine. Everything smelled of summer. Her stride matched his. Long legs. High-heeled sandals clicking on the rain-washed pavement.

Her name was not Regan with an a, she told him, but Regen with an e. A harried Ellis Island customs official had mistaken the name of her grandparents' town for their surname and had then summarily shortened it to something that sounded more 'American.' Her grandparents had come from Regensburg, in the southern part of Germany, not far from Nuremberg. His shiksa was a Jewish-American Princess.

She took off her sandals and walked barefoot in the puddles alongside the curb. He put his arm around her waist. He could feel the heat of her body through the thin summer dress. She sidled away from him. His heart was beating so fast he thought he would collapse right there on the street. There were two old ladies in house-dresses sitting on the rickety porch of her hotel, rocking, looking out at the sunshine, rocking.

'Will I see you again?' he asked.

'Maybe,' she said.

'Tonight?'

'No, I'm busy tonight.' She looked at her watch. 'In fact, I have to get dressed. He's picking me up at six.'

'Early date,' he said.

'Well, what business is that of yours?' she said.

Typical, he thought. Why couldn't she have been a shiksa?

'How about tomorrow night?' he said.

'Well, why don't you call me in the morning?'

'What's your number?'

'Look it up. There's the name of the hotel,' she said, and gestured breezily over her shoulder.

He kissed her suddenly and impulsively. The two old ladies kept looking out at the sunshine, rocking.

She broke away from his embrace. 'Hey,' she said.

She was trembling. He could see her trembling. He wanted to kiss her again.

'Just . . .' she said.

Her green eyes met his.

'Take it easy, okay?' she said.

'Okay,' he said. 'I'll call you in the morning.'

'Okay,' she said.

'Have you decided yet, sir?' the waiter asked.

David looked up at him.

'No,' he said. 'Not yet.'

The phone was ringing.

He fumbled for the receiver in the dark and then turned on the bedside lamp.

'Hello?' he said.

'David?'

'Yes, hi.'

'I'm sorry, were you asleep?'

'That's okay.'

'I just got in. Is everything all right?'

'Where were you?'

'I went to a movie.' She paused. 'With Marcia.'

'Oh. Yeah.'

'Did I tell you?'

'Tell me what?'

59

'That I was going?'

'I don't remember.'

'How is he?'

'They're going to operate again tomorrow morning. See if they can find what . . . what's . . .'

'David?'

'"Yes?' He had almost said 'what's killing him.'

'Are you all right?'

'Yes, I'm fine.'

'Where'd you have dinner?'

'A little French place up the street.'

'I'm sorry I woke you, go back to sleep. Call me in the morning, will you? After the operation. What time will they . . .?'

'First thing.'

'David? Are you sure you're all right?'

'I'm fine. Really. The air conditioning's on the fritz, but aside from that . . .'

'You poor thing,' she said.

'I'll call you in the morning.'

'Good night. I'm sorry I woke you.'

'Good night,' he said.

He lay wide awake, looking up at the ceiling.

He had left the drapes and the window open again, and the lights from his own hotel and the surrounding hotels cast a glow that illuminated the window frame. The window frame was a giant rectangle of light on the southern wall. To the east was the ocean; he could hear its rumble. To the west was the hospital, where his father was sleeping now, he hoped, before an operation tomorrow morning that had only a 50 percent chance of survival as its hidden clause. *Caveat emptor*, he thought.

What time is it, anyway? he wondered. He pressed the little button on his digital watch, illuminating the dial. Eleven forty-seven. It was never a quarter to eleven anymore. It was always either eleven forty-four or eleven forty-six or eleven forty-seven, but never eleven forty-five, never a quarter to eleven. Digital watches, he thought. Can anybody tell time anymore? She had called – what, five minutes ago? Just got back from the movies. Went with Marcia. Who the hell was Marcia?

60

He tried to think who Marcia might be. He could not think of anyone named Marcia.

That summer at Rockaway, he had not waited till morning to call her. He was sharing a rented room with a dental student who had found a girl with whom he spent virtually all of his days and nights. David was alone most of the time, in a seedy room with sticky sheets. He called Molly at ten o'clock and got no answer. He called her again at eleven, and again at midnight.

'Hello?' she said.

'Molly?'

'Yes?'

'It's David.'

'Oh. Hi.'

'How was your date?'

'Well,' she said, 'what business is that of yours?'

Goddamn Jewish-American Princess, he thought.

'How about tomorrow night?' he said.

'I told you to call me in the morning.'

'Why? How's the morning going to be different from tonight?'

'Well,' she said again, 'what business is that of yours?'

'How long will you be here in Rockaway?' he asked.

'Till Sunday. I'm going back Sunday.'

'Back where?'

'To New York.'

'Where do you live in New York?'

'Well, look it up,' she said. 'I'm in the book.' She hesitated. 'You really shook me up, you know,' she said.

'What do you mean?'

'Kissing me like that. I could hardly find my key. It took me ten minutes' fumbling in my bag to find my key.'

'Well, that's good, isn't it?'

'I'm not so sure it's good.'

'What are you wearing?' he asked.

'What?'

'What are you wearing?'

'I just got home. I'm still in my dress.'

'Do you have shoes on?'

'No.'

'Put on your shoes, and come on over. I'm all alone here.'

'No, I don't think that would be such a good idea.'

'Why not?'

'I don't need a reason,' she said.

'Then why don't I come there?'

'No.'

'It seems silly, you being there alone and me being here alone.'

'Well, I don't think it's so silly.'

'Come on over,' he said.

'No.'

'Come on.'

'No Really, now. No. Call me in the morning, okay? You really shook me up,' she said.

There was a small click on the line.

He fell asleep at last.

He awoke shivering in the middle of the night.

The air conditioning had been fixed, apparently, and the room was icy cold. He snapped on the bedside lamp, got out of bed, turned on the overhead light, and went to the thermostat. The room temperature was sixty-four degrees. He raised the thermostat setting and then searched the closet shelf for another blanket. He opened all the dresser drawers searching for another blanket. Finally, he took the quilted bedspread from the chair over which he'd draped it and threw it on the bed over the single blanket. He closed the window. He drew the drapes. Even with the drapes and the window closed, he could hear the sound of the crashing sea. He turned off all the lights again and got into bed. He was still cold.

He suddenly had to go to the bathroom.

He turned on the bedside lamp, got out of bed again, and crossed the room. The attack of diarrhea was immediate and surprising. He tried to think what he could have eaten to have caused such a sudden attack. The bland veal chop? The side order of broccoli? He thought of his father's severed intestines, his father's body fluids seeping along a soiled tube into a soiled bag.

He wiped himself several times, kept wiping himself until there was no trace of stain on the toilet tissue.

Then he went back to bed.

62

Wednesday

He awakened with a start.

He did not know where he was for a moment. The room came slowly into focus. The air conditioner was humming, the drapes were drawn, only a thin vertical line of sunlight gleamed where the separate halves met. He looked at his watch. Eleven minutes past ten! He had forgotten to leave a wake-up call, had forgotten as well to set the little alarm on his watch.

He got out of bed and went to the drapes. He fumbled in the near-gloom until he found the drawstrings and then yanked the drapes open. Sunlight splashed into the room. He blinked against it. He went to the dresser, took a cigarette from the package there, picked up his lighter, and went into the bathroom. Sitting on the bowl, he lit the cigarette. He sat smoking and peeing. The diarrhea seemed to be gone. Better get cracking, he thought. He tore a piece of toilet tissue from the roll, wiped the end of his penis with it, and then stood up. He threw the cigarette into the bowl and then flushed the toilet. He looked at himself in the mirror. He looked about the same as he had yesterday. No more surprises, he thought. For the longest time, whenever he'd looked at himself in the mirror, he'd seen a thirty-seven-year-old man. He had liked being thirty-seven. Now he looked fifty. He would not be fifty till August, but he had stopped thinking of himself as forty-nine on New Year's Eve.

Naked, he went into the bedroom and sat on the edge of the bed. He dialed twenty-one for room service and ordered an orange juice, a cup of coffee, and a toasted English muffin. *You should eat too*, Mrs. Daniels had said. *To keep your strength up*. Mrs. Daniels, whose husband had just undergone open-heart surgery for the second time and was now refusing to eat. *Keep your strength up*. He fished in his wallet for the hospital's number, dialed nine for an outside line, and then dialed the number directly.

'St. Mary's Hospital,' a woman's voice said.

'I'd like some information on a patient, please,' he said.

'The patient's name?'

'Morris Weber.'

'One moment, please.'

He waited.

'Mr. Weber is in critical condition,' the voice said.

'Yes, I know that, but he was supposed to go into surgery this morning, and I wanted to know . . .'

'One moment, please.'

He waited.

'I have no indication of that, sir.'

'Of what?'

'Of any surgery this morning.'

'Well, is there any way you can check? I simply want to know how the operation . . .'

'I'm sorry, sir, there's nothing on the computer except that he's in Intensive Care.'

'Thank you,' David said.

He lit another cigarette, looked for the slip of paper on which he had written Kaplan's number, and then dialed it. He got the answering service again, a pleasant-voiced woman who said she would give Dr. Kaplan his message and would ask him to call back as soon as possible.

'I want to know how the operation went,' David said.

'Yes, Mr. Weber, I'll give him that information.'

'Thank you.'

He put the receiver back on the cradle. The phone rang while his hand was still on the receiver, startling him. He picked it up at once.

'Hello?'

'David, it's me.'

'Hi, Molly.'

'I thought you'd have called by now. I was beginning to get worried.'

'I overslept.'

'How is he?'

'I don't know yet. I'm waiting for the doctor to call back now.'

'Did you call the hospital?'

'Yes, but their computer doesn't show anything.'

'What do you mean?'

'About how the operation went.'

'Did you ask if he was in Recovery Room?'

'No.'

65

'Why didn't you?'

'Because . . . honey, the goddamn computer didn't *show* anything!'

There was a silence on the line.

'All right,' Molly said, 'call me when you know something.'

'I will.' He paused. 'Molly, I'm sorry I . . .'

'I know you're upset,' she said, and hung up abruptly.

He stared at the receiver. This is the way it started, he thought. On the telephone. This is the way it really started. Now she just hangs up. He slammed down the receiver. The entire phone shook, the bell vibrated. Well, I shouldn't have yelled at her, he thought. Still, you don't just hang up that way. In Rockaway that summer, she didn't hang up. That summer . . .

He could not wait for morning.

He had spoken to her at midnight and then had lain awake half the night, thinking of her, wondering why she couldn't have told him last night whether she'd be seeing him tonight; was she waiting for a call from the guy who'd dated her, was she hedging her bets, playing one off against the other? The sheets were sticky. Even naked, he was hot.

There were two beds in the basement room he was renting with the dental student who was never there. There was a paisley-printed curtain hanging over the small window; it tinted the sunlight red and stained the bed. The phone was beside the bed, between his bed and the one the dental student never slept in. There was a big dental chart on the wall opposite the bed; it showed the position and gave the name of every tooth in the human mouth. David knew the names of all the teeth by heart. It was only eight o'clock; was she still sleeping? He didn't want to wake her up, but neither did he want to chance missing her. Suppose she was an early riser? Suppose she was already out on the beach, taking the sun; she said she'd be leaving on Sunday, and this was already Wednesday; suppose he missed her?

He reached for the phone.

No, he thought, pulling back his hand, give her another fifteen minutes.

He could hear the ticking of his watch.

In the backyard outside, someone was taking a shower. He heard the person singing in the shower. There was no hot water out there; how could anyone possibly sing so loud in a cold shower? He could not tell whether the person was a man or a woman, the voice was that rotten. Naked, he got out of bed, walked across the room to the thrift-shop dresser, and turned on the small electric fan there. He was still hot. He went back to the bed. It was ten minutes past eight.

He waited.

The person outside stopped singing. He heard the shower being turned off. 'Good morning,' he heard a woman chirp. 'Good morning,' someone chirped back. He looked at his watch again. In the room upstairs, he heard the floorboards creak. The fat lady who wore the shorts and halter tops. The widow lady. She'd once asked his invisible dentist student roommate if he'd like to come in for a cup of coffee. She's placed her hand on his arm and said, 'My coffee is very good, I'm told.' The dental student declined the invitation; he had already met the redheaded dancer he was sleeping with. David was tempted to wander by the fat lady's room one day, see if she'd invite *him* in for some of her very good coffee. It had been *that* kind of summer.

He looked at his watch again.

Two more minutes, he thought.

He started reciting aloud the names of the teeth on the dental chart. He had gone through all of them in the lower jaw when he looked at his watch again. Okay, he thought, here we go. He picked up the slip of paper on which he'd written the phone number for the Seaview Hotel. His hand was shaking when he dialed the number.

'Seaview,' a voice said.

'Miss Regen, please,' he said.

'Who?'

'Molly Regen.'

'Just a second.'

He waited. His heart was pounding.

'Hello?'

God, he'd woken her up!

'Molly?'

'Yes?'

'It's me. David.'

'What time is it?' she said.

67

'Eight-fifteen,' he said.

'Oh,' she said. He heard her yawning. 'Sorry,' she said. 'I was asleep.'

'I'm sorry I woke you up.'

'That's okay,' she said.

'How are you?'

'Fine.'

'Listen, I'm really sorry I woke you up.'

'Well, that's okay.'

'Have you given any thought to tonight?'

'Tonight?'

'Yeah, I . . . uh . . . you remember I asked you if you might like to go out with me tonight?'

'Uh-huh.'

'So what do you think?'

'Well, it's early yet,' she said.

'Are you waiting for another call, is that it?'

'No.'

'Then what is it?'

'I just don't like to make decisions so early in the morning. I'm lying here in bed, I just woke up, you woke me up, I don't like to have to make a decision just yet.'

Goddamn snooty Princess, he thought.

'What are you wearing?' he said.

'Why?'

'I'm curious.'

'A T-shirt,' she said. 'And panties.'

'What kind of panties?'

'Bikinis.'

'What color?'

'Blue.'

There was a silence on the line.

'Why don't you take them off?' he said.

'Okay,' she said, 'just a sec.'

He heard the telephone clattering on a hard surface. Jesus! he thought. Jesus, she's actually taking off her panties! He waited. His heart raced, his heart was going to explode.

'Okay,' she said, 'they're off.'

'Uh-huh,' he said.

There was another silence.

'So . . . uh . . . what've you got on now?' he asked. 'Just the T-shirt?'

'Yes.'

'What kind of T-shirt is it?'

'Just a T-shirt. A white T-shirt.'

'Does it have any lettering on it?'

'Yes.'

'What does it say?'

'It says "WQXR." '

'You listen to WQXR, huh?'

'Yes.'

'You like classical music, huh?'

'Is that why you asked me take off my panties? To discuss music?'

'Well, no, I . . .'

There was another silence.

'Are you blond?' he asked.

'Yes.'

'I mean . . .'

'I know what you mean. I'm blond.'

'What are you doing now?' he asked.

'Just lying here.'

'On your back?'

'Yes.'

'Are your legs spread?'

'No.'

'Spread them.'

'Okay,' she said.

'Are they spread now?'

'Yes.'

'Why don't you put your hand down there?'

'Down where?'

'You know. Down there.'

'Tell me where.'

'Between your legs,' he said.

'Where between my legs? Tell me.'

'On your . . .'

He hesitated, panicking.

69

'On my what?' she said.

'Your cunt,' he said.

'Okay,' she said.

There was another silence, longer this time.

'Are you . . . did you . . . are you . . is your hand there now?' he asked.

'Yes.'

'Are you wet?'

'Yes.' She paused. 'What are *you* wearing?' she asked.

'Nothing,' he said.

'You're naked?' she said.

'Yes.'

'Are you on your back?'

'Yes.'

'Do you have an erection?'

'Yes.'

'Is it just sticking up there?'

'Yes.'

'Just sticking up there big and hard?'

'Yes.'

'Grab hold of it,' she said.

He thought in those next ten delirious minutes, he thought, Jesus, this is impossible, she *can't* be Jewish! Her image filled his mind, the first glimpse he'd had of her, Molly turning from the sea, materializing in sunlight, stepping out of sunlight, the sea wind lifting her skirt over incredibly long legs, her hand moving to flatten it, that beautiful face with its upturned Irish nose and rampant freckles (but she's *Jewish*!), the wide mouth and sea-green eyes, the *miracle* of her! And imagined her now, as she was now, as they whispered urgently to each other now, visualized her at the Seaview Hotel on a bed in a room he had never seen, conjured her on her back with her legs spread and her hand buried in her crotch (She was using just one finger, she told him, she was getting *very* wet now), the long slender length of her on a tangled sheet, her blond hair loose on the pillow, her eyes closed (My eyes are closed, she whispered), freckles on her breasts (Do you have freckles on your breasts? he asked. Lots, she said), nipples poking the thin fabric of the white T-shirt (Are your nipples hard? he asked. Very, she said), hard nipples

70

puckering the WQXR (Are they big? he asked. My nipples? she asked. Your tits, he said. They're ample, she said), saw her writhing on that bed, crisp golden-blond moist cunt hair curling around her frantic fingers (I want to kiss your cunt, he said. Yes, I want you to, she said), his Yiddishe Shiksa, he could not believe what was happening, could not believe he had found her, could not believe the miracle of her (I'm very close, she said, and then without prompting said, Fuck me, David, oh fuck me, David, *fuck* me!).

So long ago, he thought.

What happened, Molly? What happened to the miracle?

When did we become obsolete?

He went into the bathroom to shower, worrying that he might not hear the phone if Kaplan called.

'I was waiting for you by the Emergency Room,' Bessie said.

'I came in the main entrance,' he said.

'Do you come by taxi?'

'Yes.'

'It's shorter if they drop you by the Emergency Room.'

'Well,' David said.

'What does it cost, the taxi?'

'I don't know.'

'You don't know what it *costs*?'

'Two-fifty, something like that.'

'You should have them drop you by the Emergency Room. It's shorter.'

David nodded. He did not want to be talking to Bessie about taxi fares; he did not want to be talking to her about *anything*, in fact. He wanted to know only whether or not his father had survived the operation. They were walking swiftly down the third-floor corridor; or, rather, *he* was walking swiftly, and Bessie was trying to keep up. He did not want the encumbrance of an old woman at his side. He wanted to get to the nurses' desk in the Intensive Care Unit and find out how his father was. He looked at his watch. It was five minutes to eleven. As they passed the open door to the waiting room, he said, 'Wait for me, here, I'll be right back.'

He walked directly to the door at the end of the hall and

71

stepped into the unit. He did not think anyone would chastise him for breaking in here five minutes earlier than he was supposed to. Besides, he didn't care. A strange nurse was standing behind the desk. She looked Oriental. Chinese or Japanese, he couldn't tell which. Maybe Vietnamese. That was probably it.

'I'm David Weber,' he said. 'How's my father?'

'Fine,' the nurse said, and glanced up at the clock.

'When did he get back from surgery?' David asked.

'He didn't go to surgery,' the nurse said.

'What do you mean?'

'Have you talked to Dr. Kaplan?'

'No.'

'You'd better talk to Dr. Kaplan.'

'Why? What's the matter?'

'He should be here in a little while, he called ten minutes ago. You can talk to him.'

'Where's my father now?'

'In his room.'

'The same room?'

'Number five,' the nurse said, and nodded.

He went into the room without asking permission. The clock on the wall opposite his father's bed read four minutes to eleven. His father was staring at the wall. There seemed to be more tubes attached to him, was that possible? A tube running under the sheet, alongside the one that went to the stained bag. Another tube hanging on a stand, the end of it taped to his left arm, the tube on his right arm still feeding him his three thousand calories a day. His father kept staring at the wall.

'Hello, Pop,' he said.

'Yeah, hello,' his father said. 'What's going on here?'

'What do you mean?'

'They shaved me, they washed me, they told me I'm going down for an operation, and all of a sudden I'm sitting here twiddling my thumbs. What's going on?'

'I don't know, Pop.'

'So who *does* know?'

'I called Dr. Kaplan early this morning, but he never returned my call.'

'Of course not, his father said, nodding. 'President of the United States.'

'He should be here soon, I'll find out then.'

'Got me all ready,' his father said, 'and then nothing happened.'

'Well, there must be a reason,' David said.

'The reason is they don't know what they're doing. Where's Bessie?'

'Outside.'

'Why isn't she inside? What's she doing outside?'

'Pop, I didn't learn until a minute ago that you didn't have the operation.'

'They don't tell you anything around here,' his father said, nodding. 'Go get her, would you, please?'

When Bessie came into the room, his father said, 'Hello, kiddo.'

'Hello, Morris,' she said, and went to the bed and kissed him on the cheek.

'Did you bring the scissors?' he asked.

'Oh, Morris dear,' she said, 'I forgot.'

'My nails are getting like Fu Manchu's,' his father said. 'Many man swallow,' he added, 'but fu man chew.'

'He always makes jokes,' Bessie said fondly. 'I miss your jokes, Morris, you'd better hurry up and get out of here.'

'Are you still playing cards?' his father asked.

'Every night, Morris. But it's not the same without you.'

'Nobody to cheat them, huh?'

'You don't cheat, Morris.'

'I cheat,' he said.

The Vietnamese nurse came in.

'How are you doing, Mr. Weber?' she asked.

'Why'd they call off the operation?' his father said.

'You'll have to ask Dr. Kaplan.'

'I'm asking *you*. This is the Dragon Lady,' he said to David. 'Bane of my existence. Can't get a word out of her. Inscrutable.'

The nurse pulled back the sheet.

There was a tube sticking in his father's penis. They had shaved his pubic hair and the hair on his legs. He looked very white all over. His penis looked tiny, like a boy's, the tube sticking into its

73

opening, yellow fluid seeping along the tube, bubbling along the tube. David was embarrassed for a moment by the intimacy of the situation. Bessie standing beside the bed as the nurse exposed his father so completely, he himself seeing his father's genitals for the first time since he was a small boy undressing with him in the locker room at Jones Beach. His father's penis had looked so huge and threatening then, and he had turned away, somewhat frightened. He turned away now, too, but only because he was suddenly overcome by a wave of grief so keen that it brought quick, hot tears to his eyes. The sight of his father lying there helpless and vulnerable, the nurse checking the tube as if it were attached not to his father's very masculinity but to some *machine* instead, as impersonal as any of the machines around –

'Does that feel all right?' she asked.

'Oh, it feels just fine,' his father said. 'I've always wanted to pee in a tube.' Then, forgetting he had used the same line yesterday, he said, 'You'll be the urination of me.'

'He's a very funny man, your father,' the nurse said unsmilingly, and pulled up the sheet and walked out.

David went to the bed. He took his father's hand in his own.

'I'll find out about the operation,' he said. 'I'll let you know.'

The tears were still standing in his eyes. His father looked up at him. His own eyes widened when he saw the tears. A look of surprise crossed his face. The look said: What's this? Tears? He kept looking at David in surprise until finally David turned away and left the room, hoping he had not revealed too much, hoping he had not transmitted to his father the knowledge that he was dying. Bessie came out a moment later.

'He looks terrible,' she whispered.

'Excuse me,' Kaplan said, 'but is this your mother?'

'No, she's a friend,' David said.

Kaplan looked at him. Bessie nodded expectantly.

'She can hear anything you have to say,' David said. 'What happened? Why didn't you operate this morning?'

They were standing in the corridor outside the waiting room. A long table on wheels was in front of the window streaming sunlight. Kaplan was dressed more severely today. A dark blue suit, a white shirt, a blue tie. He looked like a mortician.

'Well, we planned to,' Kaplan said, 'but we thought it best to postpone. We discovered fluid in his lungs, and we . . .'

'His lungs? I thought his lungs were okay.'

'Well, they are, basically. The fluid is something we can take care of, we've put him on medication to clear it up. His kidneys were beginning to malfunction as well . . .'

'Is that why there's a tube in his penis?'

'No, that's to facilitate emptying of the bladder.'

He looked at Bessie. Bessie looked back at him, her blue eyes unflinching. 'It would have been foolish to risk an operation until the numbers were right,' Kaplan said.

'I'm not sure we should risk an operation at all,' David said.

'Is there a choice, Mr. Weber?'

David looked at him.

'I don't think there's a choice, Mr. Weber.'

'When will you do it?'

'Tomorrow afternoon. I expect the problems will be resolved by tomorrow morning. We normally operate on infected patients in the afternoon. We try to operate on any noninfected patients in the morning.'

'But you were supposed to operate on him this morning, weren't you?'

'Yes.'

'And he was infected, wasn't he? He's still infected, in fact.'

'Yes, but we ran into the problems I just told you about.'

It was all beginning to sound like gobbledygook.

'So now you won't be operating till tomorrow afternoon. When you normally operate on infected patients.'

'Once we resolve the problems,' Kaplan said, and nodded. 'And when we're sure his heart can . . .'

'His heart?' David said. 'What's wrong with his heart?'

'He's eighty-two years old, there's fluid in his lungs,' Kaplan said. 'We want to make sure he has the optimum chance of getting through this surgery.'

'You're certain you'll be able to resolve these problems?'

'I would hope so.'

'So what time will he go into surgery? Tomorrow, I mean.'

'Shortly after noon, I would expect. If the numbers are correct.'

75

'The numbers?'

'The readings on the heart and kidneys. I've been in constant touch with the cardiologist, and I plan to update the anesthesiologist before we operate. I can assure you we won't do anything foolhardy, Mr. Weber.'

David felt mildly chastised.

'We're trying, believe me,' Kaplan said.

'Then why is he still sick?' Bessie asked suddenly.

'I wish I could tell you that,' Kaplan said wearily. He turned to meet her challenging gaze. 'My own wife died three years ago. I'm a physician, a surgeon, I *still* don't know what killed her. There are things we don't know. I wish we *did* know them. But we don't.' He sighed heavily and turned to David again. 'I wish I could get him to walk out of here tomorrow, believe me. I wish I could wave a magic wand over him and cure him. I can't. I'm doing my best.'

'I'm sorry about your wife,' David said.

Kaplan nodded.

'Will I be able to see him tomorrow morning, before the operation?'

'Yes, you can come at eleven, the usual time.'

'Will *you* be here then?'

'Possibly.'

'I'll look for you.'

'Please do.'

'What shall I tell my father?'

'The truth,' Kaplan said.

They decided it would be a great gag to lie to his father.

Tell him only *afterward* that the Molly he would automatically assume was a Regan rather than Regen (a Webb rather than a Weber, so to speak), a blond, green-eyed, freckle-faced representative of the enemy camp (right in his own living room!), wasn't Irish at all but was instead as Jewish as the Torah. A man who could change an 'earn' to an 'urn' would be thoroughly delighted by a Regan-Regen *mishegoss* — unless he died of a heart attack the moment he was introduced to her, a danger that was greater as concerned David's mother, who on many an occasion had declared her intention to stick her head in

76

the oven if he ever brought home a shiksa. His father would roar with laughter once they revealed the truth to him.

He tipped at once.

'Why'd a nice Jewish girl like you change her name?' he asked.

So much for that.

David had been seeing her for little more than a month by then; this was the fall of 1957; he was just entering his second year at N.Y.U. Law. He was not yet in love with her. That would come later. On Valentine's Day. He often wondered whether his father's stamp of approval had been necessary before he could make the transition from merely *wanting* her day and night to actually *loving* her. 'I'll tell you something,' a fellow law student once said to him. 'Men aren't into love, they're into sex. If the sex is good, they kid themselves into thinking that's love. Women are just the opposite. *First* they fall in love, and *then* they translate that into sexuality. The prosecution rests.'

But Molly –

Oh God, Molly.

She approached sex with all the innocence and all the expertise of an idiot savant. There was nothing she was unwilling to try, nothing she denied him. He asked her once if she thought about sex often, and she replied, 'Yes, all the time.' He had never known anyone like her; her appetite was so overwhelming it frightened him sometimes. He once wondered, aloud, if he had stumbled across his first real-live nymphomaniac, and Molly said, 'Nymphos don't come, David.' They made love either in his apartment on Christopher Street, six blocks from the school, or else in her smaller apartment on First Avenue, near the hospital. Often, when they were apart – even if they'd seen each other only minutes earlier – he phoned her and they masturbated the way they had that first time ('The Regen-Weber Phone Phuck,' she called it). She confessed to having begun masturbating at the age of ten, said she used to do it with a book open on her lap while her teacher prattled on about geography. That was why she didn't know where North Carolina was. She had masturbated her way clear across the United States of America, north and south, east and west. 'I also masturbated my way through civics, history, geometry, and biology – *especially* biology. I *love* masturbating, what's wrong with it?'

David could see nothing wrong with it and often encouraged her to do it in his presence. She did so eagerly and without any sense of shame or self-consciousness, slipping her panties off, spreading her legs for him ('I love you to watch me'), touching herself gently at first and then more vigorously and at last ferociously, writhing on the bed, her skirt above her waist, her legs finally closing tight around her wildly rotating hand and her violent orgasm. He once bought her a pair of red crotchless panties and asked her to put them on ('Where'd you *get* these: God, I feel so *open*!'), and she sat on a chair opposite him and, anticipating his request, placed her hand between her legs and brought herself to fitful climax within minutes, asking him seconds later to fuck her with the panties on, 'Stick that big cock in me and grab my ass, David, with me all open in these panties.'

On another occasion, he bought a vibrator for her and told her he was interviewing applicants for saleswomen to sell the 'marital aid' on a door-to-door basis, demonstrating its pleasures to any prospective customer, the sole restriction being that he could not possibly hire anyone who herself succumbed to the product's temptations. 'Oh, I get it,' she said at once, 'I'm not allowed to come, right? I don't get the job if I come.' She stood before him holding her skirt above her waist – she was wearing her nurse's uniform that day, crisply starched and white, long white stockings, white garter belt and panties – and switched on the eight-inch-long device, and became at once a shy and inexperienced virgin with a dangerous toy, rubbing the pulsating cock-shaped machine over the nylon of the white panties, and then sliding it beneath the lace-trimmed leghole ('Wow, this is really something!'), releasing her skirt for a moment to step out of the panties, and standing spread-legged before him again, one hand clutched into the bunched skirt, the other manipulating the vibrator, pulling it away each time she felt close to orgasm ('I can't *stand* it!'), and finally thrusting the entire pulsating shaft inside her, head thrown back, hips thrust forward, widespread legs quivering ('Oh, my *God*, it's like a thunderstorm!').

She called him once from the nurses' station at New York Hospital. It was three o'clock in the morning; she was working the night shift. 'I'm sitting here with a clipboard on my lap,' she whispered, 'covering my hand. The head nurse is six feet away

78

from me, across the room, half-asleep. Tell me what you'd like to do to me.' Masturbation was virtually the foundation stone of their relationship, a sexual act that achieved the status of tradition from that very first morning in Rockaway, when she'd immediately responded, 'Okay, just a sec,' to his suggestion that she take off her panties. She once rode in a taxi from her apartment to his without any panties on. 'I wanted to be wet when I got here,' she explained. She went to restaurants with him and sat demurely eating with absolutely nothing on under her skirt. She became wildly passionate whenever they made love fully clothed, she wearing everything but her panties – blouse, skirt, bra, garter belt, stockings, high-heeled shoes – he wearing trousers and shirt, 'Your big cock sticking out of your pants there,' she said, 'I *love* your cock!'

Whenever she slept in his apartment overnight (and she began doing this more and more frequently), she would fall asleep in his arms, cuddled against him, the firm flesh of her ass tight against him, rounded against him, and he would suddenly discover himself erect and would thrust into her from behind, amazed to find her wet. Whenever they made love, she moaned gutter words of lust and longing, a litany, stringing the words out without meaning, cock, fuck, give me, fuck, hard wet cunt cock, fuck me, cockcunt, fuck, give it, fuck, fuck me, fuck my cunt.

'I hate the word "cunt," ' she told him. 'I only use it because I know it excites men,' and quickly amended this to '*You*, I know it excites *you*.' They embarked on a search for a substitute noun. She detested either 'pussy' or 'box,' equally abhorred 'slit' (although 'lubricious slit' had grace and style, she thought), considered 'snatch' a good possibility and enthusiastically accepted 'quim,' which he suggested as a last resort – 'My quivering, quaking quim,' she said, and clapped her hands together in delight. He told her he wanted to fuck her cunt ('My quim,' she corrected), her asshole, her armpit, her earlobe, her nostril, the spaces between her toes, and she said, 'Yes, I want you to.' He entered her fore and aft, sideways, right-side up and upside down. He fucked her with her knees under her chin or her legs wrapped around him. He fucked her on her knees from behind; he fucked her on the bed, on the floor, in the bath-tub, or leaning over the sink. She straddled him facing him or with her

79

back to him, his hands fiercely clutching her ass. He loved her ass. The first time he entered her from behind, truly from behind, she said, 'Don't hurt me, David,' and then thrust herself deep onto his shaft moments after penetration and wriggled there and moaned her litany, bringing him to orgasm within seconds.

One night, she told him a story that infuriated him. She had been at a ski lodge with some married friends – this was only the year before – they had rented a lodge up in Vermont someplace; she didn't remember the name of the town, she was an idiot when it came to geography. The woman was six months pregnant; they were older than she was, the man must've been about twenty-nine or thirty. And they'd been drinking wine and lying before the fire, the pregnant wife on the couch and her husband lying alongside the couch, just beneath her, on the rug, you know, on the floor. And Molly was on the other side of the fireplace, also lying on the floor, on a bearskin rug they had there on the floor.

The wife fell asleep.

The fire was still going.

Molly almost fell asleep herself.

Then she heard a kind of moaning sound from across the room where the husband was lying, you know, and she opened her eyes and looked across at him, and he had his cock in his hand and he was masturbating. She watched him masturbating. And then she lifted her skirt and stuck her hand inside her panties, and *she* began masturbating, too. The two of them were six feet apart from each other, the fire crackling and spitting in the fireplace between them, and they kept looking at each other and masturbating. She watched him coming, she saw his cock spurting. They never said a word to each other; he never made a move to come over to her where she was lying on the bearskin rug across the room. And the next morning it was as if nothing had happened. Everybody went about his or her business as usual. But it was the best orgasm Molly had ever had in her life.

'Come here,' he said.

'Are you angry?' she said.

'Yes.'

'What are you going to do? Spank me?'

'Yes,' he said.

80

'I want you to,' she said.

She lay obediently across his knees. Her yanked up her skirt and pulled her panties down onto her thighs. Her legs were trembling slightly. He was suddenly very hard. He raised his hand, hesitated a moment (she trembled again), and then brought it down sharply. She moaned. He slapped her again, harder this time. And again. She lifted her buttocks to him, anticipating each slap.

'My handprints are all over your ass,' he said.

'I want them there,' she said.

She thrilled him, she delighted him, she shocked him sometimes, but he had not yet told her he loved her. 'I love your mouth,' he said, 'I love your ass, I love your breasts, I love your cunt ('My quim, my quim'), your *quim*, I love every inch of you,' but he never said, 'I love *you*.' Perhaps he didn't love her; perhaps he loved only the sexual fantasy she represented. Or perhaps he was *afraid* of loving her. In any event, he never said the words, and she never asked him to. Nor did she reveal herself completely to him. Revealing herself, the complicated and very important self who was the true Molly Regen, would come only later, when she was more certain of him. For now, she was only what he wanted her to be – herself, to be sure, but not her *complete* self.

He asked her one night to dress for an orgy, to put on whatever she thought she might wear to an orgy if ever they were lucky enough to get invited to one. He had in mind black garter belt and panties, lacy black bra, perhaps a black chemise. He guessed he had in mind spread-eagling her on the bed, tying her hands and feet to the corner posts, vulnerable white thighs pale above the ribbed tops of her black nylons, tufts of blond hair curling around the edges of her panties – your average red-blooded American boy's fantasy of male dominance. She disappeared into the bathroom at the end of the hall and was gone for an hour. He lay on the bed, listening to the sounds of the traffic downstairs on First Avenue, visions of sugarplum fairies dancing in his head. When at last she came into the bedroom, she scared him half to death.

She had done herself up like a Charles Addams character. Her face was powdered a deadly white, her cheeks faintly rouged, lips glowing with lipstick dark as blood, eyelids shadowed with a green deeper than her eyes, their slant exaggerated by lines of mascara that swept upward from the outer edges, blond hair cascading on either side of her face. She was wearing a black cape he'd seen hanging in the closet of her living room, something she'd picked up in a thrift shop someplace and had never worn till that moment. A single ornate catch held it fastened at the throat.

As she walked into the room, the cape flared.

She was naked above the waist, her large nipples rouged with bright crimson, a knotted strand of pearls hanging between her freckled breasts. She was wearing black tights and black high-heeled pumps. She drew the cape closed around her and came to the bed and sat on the edge of it. She stared at him. She said, 'I won't take off the cape,' and he was suddenly erect.

She held the cape wrapped tightly around her while he kissed her blood-black lips and her closed eyes, kissed the hollow of her throat above the ornate catch, kissed her temples and her hair, her hands hidden somewhere deep in the folds of the garment, clutching the heavy wool to her. This was the beginning of September, the nights were still warm; a thin sheen of perspiration beaded her upper lip, but she would not remove the cape; she lay within it like a butterfly in a cocoon, unyielding, a chrysalis that finally opened black wings against the white sheet. Her breasts were covered with sweat. She had slashed open the crotch of the tights and rouged her nether lips, the black nylon framing in parentheses a dazzling female autumn, golden pubic hair and crimson vulva; he entered her trembling.

David's law student friend once posed the riddle, 'What's the difference between Jewish girls and cancer?' David pondered it: he had always loved riddles, especially his father's. At last he gave up. 'What?' he said. His friend grinned. 'Cancer sucks,' he said.

Wrong, David thought.

Molly's mouth was a thirsting abyss that engendered and enlarged, enhanced and engaged, employed and enjoined, enfolded and engulfed, englutted and engorged, enraptured and enravished, enfeebled and enslaved – he got carried away just *thinking* about her mouth!

'Where'd you learn how to do this?' he asked her.

'Well, what business is that of yours?' she said.

Before Molly, he had never particularly enjoyed being the

donor when it came to oral sex. But Molly – ah, Molly. He loved the *look* of her down there, the pale crisp pubic hair curling around her pink interior lips, fold upon secret fold, a mysterious female labyrinth. He loved the scent of her as well. 'Once you get past the smell, you've got it licked,' his law school friend said in a rare foray into Morris Weber territory. Wrong again, David thought. Gently parting her lips with his fingers, unfolding her secrets to him, bringing his mouth to where she waited expectantly open to him, the glistening coral moistness of her, the summery bouquet of her, the sight of her, the fragrance of her, caused his senses to reel, and he became confused and grew dizzy in her proximity and thought he could hear in the distant reaches of his memory the echo of a scratchy phonograph record on a windup machine, could see a lonely strand of endless beach, a single drifting cloud, could feel moist sea wind on his face.

She tasted of silver and salt.

He probed her with his tongue, her back arched to him, her hands resting lightly on either side of his face, her fingers tightening as he explored her more relentlessly and discovered at last ('Yes, that's it') the miniature pink replica of his own spiring tower beating against the tortured sheet, the damp salt air, the silvery splintered sunshine. Dizzily he lapped at her, devouring her, consuming her, licking her quivering, quaking quim, tonguing her to dissolving oblivion, her litany echoing in his ears, bigcock, suckcock, wetcunt, *eat* me! Fuck Freud and his vagina dentata, David thought; Freud never went down on Molly Regen.

David's father tipped to her sensuality as quickly as he had to her ethnicity. He became flirtatious, almost seductive. He had always played the fool for David's mother, and he played the fool for Molly as well at their first meeting in that fall of 1957. One of his father's specialties was the sophisticated pratfall. He would seemingly trip going up a flight of stairs, plunge headlong toward the steps, come up holding his hand to the famous Weber proboscis, and then smilingly pull the hand away to reveal his uninjured beak. Similarly, he would walk into walls or open doors, the hand coming up immediately to cover the supposedly violated nose, and then unmasking it (again the roguish smile) unbloodied and unbent. By David's count, he walked into six

83

doors before dinner that night. Molly giggled in delight each time. David was beginning to feel a little jealous.

His father punned unmercifully for her; she found *this* delightful, too, although David's own puns over the past month had left her seemingly unmoved. 'Would you please pass the bread, kiddo?' he said to David's mother, and then winked at Molly and said, 'I'll bet bakers make a lot of dough.' Molly giggled. As he ladled out the soup, he asked, 'Who was that ladle I saw you with last night?' and then immediately supplied, 'That was no ladle, that was my knife.' Molly giggled. David looked at her. In recounting the history of all his failed businesses (he made them all sound like enormous successes he had abandoned on whims), he said, 'I used to be in ladies' underpants, too; pulled down a hundred a week,' and Molly giggled, and David thought of her own underpants and wondered if she was wearing any. (Besides, his father had *never* been in ladies' underpants.)

His success with this mild sexual innuendo led to a bolder pun. Glancing covertly at Molly's low-cut blouse, ostensibly commenting on the giggle that erupted girlishly each time he delivered another of his little bon mots (which David had only heard a thousand times already), he said, 'I love your titters, Molly,' and then rolled his eyes heavenward as though he'd shocked even himself. Molly tittered. 'A little more breast?' his father asked, extending the platter of chicken to her, compounding the felony. 'You eat like a bird,' he said, and then immediately, 'You chicks are all the same,' priding himself on what he thought was youthful jargon, even though the expression had gone out of style fifteen years ago. 'You'll waist away to a shadow,' he said, and spelled 'waist' for her, lest she miss his cleverness, and then mysteriously added, 'The Shadow knows,' to which Molly inexplicably giggled even *before* he touched the Weber legacy with the tip of his finger and amended his earlier remark to 'The Shadow's nose,' eliciting yet *another* giggle – was she losing her *mind*? 'I once auditioned for a job as a r-r-r-radio an-an-announcer,' his father said, imitating a stutterer, 'b–but they t-t-turned me down. Anti-S-S-Semitism!' he said, and laughed triumphantly when Molly almost choked on her chicken.

He dubbed her 'The Shiksa' that night.

It would become a private and personal endearment over the years.

He wanted The Shiksa to have his ring when he died.

The first meeting between them took place in September of 1957; it was not until February of 1958 – on St. Valentine's Day, to be exact – that David knew he truly loved Molly. He wondered now if his father hadn't fallen in love with her first.

The people in the waiting room were becoming family.

Lacking the proximity of his own family, deprived of anyone who might empathize and sympathize, he began thinking of these people as kindly relatives who understood and shared the pain and the suspense. He could have been a young boy again, surrounded by his Uncle Max, his Aunt Anna, his cousin Shirley, his cousin Rebecca.

'He'll probably be wearing different clothes tomorrow,' Di Salvo said, and unconsciously stroked the mustache he was growing. 'He's finally going to bed. Tomorrow we'll see him waking up in the morning, the tuxedo'll be draped over the chair there.'

'Things take forever on the soaps,' Mrs. Daniels said. She was not wearing her wedgies today. She had on sandals instead. Her toenails were painted a bright red. She looked paler and thinner than she had yesterday. Her husband still refused to eat, she had told David, even when she and her daughter had tried feeding him.

'Usually on these soaps, the *girl* goes to bed with them,' Mrs. Horowitz said. Her face still looked flushed and excited. She was smoking a cigarette. 'They get right into bed together. You can see their shoulders, they're supposed to be naked.'

'Anything goes on television these days,' Mrs. Daniels' fat daughter Louise said. Her own daughter was with her today, a thin, dark little girl, eight or nine years old, David guessed. Her ballet recital yesterday had been a great success, but when Mrs. Horowitz asked her more about it, she turned away shyly and buried her face in her mother's bosom. 'I'll bet she has the biggest minnies in the entire world,' his cousin Shirley had said about their grandmother an eternity ago. He wondered where Shirley was now. The last he'd heard, she had divorced her second husband to run off with an insurance salesman.

'Hey, look, there he goes!' Di Salvo said. 'He's taking off his jacket!'

'He'll be taking off his *pants* next,' Mrs. Daniels' daughter said. 'They can do anything they want on television nowadays.' She was wearing dangling red earrings today; they spilled from her short platinum hair like bloody teardrops, matching the lipstick slash across her mouth.

'Now, he's lowering his suspenders,' Di Salvo said.

'He's keeping us in suspenders,' David said.

'That's very good,' Mrs. Daniels said. 'A smile every now and then, Mr. Weber. It can't hurt.'

'Neither could a little chicken soup,' Mrs. Horowitz said, and suddenly winked at David, as if certain he would understand her reference to the old joke. He nodded to her, acknowledging her surmise.

'I'll be happy to see the end of that tuxedo,' Di Salvo said.

'I'll be happy to see the end of this *room*,' Mrs. Horowitz said.

'What room *is* this, Mommy?' the little girl asked Louise.

'It's Intensive Care,' Louise said. 'The waiting room.'

'Is it the hospital?'

'It's the hospital.'

'Be quiet now, Charlene,' her grandmother said.

'She's not supposed to visit unless she's twelve, you know,' the pink lady said.

'She's not visiting,' Mrs. Daniels said. 'She's only sitting here. She won't go in, don't worry.'

'I'm only telling you what the rules are,' the pink lady said. She was a new one; David had never seen her before. She sat behind the desk, tapping a pencil.

'I know the rules better than you,' Mrs. Daniels said. 'I've been coming here half my life now, I think I know the rules.'

'It's better *I* should tell you than one of the nurses.'

'Let the nurses tell me,' Mrs. Daniels said.

'There are sick people here, you know,' the pink lady said, and Mrs. Horowitz suddenly burst out laughing. Di Salvo looked at the pink lady in surprise, as though he could not believe what she had just said. He began laughing, too. Even Mrs. Daniels, who a moment before had seemed ready to strangle the pink lady, started laughing. The pink lady kept tapping her pencil. Everyone in the waiting room was laughing now.

'What's funny?' the little girl asked.

'They think it's funny, darling,' the pink lady said.

'Don't call me "darling," ' the little girl said. 'My name is Charlene.'

The clock on the wall read one minute to se .

'So?' his father said. 'Is it still on, or what?'

'It's still on, Pop.'

'They're sure this time?'

'Positive.'

'What time tomorrow?'

'Shortly after noon.'

'Will you be here?'

'I'll be here even before you go up.'

'Let's hope I won't be going *down*,' his father said. 'For the ten-count.'

'Well, this isn't a prizefight,' David said, and smiled.

'We used to get in fights with the goyim all the time, Max and me,' his father said. 'Did you talk to your uncle? Does he even know I'm in the hospital?'

'I planned to call him tomorrow. After the operation.'

'Maybe you ought to call him tonight. Give him my final regards.'

'Come on, Pop, don't talk that way.'

'Tell him I said to keep his shoulder ducked. He'll know what I mean. Will you tell him that?'

'Yes, Pop.'

'Do you remember when Louis beat Schmeling? That Nazi? You were just a little kid.'

'I remember.'

'That was some fight.' His father paused. 'They have hard heads, niggers.'

David said nothing.

His father closed his eyes.

'Be a bigger fight than Louis ever had in his life,' he said. 'Tomorrow. When I go under the knife again.'

David looked at him.

87

'I'm scared to death,' his father said, and opened his eyes.

He took his father's hand between his own.

'No, don't be scared, Pop,' he said.

'I don't want to die on the table.'

'You won't. You're not going to die at *all*. They're going to find what's wrong, and you're going to be okay.'

'I hope so,' his father said.

'That's the way it'll be,' David said, and nodded. His father was staring at him. He forced himself to look directly into his father's eyes. 'You'll see.'

'You wouldn't kid a kidder, would you?' his father said.

'I'm telling you the truth.'

'Uh-huh.'

'I am, Pop.'

'Uh-huh.'

'I am.'

His father was silent for a moment. Then he said, 'Did you find that tax form for me?'

'What tax form?'

'The one you have to send in. What's it called?'

'What do you mean, Pop?'

'In April. When you pay your taxes.'

'The Ten-Forty, do you mean?'

'Yeah. Did you find it? The copy the accountant gave me?'

'Was I supposed to look for it?'

'Didn't I tell you to go find it?'

'No, Pop.'

'I can't remember if I paid it.'

'Well, don't worry about it. The IRS won't . . .'

'I usually pay them right on the dot, April fifteenth, but I can't remember now. If I paid it, there'll be a copy. The accountant gives me a copy, and I have the check Xeroxed at the bank. You go look for it, David.'

'Where, Pop?'

'My apartment. In the bedroom someplace. One of the drawers there. Bessie has the keys, ask her for the keys.'

'Okay, Pop.'

'I don't want to die with them thinking I didn't pay my taxes.'

'You're not going to die, Pop.'

'Can you get me a glass of water? They never give you any water here. You'd think it was the Sahara Desert here, you've got to beg for a drop of water.'

He went out into the corridor and asked the Vietnamese nurse for a glass of water. She gave him a plastic cup with a flexible straw in it. He carried it back into the room.

'Is it cold?' his father asked.

'It feels nice and cold.'

'Not too cold, is it?'

'No, just right, I think.'

'Because if it's *too* cold . . .' he started, and then shook his head.

'Do you want it now?'

'Yes, please.'

He held the bent straw to his father's lips. For the first time, he noticed that the inside of his father's mouth looked raw, almost excoriated. His father took the straw between his lips and began sucking on it before his lips were fully closed. There was the hissing sound of air.

'Just a second, Pop.'

He seated the straw more firmly between his father's lips.

'Okay?' he said.

His father nodded, inhaled on the straw, and then exhaled. The water in the cup bubbled.

'Try not to breathe out,' David said.

His father nodded.

'How's that?' David said. 'Okay?'

His father nodded again, and then turned his head away from the straw.

'Enough?'

'Yes,' his father said.

'You're sure you don't want anymore?'

'It was too cold. They either give you *pyok* water or water so cold it could freeze your belly. Who's out there, the Dragon Lady?'

'Yes,' David said.

'This is her idea of Chinese torture,' his father said. 'I'm surprised she isn't dripping it on my forehead.'

David smiled.

89

'He thinks I'm kidding, my son,' his father said.

'I'll put this on the sink,' David said. 'If you want more, just press your buzzer.'

'Sure. Press your buzzer, they'll all go out dancing. Nobody comes in here. You could press the buzzer till your finger wore out, nobody comes. They're too busy out there.'

His father was silent for a moment.

Then he said, 'Does The Shiksa know they're operating again tomorrow?'

'I haven't told her yet,' David said.

'I'm curious about what she'll say.'

'I'm sure she'll think it's for the best.'

'You think so, huh? You don't know Molly.'

'I'm sure it *is* for the best, Pop.'

'Because if they don't do it, I'll die anyway, right?'

'No, who told you that?'

'Who has to tell me? If a man gets to be eighty-two and he isn't his own best doctor, then he ought to go see a doctor.'

The clock on the wall read a quarter past seven. The pink lady had undoubtedly been intimidated by all the laughter at her expense; she was allowing the visitors a grace period. David felt he ought to say something more before his time was up. Well, I've got tomorrow morning, he thought. I'll tell him then. I'll see him before the operation and tell him then.

He did not know what he wanted to tell his father.

'Cat got your tongue?' his father said.

'I hope you know I love you,' David said.

'Why wouldn't I know that?' his father said.

Maybe because I'm not sure myself, David thought.

The British girl was sitting in the lobby when he came back from dinner that night. She was reading a paperback book, sitting in one of the brocaded chairs that faced the registration desk. Her hair was loose again. A small sprig of flowers was fastened to the right side of her head, tiny blue flowers against the blond hair. She glanced up as he passed her.

'Hello again,' she said.

'Hello there.'

90

She closed the book. He hesitated a moment, and then took the chair opposite hers.

'How are you?' he asked.

'Fine, thanks. And you?'

'Fine.'

He reached into his pocket, found his cigarettes and offered her one.

'No, thank you, I don't smoke,' she said.

He thumbed his lighter into flame and suddenly remembered one of his father's puns. Smiling, he lit the cigarette and realized the girl was watching him.

'Yes?' she said.

'I was just thinking of something funny,' he said.

'Share it with me, won't you?'

'I'm not sure you'd appreciate it.'

'Give it a try.'

'Well, when I was a boy, my father would allow me to snip off the end of his cigar for him – he had one of those little cigar cutters, you know – and then he'd put the cigar in his mouth and hand me his lighter, and while I lit the cigar for him, he'd say, "And now for the lighter side of the news." '

The girl smiled.

'I warned you,' he said.

They were silent for a moment.

'Are you here on vacation?' he asked.

'Heavens, no,' she said. 'Oh, *do* forgive me. Are *you*?'

'No,' he said.

'Are you here on business then?' she asked.

'No.'

'Or would you rather not say? You're not one of those horrid drug dealers, are you?'

'No, no,' he said, and smiled. 'My father's in the hospital here.'

'I'm so sorry,' she said.

'Well, he'll be okay.'

'I'm sure.'

There was another silence.

'Are *you* here on business?' he asked.

'Yes,' she said, and pulled a face. 'Unfortunately.'

91

'What sort of work do you do?'

'I'm a travel rep.'

'What does a travel rep do?'

'Just at the moment, I'm preparing the way for a thundering herd that should arrive next Friday. Arranging all the nightclub tours, and the expeditions to safari parks, and the boat rides, and the excursions, and so forth.' She shrugged. 'Sunniworld's five-hundred-pound, all-inclusive wonderful week of fun and adventure in Miami Beach, Florida.'

'Sounds interesting,' he said.

'It's really rather tedious,' she said. 'I shouldn't even *be* here, actually, except that we were obliged to sack our on-the-spot rep. I'm filling in, so to speak. Just when I was about to leave on holiday myself.'

'That's a pity,' David said.

'Really,' she said. 'Miami Beach rather than Marbella.' She smiled. 'Have you ever been to Spain?'

'Never.'

'It's lovely. And cheap as dirt. Well, perhaps not so much so now, with the pound in such bad straits again. Of course, the pound doesn't matter all that much to you, does it?'

'Not really.'

'My name is Hillary Watkins, by the way,' she said, and extended her hand. The fingernails were long and painted a very bright red. He took her hand.

'David Weber,' he said.

'Pleasure to meet you.' She paused. 'What do *you* do?' she asked. 'When you're not in Miami, that is.'

'I'm a lawyer.'

'Ah? Where?'

'New York.'

'I *adore* that city,' she said.

'I prefer London.'

'Do you *really*? You're not serious! Are you from New York originally?'

'Born and raised there. Lived there all my life.'

'Perhaps it's paled for you then.'

'Perhaps.'

They both fell silent again. She looked at her watch.

'I think I'll have a drink before I turn in,' David said. 'Would you care to join me?'

'Thank you, no, I have to get an early start tomorrow.'

She picked up her paperback.

They both stood up.

'Any good?' he asked.

'The book? A bit raunchy,' she said, and smiled. 'Well, good night,' she said, 'it was nice talking to you.'

'Good night, Hillary.'

'David,' she said, and extended her hand.

They shook hands.

'Good night,' she said again.

He watched her as she walked to the elevators. Before the doors closed on her, she smiled again and waved at him.

He had three drinks in the disco bar, and then went back up to the lobby and rang for the elevator. He felt a bit woozy. Hell with it, he thought. The elevator arrived, and he got into it and pressed the button for the fifteenth floor. The elevator always stopped on the twelfth floor. There was never anyone waiting there when the doors opened. They were doing renovations on the twelfth floor. The workmen probably had the elevator fixed somehow so it would stop there automatically. It stopped there now. The doors closed again. He pressed the button for fifteen again. The fifteenth-floor corridor was empty. He walked down to his room, unlocked the door, took off his shirt, and threw it onto the chair near the window. He would have to call Molly. He had put off calling her again today, but he knew she'd be waiting. And probably angry that he hadn't called sooner. Sighing, he dialed eight for long distance and then direct-dialed the number of New York. He looked at his watch. It was almost nine-thirty. She picked up the phone on the third ring.

'Hello?'

'Molly, it's me.'

'Is everything all right?' she said at once.

'Yes, fine.'

'How'd the operation . . .?'

'They didn't do it today.'

'Why not?'

He explained the problems to her. He told her they would be

operating shortly after noon tomorrow. She listened without saying a word. Molly Regen, R.N., he thought. When he finished, she said, 'Why didn't you call me sooner?' She paused. 'Have you been drinking?'

'Yes,' he said.

'I wish you . . . have you had dinner yet?'

'Yes. You sound like Mrs. Daniels,' he said.

'Who's Mrs. Daniels?'

'A woman at the hospital. Her husband won't eat.'

'I want you to call me as soon as you know tomorrow. Will you promise me that?'

'I promise.'

'Are you sure you don't want me to come down there?'

'What would you do down here?' he said.

'I don't think you should be going through this alone.'

'I'm managing,' he said. Where the hell were you the *last* time I needed you? he thought. The last *two* times, he thought. 'I'll be fine,' he said, 'don't worry.'

'Well, all right, then,' she said. She sounded relieved.

There was a long pause on the line.

'Do you think he's going to die?' she asked.

'Yes,' he said without hesitation.

'Are you in favor of this operation?'

'Yes, I think so.'   .

'I'm not,' she said.

'Well . . .'

'Why don't they just let him die in peace?' she said.

He sighed heavily. 'I'll call you tomorrow,' he said.

'Please,' she said, and hung up.

He lowered the receiver gently onto the cradle and stretched out on the bed. His father had known what her reaction would be. Maybe his father knew her best, after all. *You don't know Molly*, his father had said.

Ah, but I *do* know her, he thought. Or *believed* that I knew her, or at least was *starting* to know her. As far back as the beginning . . . well, almost the beginning. Her apartment that day, the clutter of packed cartons and things waiting to be packed into yet more cartons. It was very cold, wasn't it? I'm sure it was cold. I'm forgetting. It *had* to be cold in February, didn't it? It was cold, I'm sure of that. We were both working in overcoats, yes. Molly was wearing a bright green muffler around her throat, a matching green watch cap on her head, green woolen gloves. Her blond hair was pulled back into a ponytail. Our breaths plumed from our mouths as we worked. It was already 8:00 A.M., and the moving van was coming at nine. Molly was moving.

I'll *never* forget, he thought.

They talked as they worked. Molly directed him to her dishes and cups and saucers. He wrapped each of the items in newspaper. She packed them into the cartons. She told him the move from First Avenue to York would bring her closer to the hospital. Besides, she'd be able to see the East River from the new apartment. She liked the sounds on the river, she said. All those boats, maybe even ships coming from faraway places over the sea. He told her he hadn't forgotten it was St. Valentine's Day. In fact, he'd been walking past Tiffany's yesterday and had seen a fat gold heart in the window and almost bought it for her. 'For Valentine's Day,' he said, and smiled.

'Almost?' she said.

'I didn't have any money with me, he said. 'It cost two hundred dollars.'

'Almost?' she said again.

'I'll pick up something later today,' he said.

'Why is it always *almost*?' she said, and suddenly she was weeping. She stood in the middle of the kitchen floor, cartons and dishes and saucers and cups everywhere around her, stood in her long dark overcoat, wearing the green watch cap and muffler, and she covered her face with her hands and wept into her green woolen gloves. 'All anybody does is *take* from me,' she said, weeping.

He was crouched near one of the cartons, a newspaper-wrapped saucer in his hand. He looked at her weeping in the center of the kitchen and wondered what she wanted from him. A lousy little heart from Tiffany's? I'll buy the heart this afternoon, he thought. I'll run over there and buy it. He got to his feet. He put down the saucer. He tried to take her in his arms.

'No, don't,' she said.

'Molly . . .'

'Please,' she said, 'I don't care, really, I don't. I know you don't love me, it doesn't matter whether you buy me presents or not.'

'But I do love you,' he said. It was the first time he'd ever said the words to her.

'No, you don't. Oh, please, David, you love *fucking* me is all, please.'

'Molly . . .'

'I'm a person,' she said. She wiped one gloved hand under her runny nose, and shook her head and looked at her watch. 'I have to pack,' she said, 'I have to get out of here.'

'I know you're a person,' he said.

'No, you don't! You think I'm a quivering, quaking *quim* is all. I don't care, really, I don't. But, Jesus, isn't *anyone* ever going to see me for what I am? Isn't anyone ever going to treat me like somebody?' she said, and burst into fresh tears.

'I know you're somebody,' he said.

'Who am I then?' she said, sobbing.

'Someone I love.'

'That isn't true.'

'I do love you, Molly.'

'Please,' she said, sobbing. 'When I was in Bloomingdale's the other day, looking for your Valentine present . . .'

'Molly, I'm sorry, really. I'll go buy the heart this afternoon.'

'Who needs the heart?' she said. 'If you *almost* bought it, then you *didn't* buy it, so what difference does it make? That's not why I'm telling you about Bloomingdale's, you're not even *listening* to me.'

'I'm listening, Molly.'

'There was this girl there?' she said, sobbing. 'And she was trying on dresses? And her mother was looking them over? She'd come out and show the dresses to her mother? And she came out in one dress and showed it to her mother, and she said, "Mom, make believe I'm *somebody*. How do I look?" And I burst into tears right there in the store because nobody in the world knows *I'm* somebody, either.'

She began crying more bitterly, her face in her gloved hands. He watched her helplessly. Whatever had gone before, whatever they had done together in bed, seemed suddenly unimportant, an act even monkeys in the zoo could perform with expertise. She had given him her body completely, and he had taken it

96

unashamedly, greedily accepting her extravagant gift, taking from her with both hands, and giving nothing but his own lust in return. Now, here in this cluttered kitchen, she was giving him more than she had ever given him before. She was daring to expose herself. She was trusting him with her tears.

He turned wordlessly and left the apartment. He raced down the steps. He ran into the street. His bank was downtown in the Village. He had only eight dollars in his pocket, but he blew almost all of it on a taxi downtown. There was $512 in his account, all he'd been able to save from his monthly G.I. Bill checks. He withdrew all of it but five dollars. He took another taxi uptown. He found a flower shop a block from Molly's new apartment. He put $500 in cash on the counter and told the startled florist what he wanted.

Molly told him later that the first dozen roses were waiting outside the door to the new apartment when she got there at nine-thirty. The movers had not yet arrived. She picked up the roses in their pressed cardboard vase and opened the little envelope hanging there and looked at the card. It read, 'Molly, I love you.' No signature. She told him later that she'd hoped the roses were from him but that she was singularly unimpressed. A dozen red roses were *not* the same as a fat gold heart from Tiffany's. She unlocked the door and went into the empty apartment. She put the vase of roses on the kitchen counter top because her furniture wasn't there yet, and there was nothing else to put them on. The next dozen roses arrived at ten o'clock, a half-hour later. The same card. 'Molly, I love you.' She smiled. The movers arrived just about when the third dozen roses were delivered at ten-thirty. She rummaged in a carton she had marked GLASS and found *real* vases for all three dozen roses. She did not expect any more roses. She would have called him at his apartment to thank him, but she didn't yet have a phone. Besides, she wouldn't have been able to reach him; he was downstairs outside her building, watching for the delivery boy, making certain the roses kept coming.

She was telling the movers where to put her furniture when the fourth dozen roses arrived at eleven o'clock. She had run out of glass vases, so she left them in the cardboard vase. She told him later that she'd frankly hoped *this* batch would be the last of them.

But the roses kept coming. Every half-hour. The same card each time. 'Molly, I love you.' By one o'clock, when the movers finally left, there were seven dozen roses in the apartment and a boy standing at the front door with yet *another* dozen. By three o'clock, there were twelve dozen roses. When David walked into the apartment at five o'clock, there were sixteen dozen roses on the kitchen counter and sitting on top of unopened cartons and on all the tabletops and windowsills and even on the floor.

'Hi,' he said.

She ran into his arms.

'You dope,' she said.

The roses kept arriving. The flow of roses didn't stop till nine that night, when the florist closed and the money David had left with him ran out. By then, they were making love in Molly's big bed in the bedroom with its windows facing east. They could hear the sound of tugboats on the river. There were roses all over the bedroom. She wore a rose in her hair and nothing else.

'I have an idea,' he whispered.

'Yes?' she whispered.

'Since we already have the flowers, why don't we have a wedding?'

'When?' she said at once.

He woke up at three in the morning.

He blinked into the room. He could not remember when he'd fallen asleep. He was still wearing everything but his shirt. The window rectangle was illuminated with a soft glow. He could hear the ocean nudging the shore. He went to the window. In the distance, in the west, he could see the lighted walls of the hospital. He wondered if his father was sleeping. *I'm scared to death*, his father had said. So am I, David thought. He took off his shoes and socks, his pants and undershorts. He went to the drapes and closed them. He went back to the bed. Stretched out on the bed in the glow of the bedside lamp, he thought, *If he dies tomorrow* . . .

Well, don't think about that.

But if he dies tomorrow, and if the old Like Father, Like Son adage applies, then I myself might be able to count on another thirty years at best. Like father, like son, he thought. Ike and

Mike, we look alike. Except in the case of Stephen and – well, he didn't want to think about *that* either. There was no sense thinking about *that*. Nothing made sense about *that*, the unfairness of *that*!

The buck stops here, he thought. No more sons, Pop. This is the end of the line. Morris Weber will be closing his last business. Where was the sense of it? First Stephen (ah, Jesus, *please* don't think about it) and then his mother. Well, she was almost seventy. Still, that was young. Is seventy all we can hope for? Phone call at two in the morning. *Your mother is dead.* Will all you men whose mothers are still living take one step forward? Not so *fast*, Seaman Shavorski! All the little jokes about death and dying, *I'm scared to death.* There's nothing funny about death, he thought, nothing funny about the way Stephen – well, look, get *off* that, will you, please?

The tube in my father's penis.

I wish Molly was here to suck my cock.

I should have told her to come down. Is that a pun? *I can almost come sucking your big hard cock, do you know that?* Molly Regen, circa 1958, 1959. I believe it, he thought. *Used* to believe it, anyway. What's left to believe? Lies?

All the lies and all the lying, he thought. Is that another pun? Five long years of lies and lying. Fireworks against the nighttime sky. The phone ringing. Always on the goddam telephone. David, it's for you. Who knows me in East Hampton? Molly screaming. And everything stopping. All time stopping from that day forward. That memorable Fourth of July. That Glorious Fourth, the two-hundredth anniversary of our liberated nation. Molly in white. White dress and white scarf, Nurse Regen. Cocktail chatter, party voices, surrounded by strangers on the edge of the sea while their fifteen-year-old son was crashing a car into a –

He squeezed his eyes tightly shut.

He turned off the light and tried to sleep.

Thursday

His father's room was empty.

He went immediately to the nurses' station.

'Where's my father?' he asked.

She was a nurse he had never seen before. Little red-headed thing sipping at a Coca-Cola.

'His name, please?' she said.

'Morris Weber.'

'I think he went up to surgery,' she said.

'What do you mean? This *morning*, do you mean?'

'Yes, sir. He was scheduled for nine o'clock surgery,' she said. She was consulting a clipboard now.

'Dr. Kaplan said this afternoon.'

'He went up at nine,' the nurse said.

'Is he still there?'

'I don't know, sir.'

'Well, how do I find out?'

'If you'll wait outside, sir, I'll notify you as soon as I have any word.'

'Would he be in the Recovery Room yet?'

'You couldn't go there in any event, sir.'

'Would you try to find out, please?'

'Yes, sir. If you'll wait outside, sir . . .'

'Thank you,' he said.

The waiting room was empty of visitors. The television set was on. There were two pink ladies behind the desk. Both of them in their seventies, David guessed. He took a seat on one of the leatherette couches and lit a cigarette. He wondered where they all disappeared to during visiting hours, this waiting-room family of his. Through the door at the end of the hall and then into all the little warrens that sheltered their sick and dying. He did not know which visitor belonged to which patient. The patients in there were anonymous. It suddenly occurred to him that his father was anonymous, too. Except to David. And perhaps to him as well.

'Excuse me,' one of the pink ladies said. 'Do you have a patient in Intensive Care, sir?'

'I do,' David said.

'His name, please?'

'Morris Weber,' David said.

She consulted a clipboard and said to the other pink lady, 'You have to check their names on the sheet here. Otherwise, people try to come in who don't have patients here.'

David wondered who might possibly want to go in if he didn't have a patient here.

'I copy them from the sheet onto a separate piece of paper,' the woman said to the other pink lady. 'I copy them in alphabetical order. It makes it easier to check up on them.' She was training the other lady, David realized. On-the-job training. She turned to David. 'Are you a relative of Mr. Weber?' she asked.

'His son,' David said.

'You have to check if they're relatives or not,' she said to the other woman. 'Only relatives are allowed to visit.'

Where does that leave Bessie? David wondered.

'You can go in now if you like,' the woman said to him.

'He's in surgery,' David said.

The woman nodded. She turned to the trainee. 'Sometimes they try to go in before the hour. You just keep your eye on the clock. They're not supposed to go in until eleven, two, four, and seven o'clock – sharp! Not a minute before. When the ten minutes are up, you go in and get them out. Otherwise, they'll try to stay all day.'

'Ten minutes each time,' the trainee said. Her eyes were glued to the television screen. She seemed more interested in the soap than in the other woman's instructions.

Bessie appeared in the doorway.

'I'm sorry I'm late,' she said, 'the bus was late.'

'Excuse me,' the bossy pink lady said, 'do you have a patient in Intensive Care?'

'Yes, Morris Weber,' Bessie said.

'Are you a relative?'

'I'm his sister,' Bessie said. 'My name is Bessie Goldblum.'

She had learned the rules, David thought. Smart lady, Bessie.

'You can go in now,' the pink lady said by rote.

'He's in surgery,' David said.

'What do you mean?' Bessie said. 'They took him down this *morning*? I thought it was this afternoon.'

'They make their own rules,' David said.

'The doctors know what's best for the patients,' the bossy pink lady said, reprimanding him.

'I'm sure,' David said.

'What's wrong with your father?' she asked.

'Everything,' he said. He did not want to get into a long conversation with her about his father. Or about *anything*, for that matter.

'If he's in surgery, there's no sense waiting,' the pink lady said. 'Visiting time is up in three minutes. He won't recognize you, anyway.'

'If you don't mind, I'd *like* to wait,' David said.

'Suit yourself,' she said. She turned to the trainee. Officious damn biddy, David thought. 'Let me show you how to make the coffee,' she said. 'You make the coffee first thing in the morning, when you come in. If you're here in the afternoon, you have to clean the pot, and empty the grinds, and lock up the coffee maker in the cabinet before you go. That's after the four o'clock visit. At four-ten – sharp! If you don't lock it up, they steal it.'

David wondered who 'they' were. The visitors? The patients? The hospital staff? He visualized a huge band of coffee-maker thieves operating right here out of St. Mary's.

'The key to the cabinet is in an envelope in the top drawer of the desk here,' she said. 'Be sure to put it back in the envelope after you've locked up, and then take it downstairs to Mrs. Thorpe in the Volunteer Section and give it to her before you leave the hospital.'

'Do I lock the door, too?'

'What door?'

'Here to the waiting room.'

'No, that stays open all the time. They come in after we leave, you know. For the seven o'clock visit. We leave at four.'

'Four-ten, you mean,' the trainee said.

Touché, David thought.

'Mr. Weber?'

His appearance startled David. He was wearing a green surgical gown and cap. A green surgical mask dangled loose around his neck. It was as though, quite suddenly, David was privileged to see him wearing the garments of his trade. In that

104

moment, Kaplan became a *surgeon*, and not someone mouthing unfathomables about mysterious infections. He got to his feet at once and joined him in the corridor. Bessie, inexplicably, sat just where she was, unmoving, her head bent, her hands clasped in her lap as if in prayer.

'How is he?' David asked.

'Fine, they're closing him up now,' Kaplan said. There was that same sorrowful tone in his voice, that same grieving expression on his face.

'What'd you find?'

'Nothing,' Kaplan said, and shook his head. 'Clean as a whistle.'

David looked at him. Please don't tell me it's all very baffling, he thought.

'It's all very baffling,' Kaplan said.

'So what now?'

'Now we see,' Kaplan said.

'Now he dies,' David said.

'Not necessarily. He may fight back. There's always the chance that his will to live will overcome whatever is causing his problem.'

'When can I see him?'

'He won't be back down for a while yet.'

'Shall I wait for the two o'clock visit?'

'Four would be better. In fact, Mr. Weber, why don't you take the day off? Relax, get some rest. If you can come tonight at seven, that would be fine.'

'What if . . .?'

'Nothing's going to happen to him. Seven will be fine.'

'Are you sure?'

'I'm positive.'

'You'll keep me informed, won't you? If anything should . . .'

'Yes, of course,' Kaplan said.

He wondered if he should shake hands with the doctor. Kaplan nodded briefly and walked off. David went to where Bessie was sitting, her head still bent, her hands clasped in her lap.

'Did you hear?' he said.

'I heard. So they found nothing.'

'Nothing.'

'So what was the use?' She shook her head. 'He wants us to come back at seven?'

'That's what he said.'

'I'll come back at seven,' she said, and sighed. 'Where are you going now, the hotel?'

'I thought the apartment first. He wants me to look for his Ten-Forty.'

'His what?'

'His tax declaration. He's not sure he paid his income tax.'

'His mind wanders,' Bessie said. 'He forgets what he paid, what he didn't pay.' She paused. 'If you're going to the building, pick up the mail, too. He gets a lot of letters, there's a whole stack of mail there.'

'Okay, I will. Do you have the keys? He said you have his keys.'

'He gave me all what he had in his pockets,' Bessie said. She unclasped her handbag. 'There are four keys altogether,' she said. 'The little one is for the mailbox, but the mailman is holding all his stuff in the room they have there in the building, where he sorts the mail. The other keys, there's two locks on the door and also a chain you have to open with a key. That's the smallest key, the chain key. You can fit your hand in after you open the other two locks, and then you can get at the lock on the chain. It just falls down when you open the lock.'

'Thank you,' he said, and put the keys in his pocket.

He fumbled with the keys for several moments, trying to learn which key fit which of the door locks. He finally managed to get both locks open and then to unlock the chain lock. The chain dropped out of its holding bracket the moment he turned the key, just as Bessie had promised. He swung the door open.

His father had been living in this apartment for more than three years now. David had never come down to Miami Beach because his father made semi-annual visits to New York, and he'd felt no need to see him more often than that. He called him every other Sunday morning, ascertained that he was in good health and keeping busy, and that was that. He had never been inside this apartment, and he was totally unprepared for what he found here now.

A long narrow corridor leading to the living room was stacked with cardboard cartons on its left side, barely allowing passage between the boxes and the closets on the right. In the living room, a table covered with a soiled cloth was stacked high with envelopes, some of them sealed, some of them opened. Scattered on the tabletop were marking pens, sheets of paper with figures and dates on them, scissors, masking tape, cellophane tape, a magnifying glass, ashtrays brimming with cigar butts. There were more cartons in a haphazard circle around the table. Two facing sofas in the living room were stacked with narrow boxes some twelve inches square. A television set was piled high with shoe boxes, old *TV Guides*, and newspapers. A sweater, a shirt, a pair of undershorts, and an old hat were resting on the seat of a chair drawn up close to the television set.

The apartment was stiflingly hot.

David took a deep breath, went to the window air conditioner and turned it on. From where he stood at the window, he could see into the kitchen. Pots and pans, dirty dishes, cups and glasses were piled in the sink and on the drainboard. A stepladder was leaning against the kitchen door that opened onto the outside hallway. Even from here, David could see that the only locks on the door were the push-button one on the knob and a chain hanging at eye level. His father had barricaded his front door but had neglected to take the same precaution with his kitchen door.

He had to begin looking for the duplicate copy of the tax form.

His father had said, 'In the bedroom someplace. One of the drawers there.'

He walked out of the living room, toward the entrance door, and then turned left into the corridor there. More cartons were stacked along either wall, making passage almost impossible. He looked into the bathroom on his right. A sign on the partially open door, hand-lettered by his father, read THIS IS IT! A sign over the toilet-paper roll, again hand-lettered, read FREE! Bottles of medicine, tubes of toothpaste and ointment cluttered the counter around the sink. There were soiled towels on the floor. An enema bag hung on a wire hanger from the sliding doors that enclosed the bathtub. One of the doors was open. Stacked in the bathtub, almost to the ceiling, were more of the twelve-inch-square boxes he had seen on both sofas. His plates, David thought. His plate collection.

He went into the bedroom.

A pair of twin beds faced a big dresser with a mirror over it. Photographs of people David didn't know lined the mirror. A smaller dresser was beside the bed closest to the door, near the closet. A third and yet smaller dresser stood against the wall between the closet door and the entrance door to the bedroom. Each of the dresser tops was covered with stacks of newspapers and magazines. On top of another television set, on a trolley near the windows, there were more stacks of *TV Guides*. One of the beds, presumably the one his father did not sleep in, was piled high with cartons, envelopes, manila folders, and dirty clothes. At least a dozen pairs of shoes were scattered all over the bedroom floor. Pictures clipped from magazines and newspapers were Scotch-taped to every inch of the wall space.

David stood dumbfounded in the middle of the room.

He was closest to the big dresser, so he tried that one first. The top drawer was full of his father's socks, handkerchiefs, undershorts, and undershirts. The second drawer contained his shirts and sweaters. David opened the third drawer. It was full of bank statements still in their envelopes and rubber-banded together. Under each rubber band was a hand-lettered slip of paper identifying the year in which his father had received the statements. Even at a glance, David saw that some of the statements went back ten years. Didn't he ever throw anything away? The bottom drawer of the dresser contained bills and receipts for all the businesses his father had opened and closed, evidence of his failures, each marked with the name of the business and the years through which it had struggled for survival. I'm looking at the history of his life, David thought, and suddenly felt like an intruder.

He was here to find a duplicate tax form.

He went to the dresser near the twin bed stacked high with cartons. The top drawer of the dresser was stuffed with postage-free return envelopes and postage-free cards torn from magazines, each marked with a date. Are these valuable? David wondered. Is there anyone on earth who collects postage-free envelopes and cards except my father? The second and third drawers contained cigar boxes. He opened one of the boxes. It was full of cigar bands. He opened another box. More cigar bands. Did people collect cigar bands? He supposed they did. He supposed people collected anything, including other people. When he was a boy, his father used to unwrap a cigar and then slip the band onto David's ring finger. He opened another box. It was stacked with gum wrappers, matchbook covers, and bottle tops. Another box contained cancelled postage stamps. Another was brimming with pennies. Another had baseball trading cards in it. Yet another was full of dice. Red dice, ivory dice, green dice, a single die on a key chain, another huge one with rounded corners. And dominoes. Three dominoes. In a box he recognized as having contained the cigars he'd sent from Dunhill's last Father's Day, David found yet more cigar bands and, buried under the heap, a passbook for the United First Federal Bank. He slid the passbook out of its plastic holder and opened it. The name on the account was MORRIS L. WEBER ITF/DAVID WEBER AND MOLLY WEBER. His father had withdrawn $600 in March, probably for his trip north, leaving a balance on that day of $1075.62.

The discovery of the passbook in a cigar box which could easily have been overlooked in a clutter of similar cigar boxes containing canceled postage stamps, gum wrappers, matchbook covers, bottle tops, baseball trading cards, cigar bands, dice, and three goddamn *dominoes* made David suddenly angry. How could his father have been so careless? He put the passbook back in the cigar box and closed the drawer. Still annoyed, he turned to the last of the bedroom dressers, the smallest one. Let me find the damn tax form, he thought. Let me get out of here. He opened the top drawer.

Photographs.

Photographs heaped haphazardly in no particular chronological order. A brown eight-by-ten picture in a professional photographer's studio folder, his Uncle Max's wedding day. Dashing Uncle Max beaming at the camera, his dark-haired, dark-eyed Rachel by his side smiling. David's mother and father

109

on their left, the matron of honor and the best man. He closed the folder. There were pictures of his mother and father standing in front of the Eiffel Tower on the European trip David's trust fund had made possible. There were pictures of his mother when she was pregnant with David. There were pictures of David as a young boy in a sailor suit sitting on the running board of Uncle Max's Studebaker. There were pictures of David in Army uniform. There was a picture of David in the dining room of his New York apartment, carving a Thanksgiving Day turkey while the rest of the family sat around the table. There was a picture – ah, Jesus – of David with his infant son in his arms, David's inherited famous Weber nose flattened against his son's plump cheek as he planted a kiss, Stephen grinning at the –

He closed the drawer.

He turned away from the dresser for a moment.

He took a deep breath.

I don't want to be here, he thought. Not yet.

I don't want to be rummaging through my father's life this way. The tax form, he thought. Death and taxes. Sighing, he turned to the dresser again. The middle drawer was stacked with letters. In one corner of the drawer, near the back, he found a bundle of envelopes tied with string. Handwritten on a sheet of paper and slipped under the string were the words PRIVATE! HANDS OFF! He was tempted to break the string and read the letters. He did not. His father wasn't dead yet. Searching through the drawer for the tax form – wasn't it possible he'd put it with the *rest* of his correspondence? – he found an envelope with his own handwriting on it. The handwriting read: *To Mom, with love, David*. He opened the envelope, expecting to find an old birthday card in it, something he had presented to his mother years ago, accompanying a small gift perhaps. There was a letter in the envelope. He unfolded the letter and recognized his mother's small, neat handwriting. He began reading.

Dear Morrie,

I am writing this because when I talk I get too excited and of course it stands to reason. I honestly was giving you a fair chance but I guess you did not want it as you are still lying to me. Even this week if I did not ask you about how much money the store made Wednesday, you would not have told me you had taken the day off as you said to go to your brother's in New Jersey.

So please this is such a simple request, I am asking you please . . .

He folded the letter again. The edges of it were brown, the ink was fading. He did not want to read it. He did not want to know anything more about his father. But he slipped the letter into his jacket pocket. And then decided to put it back in the drawer with the other letters. But left it where it was in his pocket.

The bottom drawer of the dresser was full of greeting cards his father had undoubtedly bought from a mail-order house. Birthday cards, Easter and Christmas cards for his gentile friends, Chanukah cards, get-well cards, St. Valentine's Day cards, anniversary cards, graduation cards, even St. Patrick's Day cards. There was a clipboard in the drawer, a lined yellow pad attached to it. On the pad were listed the names and birth dates of his father's relatives and friends. He had kept a list over the past ten years of anyone he'd ever sent a birthday card to. David scanned the list. He found his own name and his birth date beside it. According to his father's check marks, he had received a card from him like clockwork every August for the past ten years. He looked for Molly's name. He looked for his Uncle Max's. Both had routinely received cards from his father.

There was another clipboard in the drawer, resting on a pile of what appeared to be cards his father had received over the years. Lettered in his father's hand across the top of a sheet of paper was the word CHANUKAH. Beneath the word, lettered neatly onto another line, were the words CARDS SENT. Below that was a list of names with dates beside them. On the opposite side of the page, his father had lettered CARDS RCVD, and below that was another list of names and dates. The word DELINQUENTS was handlettered close to the bottom of the page. There were a dozen or more names under this word, those friends or relatives who hadn't sent him a card for the holidays. David's name was on that list. Delinquents, he thought.

He found the tax form tucked into a sheaf of rubber-banded envelopes containing discount coupons for supermarket items. Great place to file a tax form, he thought. Terrific, Pop. A Xerox

111

copy of the check his father had made out was stapled to the form. His father had indeed paid the amount due the United States Government on April 15, right on the dot. David slipped the form back into the accountant's envelope and then put the envelope into the pocket containing his mother's letter. Again, he debated returning her letter to its place in the middle drawer of the dresser. But it was still in his pocket when he turned off the air conditioner and left the apartment, carefully locking all three locks behind him.

He felt as if he'd been released from prison, pardoned by the governor at the eleventh hour. He was back at the hotel by a quarter to one, the whole day ahead of him (until seven o'clock, at least), no rigid timetable demanding that he return to the hospital. His father had come through the operation alive, his father was safe for the time being; he had only to call Molly, and then he was free till seven o'clock.

'Hello?' she said.

'Molly, it's me,' he said.

'Tell me,' she said.

'They operated on him this morning. He's all right, but they didn't find anything. They still don't know what the problem is.'

'Have you seen him?'

'Not yet. I'll be going back to the hospital at seven.'

'What will you do until then?' she asked.

'Have a good lunch,' he said, 'take a long walk on the beach, swim awhile, sun awhile, relax.'

'Good,' she said.

Floating on his back in the tepid water just off the hotel, the afternoon sun beating down on his chest and his belly and his legs, he felt his first pang of guilt. What if his father never came out of the anesthesia? What if his father died while he was here enjoying the sun and the sea? No, he thought, he'll live. He'll be there when I get there at seven o'clock, the anesthesia will have worn off completely by then, he'll recognize me, he'll be alive. Who was it who'd said – someone, some kid in Korea, a nineteen-year-old like himself, freezing his ass off and fighting a war he neither understood nor trusted – who had it been? The real

112

danger is living, he'd said, and David had thought it enormously profound at the time. Nineteen years old, what the hell, everything sounded profound. When you got to be twenty-nine, and then thirty-nine –

'Hello there!' she called. 'David! Is that you?'

He recognized her voice, the English cadences, the youthful timbre. He lowered his legs, treading water, and looked toward the shore. She was wearing the same minuscule black bikini he'd seen her wearing on Tuesday, when he'd watched her taking her solitary early-morning walk on the beach. Her hands were on her hips.

'Is it *safe* out there?' she shouted.

'Safe? What do you mean?'

'Are there *sharks*?'

'I don't think so,' he said.

'I'm afraid of *sharks*!' she shouted.

'No, I don't think you need be.'

'Wait for me,' she said, and went back to where she had spread a towel on the sand. He saw her taking off her watch. He wondered what time it was; he had left his own watch in the room. She walked down to the water's edge, hesitated a moment, and took a tentative step forward.

'I'm terrified,' she said.

'No, don't be.'

She came slowly into the water, her hands raised as if in defense, hovering near the full breasts in the scanty bikini top, fingers fluttering. A faint sea breeze caught her long blond hair, blowing it across her face. She brushed it back with her hand, took another step into the water.

'It's very *warm*, isn't it?' she called. She sounded surprised.

'Lovely,' he said.

When she was in the water to her waist, she took a deep breath, hesitated, and then made a clean dive. He waited. She surfaced some three feet from where he was treading water and immediately looked out past him, scanning the surface. 'What's *that*?' she said, alarmed.

He turned to look.

'Coconut shell,' he said.

'Not a fin?'

113

'No.'

'I'd hate to get eaten by a shark,' she said. 'Let's move in where we can touch bottom. Sharks don't like shallow water, do they?'

They swam in closer to the shore and stood together hip–deep in the shallow water. The water moved gently against his belly. She made tiny circles on the water with her hands. Her hands moved restlessly on the water.

'When do you go back to London?' he asked.

'London?'

'I thought you lived in London. Didn't you say . . .?'

'No, no. Oxford.'

'Ah,' he said.

'Do you know Oxford?'

'I've never been there.'

'It's quite lovely.'

'Where is it? On the coast someplace? Near Birmingham?'

'Birmingham? Birmingham's almost in the exact center of England!'

'What am I thinking of then?'

'Well, I really couldn't say. There are quite a few coastal cities, you know. We're an island, you know. Do you *really* not know where Oxford is?'

'I really don't.'

'That's like asking where . . . I don't know . . . New *Haven* is.'

'Do you know where New Haven is?'

'Of course I do.'

'Well, I'm sorry,' he said, smiling, 'but I honestly do not know where Oxford is.'

'It's north and west of London,' she said.

'But not on the coast.'

'Not on *any* of the coasts. It's inland, actually. Some fifty or sixty miles from Southampton.' She paused. Her hands made idle circles on the water. 'I suppose an American wouldn't consider that very far.'

'Not very. Where's Southampton?'

'You're *joking*!'

'Where is it?'

'On the Channel. It's an *enormous* port, do you *really* not know

114

where it is?'

'Haven't the foggiest.'

'You're teasing me, I know you are.'

'I'm not.'

'Then your ignorance is shameful,' she said, and they both laughed.

'In any case, when *are* you going back?'

'Saturday, Sunday, as soon as I've finished here. And you?'

'I'm not sure yet.'

'Of course not. It all depends, I suppose, on . . .'

'Yes.'

'Let's swim out a ways now, shall we?' she said. 'I feel much more secure now.'

They swam out into the deeper water, side by side. She had a strong, clean stroke; he found it difficult to keep up with her. He thought of his father in the hospital, and then put it out of his mind. He put everything out of his mind. There was only the sea now, and the sun overhead, and the girl swimming by his side. The sea glistened everywhere around them; the sun was strong overhead. *All that gold, the diamonds, the diamonds.* They swam out very deep. When at last they stopped to rest, treading water, they were both out of breath.

'That was marvelous,' she said.

They were very far from the shore.

'We still have to get back,' David said.

'Oh, we will,' she said. 'Not yet, though. Let's rest a bit. Let's lie on our backs, and float, and drift, and rest.'

They floated free on their backs in the water. They bobbed on the surface, legs akimbo, arms spread. Their hands almost touched.

'If this were Marbella,' she said, 'I'd have my top off in a wink.'

He said nothing.

They floated. The sun beat down on them.

'Do I dare here in America?' she asked.

Without waiting for an answer, she righted herself in the water and reached behind her to unclasp the bikini top. She floated on her back beside him again, the black top in one hand, trailing on the water. He did not turn to look at her.

'I hope sharks don't like English breasts,' she said, and

115

laughed. Her laughter splintered on the sunlit air, drifted. The water murmured around them. They floated.

'Delicious,' she said.

They drifted.

'Here in the sea,' she said, 'it *could* be Spain, couldn't it?'

'Yes.'

'Or *anywhere*, actually. France, Italy . . .' Her voice drifted.

They floated.

'Have you ever been to Italy?' she asked.

'Yes,' he said.

She was silent for a moment.

Then she said, 'Are you married, David?'

He hesitated. 'Yes,' he said. 'Are you?'

'I used to be.'

'Divorced?'

'Yes. Why did you hesitate?' she asked. 'Were you about to lie?'

'No, I don't think so.'

'Then why did you hesitate?'

'I guess . . . well, I'm not used to this sort of thing.'

'What sort of thing?'

'Meeting a young girl . . .'

'Young? Why, *thank* you.'

'You are,' he said.

'Twenty-nine,' she said.

'When a man's fifty, twenty-nine seems . . .'

'Are you fifty?'

'I'll be fifty in August.'

'That's still forty-nine.'

'Well.'

'Well, isn't it?'

'It feels like fifty.'

'Anyway, *do* go on, please. About meeting a young girl, please don't leave out the *young* part.'

'And . . . talking this way . . . sharing an afternoon this way . . .'

His voice trailed.

'How long have you been married?' she asked.

'Almost twenty-two years.'

'That's quite a long time.'

'Yes.'

'Do you have any children?'

'No,' he said.

They floated in the sea, he and Molly. The sun was strong overhead.

'This is the only way to live,' she said.

'Who needs money?' he said.

It was three o'clock in East Hampton. In Connecticut, his son was just getting off the train at the Darien station. Three P.M., his friend later said. That was when Stephen had arrived. His friend was waiting for him in the Jaguar that later killed him.

'We've never done it in the ocean,' Molly said. 'Do you realize that?'

'Shrivels up in the water,' David said.

'Let's do it,' she said.

'They'd see us,' David said.

'We'll charge admission,' Molly said, and laughed.

'Make a fortune,' David said.

All the television newscasters had warned their viewers to keep away from Lower Manhattan today. Biggest celebration in the history of the city. Two hundredth anniversary of American independence. The crush would be unbelievable. They had decided to trust the dire forecasts. At first they thought they might stay in the apartment part of the day, away from the crowd. Mix some drinks, watch the festivities on television. But David's partner called early in the morning, inviting them out to the Island, one of his famous last-minute invitations. Big fireworks display tonight, he'd promised. Parties all over town. Stephen was packing to leave for Connecticut, to visit with a schoolmate there. He would not be back till late Monday sometime. They had not known he would *never* be back. They accepted the invitation.

They floated, they drifted.

'Do you know who loves you?' Molly said.

'Haven't the foggiest.'

'Three guesses. If you guess wrong, I'll wave my magic wand and turn you into a toad.'

'Sophia Loren, he said.

'Wrong.'

'Jane Fonda.'

'One more guess.'

'Alice Reardon.'

'Who's that?'

'Girl I knew in the third grade. Irish girl.'

'*I'm* your Irish girl,' Molly said.

'My Yiddishe Shiksa.'

'Where's that thing?' she said, reaching for him.

'Come on, *hey!*'

'Where's my magic wand?'

Her hand groped for the front of his swimming trunks. He was aware of the people on the beach. He could hear the murmur of voices hanging on the air, floating, drifting. Somewhere there was the echo of a scratchy phonograph record on a windup machine. A single cloud drifted overhead. He could feel moist sea wind on his face. Laughing, he swam away from her. She swam after him. He splashed water at her. She splashed water back. He wiped his face. Laughing, he was ready to splash her again when he realized she was no longer giving chase. She treaded water some five feet away from him. Her hand broke the surface.

'Interested, baby?' she asked him with a lewd wink, and waved her bikini bottom at him.

'Put that back on,' he said.

'Free show, free show!' she yelled to the beach.

'Molly, come *on!*' he said, glancing over his shoulder toward the beach.

'Race you back,' she said, the bikini bottom still in her hand. She broke into a fast crawl. He swam after her. He caught her. He pulled her to him.

'Put on your pants,' he said.

'Take yours off,' she said.

She moved closer to him in the circle of his arms.

'Let's fuck in the water,' she said.

He was already hard.

'Save it for later,' he said.

'Promise?'

'Solemn oath.'

'Who loves you?' she said.

118

'You love me,' he said.

She kissed him.

'You're supposed to say something in return,' she said.

'I love you, Molly. I love you to death.'

She put on the bikini bottom.

'We'll do it in the tub later,' she said.

'Let's go do it in the tub *now*', he said.

'Can't. Big party at four o'clock.'

'How am I supposed to walk out on the beach with this thing?' he asked.

'Your own fault,' she said. 'I could have taken care of it in a minute.'

'They'll arrest me for indecent exposure. I'll be disbarred.'

'Just let it shrivel, darling,' she said airily, and began swimming back toward the beach.

The round of parties started at four o'clock. At about that time, according to Stephen's friend, the kids were sitting around drinking beer, smoking a little pot, bullshitting the afternoon away. There was supposed to be a parade in town later in the day. The kids all planned to go to it. And fireworks that night. There would be fireworks all over America tonight.

Molly looked stunning. She wore a white backless dress and a white scarf across her forehead and tied at the back of her head. Her blond hair cascaded from it. He called her Nurse Regen.

'That scarf makes you look like an old-fashioned nurse,' he said.

'I *am* an old-fashioned nurse,' she said.

'Florence Nightingale,' he said.

'You can be my patient later,' she said.

'I'm getting impatient,' he said.

'Thank you, Morris Weber,' she said.

There was the usual East Hampton crowd at all of the parties. Writers, artists, actors, television people, movie people, and all the lawyers who represented them.

'Lawyers are boring,' Molly whispered.

'*I'm* a lawyer,' he whispered back.

'You're a very *special* lawyer,' she said. 'If I'm any judge.'

'Thank you, Morris Weber,' he said.

The fireworks started shortly after dark. They realized later that Stephen must have been getting behind the wheel of the car at about that time. Molly ooohed and ahhhed as the fireworks erupted against the black sky. He held her hand. She squeezed his hand each time there was another explosion, another flash of color against the black. The Jaguar had been a birthday present to Stephen's friend. His friend would be a graduating senior next semester. He was seventeen years old. Stephen was fifteen. He would have been a sophomore in the fall. If he'd gone back to school. His friend had allowed him to take the Jaguar for a spin. Stephen did not have a driver's license. On the phone later, the state trooper would mention that Stephen did not have a driver's license. Exoneration for the state of Connecticut. The fireworks exploded against the blackness. Everyone ooohed and ahhhed.

The call did not come until almost ten-thirty. There was another party in progress, this one at David's partner's beach house. It was David's partner who called him to the phone.

'Mr. Weber?' the voice on the other end said.

'Is it Stephen?' Molly called from across the room. They had given him the number here before he'd left for Connecticut.

'This is Mr. Weber,' David said.

'Is it Stephen?' Molly called again.

'This is Trooper Harrington of the Connecticut State Police,' the voice said. 'We've been trying to get you at home, Mr. Weber, we only just now found the slip of paper in your son's wallet.'

'Slip of paper?' David said.

'With this number on it. Am I talking to Mr. Weber?'

'This is Mr. Weber. My son's wallet?'

'Mr. Weber, I'm sorry to have to tell you this . . .'

'No,' David said.

'What is it?' Molly said. She was standing by his side now.

'Mr. Weber,' the trooper said, 'your son's been in a car accident. Mr. Weber, I'm sorry, but your son is dead, sir. He was driving without a license, sir, his car ran into . . .'

'No,' David said. 'He's not dead.'

Molly screamed.

Outside the house, the ocean crashed in against the shore.

'You're not falling asleep, are you?' Hillary asked.

'No, no,' he said.

'Good way to drown,' she said. 'Are you ready to go back in? The sun seems to be deserting us.'

'Whenever you are,' he said.

'I'd best put this on,' she said.

Treading water, she cupped her breasts into the flimsy bra top. Her nipples were puckered. Her breasts were spattered with freckles.

'Do they suit you?' she asked, and smiled.

They swam back toward the beach together.

'Morrie, it's me!' Sidney shouted. 'Your cousin Sidney! Do you recognize me, Morrie? If you recognize me, blink your eyes once. If you don't recognize me, blink your eyes twice.'

His father's eyes looked glazed. He lay flat on his back, looking up at the ceiling. His eyes drifted, floated.

'Morrie? Can you hear me?'

'Lower your voice,' David said.

'I don't think he can hear me. Morrie, if you can hear me, blink your eyes once.'

There was a tube in his father's mouth, a thicker one than all the others. A strip of adhesive tape held it in place, partially covering his chin and his lips. There was moisture inside the tube. The tube looked clouded over on the inside. His father's eyes kept floating, drifting.

'Morrie, can you blink? If you can hear me, blink once,' Sidney said. David wanted to strangle him. 'Morrie?'

His father blinked his eyes.

'See?' Sidney said triumphantly. 'He can hear me. Morrie, if you know who I am, blink your eyes again.'

'He knows who you are,' Bessie said. She was standing beside the bed, holding his father's hand between both her own. 'Never mind blinking, Morris. Just rest,' she said.

'How will I know if he knows I'm here?' Sidney said.

'We'll tell him later,' David said.

'What good will *that* do?' Sidney said. 'If he doesn't know I was *really* here?'

He was looking for Brownie points, the son of a bitch!

'Are you in any pain, Pop?' David asked. 'I know you can't talk with that tube in your mouth, but if you can just . . .'

His father slowly shook his head.

'No pain?'

His father shook his head again.

'Good,' David said.

His father's floating brown eyes shifted, came to rest on David's face, seemed to focus there questioningly.

'The operation's over and done with,' David said.

His father's eyes stayed on his face, waiting, questioning.

'They found what they were looking for, Pop,' he said. 'The cause of the infection. They got it, Pop! It's all gone now.'

Bessie looked at him.

'There's nothing to stop you from getting well now,' David said.

His eyes met Bessie's. Bessie turned away. She leaned over the bed, close to his father's ear.

'That's right, Morris,' she said. 'They found it, and now you'll get better.'

His father nodded.

'What did they find?' Sidney whispered. David shot him a look. 'Well, *what*?' Sidney asked.

'Pop,' David said, 'we want you to rest now, do you understand? We'll come back tomorrow morning, okay?' He looked up at the wall clock. 'It's almost a quarter past seven, Pop, we have to go now. We'll be back at eleven in the morning. Okay, Pop?'

His father slowly raised his hand from the sheet. His eyes focused on his hand. He extended his forefinger. He made a downward slash on the air with his forefinger.

'What's that, Pop?'

He made the motion again.

'I don't understand, Pop.'

Again a single stroke on the air.

'Are you trying to spell something?'

His father nodded.

'Is that a letter?'

His father nodded.

'Do it again.'

His father's shaking finger made the downward stroke again.

'I?' David said.

122

'He's trying to say "I love you," ' Bessie said.

His father shook his head.

'Is it the letter "I"?' David asked.

His father nodded. He made another downward stroke, a loop, a tail.

'R?' David said. 'I, R?'

His father nodded. His finger trailed serpentinely on the air, shaking.

'S,' David said. 'I, R, S. Oh, the *tax* form. I found it, Pop, it was in one of the bedroom drawers, just where you said it was. You don't have to worry, you paid it when it was due.'

His father nodded. He closed his eyes. Bessie went to the bed. 'I'll see you tomorrow morning,' she said.

'You rest now,' David said.

Bessie leaned over the bed.

'Sleep well, Morris,' she said, and kissed him on the cheek.

'I was here, Morrie,' Sidney said. 'I'll see you Tuesday. So long, Morrie.'

David went to the bed and kissed his father on the forehead. He still felt damp and hot. He turned away from the bed. Bessie and Sidney had already gone out into the corridor. He stopped at the nurses' station. The Cuban nurse was on duty this evening.

'How's his temperature?' he asked her.

She looked at his chart. 'A hun'red an' one,' she said. 'But tha's rectal, it's not so high.'

'Everything else okay? His heart? Is his heart okay?'

'Yes, fine,' she said. 'Please don' worry, Mr. Weber, we takin' good care of him.'

'I know that,' David said. 'Thank you.'

Bessie and Sidney were waiting just outside the door to the unit.

'What was it they found?' Sidney asked at once.

'A small abscess,' David lied. 'They drained it. He'll be fine now.'

Sidney looked at him.

'He doesn't *look* like he'll be fine,' he said.

'He's still groggy,' David said.

'But he looks lousy. I never seen him look so terrible. Even after the *first* operation, he looked better than he does now, am I right, Bessie? I picked you up that day, you remember? Drove all the way from Lauderdale, stopped at the house to pick you up, drove you here, we were here right after the operation. He was groggy then, too, but he looked a hell of a lot better than he does now, this was before I started having all the trouble with my buggy, he looked *much* better than he does now. You want my opinion, Davey, I'd ask the doctor to amplify on what he told you, find out just what it was they discovered in there, putting an eighty–two–year–old man under the knife for the second time in a month, he's no spring chicken, your dad. I'd find out just *why* they went in, and just what they discovered in there, what it was they *did* in there. I'd ask for amplification, Davey, you know what I mean?'

'I'll do that, Sidney,' David said. 'When I talk to the doctor later.'

'I'd do it *now*,' Sidney said. 'I'd go right in the waiting room and use the phone on the desk there and call the doctor and find out whether they got everything they went in for. Otherwise, they'll want to go in again in two, three weeks, there's only so much shock the human body can take, he's eighty–two years old, you know, that's not a spring chicken. Even when Lillian, your cousin Lillian, went in to have her plumbing fixed, it was a tremendous shock to the body, simple little thing like a D and C, am I right? She's only forty–eight years old, never been sick a day in her life, still it was very upsetting to the entire system. Your dad looks terrible, Davey, I never seen him look so bad, I don't even think he knows I was here today, you know that? He didn't blink his eyes when I told him to, when I asked him if he recognized his own cousin who takes him wherever he wants to go in a car that's falling apart already, I don't think he knew it was Sidney there talking to him. Well, you tell him I was here, willya? Convince him I was here. I don't think he realizes it, I mean it. I don't *have* to be in Miami on Thursdays, you know, I only came to see your dad, I don't think he even knows I was here. Well, listen, I'm not asking for a medal. Just tell him I was here, okay? Tell him I'll be back on Tuesday, will you still be here on Tuesday? When are you going home?'

'I don't know yet.'

'Well, it all depends, I guess, don't it? I'd stay here as long as

124

possible, Davey, you never know.'

'Yeah,' David said.

'So that's it,' Sidney said, 'I gotta get back to Lauderdale, there's a leak in my swimming pool, the guy says he can fix it for six hundred bucks, how do you like that? I'm gonna drain the damn thing myself, patch it up myself, who needs him? Six hundred bucks? What does he think I am, the Chase Manhattan? I can fix it myself, the hell with him. Well, I'll see you, Davey, let's hope he makes it through the night, huh, the way he looked in there.' Sidney shook his head. 'I'd drop you off, Bessie, but I gotta go in the opposite direction, pick up some venetian blinds Lillian ordered, your cousin Lillian, Davey. So I'll see you, okay?'

He limped away, up the corridor, and turned the bend out of sight.

'What do you think?' Bessie said.

'I don't know.'

'You think it was right to lie to your father?'

'I think so. If I'd told him they found nothing . . .'

'I guess you're right,' Bessie said. She thought this over for a moment. 'I guess so. If he *thinks* he's getting better, maybe he *will* get better.'

'Yes,' David said.

'So,' Bessie said, and sighed. 'Did you pick up his mail? When you were at the building?'

'Damn it, I forgot,' David said.

'You forgot the mail,' she said, 'I keep forgetting the scissors. Don't worry about it, I'll stop by the building tomorrow morning. He might want to see his mail before he . . .'

She let the sentence trail.

'Just the first-class stuff,' David said. 'If it isn't any bother.'

'It's no bother,' Bessie said. 'I do the best what I can.' She sighed deeply. 'I'll pick up the mail. I'll see you tomorrow,' she said, and hesitated. 'You're getting enough to eat?' she asked.

'What?' he said.

'Because . . . it wouldn't be much . . . but if you want me to cook something for you . . .'

'No, that's all right, thanks,' he said at once.

'I could make you something,' she said.

125

'Thanks,' he said, 'I'll be okay.'

She shrugged, as though she'd been expecting him to refuse her invitation and was not terribly surprised or disappointed now that he had. He thought, Hey, come on, I hardly *know* you lady. I mean, go cook *his* meals, okay? Whoever *he* may think you are, you're not my mother.

'All right,' she said, 'I'll meet you by the Emergency Room, ten-thirty tomorrow. I know you like the Main, but I like the Emergency.'

'Yes, fine,' he said.

'Good night,' she said, and sighed again.

'Good night, Bessie,' he said.

He sat alone in the disco bar, drinking.

He had already drunk two martinis. He was on his third martini. The bartender came up to him. The lights over the dance floor flashed and beeped. Beep, beep, beep. Like the little lights on the machines all around his father's bed.

'How are you doing here?' the bartender asked.

'Fine,' David said. Fine and dandy, he thought.

'You all alone down here in Miami?' the bartender said.

'All alone,' David said.

That wasn't quite true. He had his father. But that was the same as being all alone, wasn't it? Hell with it, he thought. I'm not under oath here.

'You interested in somebody?' the bartender asked.

'I'm interested in *every*body,' David said. That was true. He was an interested observer of the entire world, officer of the court, minion of the law.

'You want somebody?' the bartender asked.

'I want another martini,' David said.

'Beefeater martini, two olives,' the bartender said, and walked away.

Do I want somebody? David thought. Yes, I want somebody. Who do I want? Whom, excuse me. My mother, he thought. I want my mother. Your mother is dead, somebody said. His father. The somebody was his father, at two o'clock in the morning. On the telephone. It always came on the goddamn telephone. Your mother is dead, his father said.

126

The bartender put the fresh drink before him.

'Seriously,' he said, 'you interested in somebody?'

David looked at him.

'Black, white, Chinese, you name it,' the bartender said.

'Golden,' David said.

'What?' the bartender said.

'Labrador retriever,' David said.

'I'm serious,' the bartender said.

'Am I to believe, sir,' David said, 'that you are offering me a lady of the *night*?'

'What?' the bartender said.

'A *hooker*?' David said.

'These ain't hookers,' the bartender said.

'Then what are they?'

'Women who will offer you their comfort.'

'In that event, I'll take two of them,' David said. 'I need all the comfort I can get.'

'Two would be easy,' the bartender said.

'Then make it three.'

'Three would cost you,' the bartender said.

'How much would it cost me? Do you know how much it costs to go to the hospital four times a day? Eleven, two, four, and seven?'

'What's those figures? Is that what it costs?'

'Those are the hours.'

'This would cost by the hour,' the bartender said, nodding.

'Terrific,' David said. '*I* charge by the hour, too.'

'You really want a couple of girls?'

'Three, I said.'

'You think you can handle three?'

'No.'

'So how many you want?'

'How many colors you got?'

'Colors?'

'I want a rainbow.'

'Why you going to the hospital four times a day? You sick?'

'Very,' David said.

'What've you got?'

'Terminal shittiness.'

'What's that?'

'It's what you get when you're fifty,' David said.

'I'm fifty, and I ain't got it,' the bartender said.

'Lucky you,' David said, and sipped at his drink.

'Seriously, you want two black girls?' the bartender asked.

'I want an Indian girl,' David said.

'Indian girls are a little difficult down here,' the bartender said. 'I can get you a Cuban, some of them got Indian blood.'

'I want a pure-blooded Indian. American Indian. Mohican,' David said. 'I want the last of the Mohicans.'

'You want a Chinese girl?' the bartender said.

'I want a Hindu.'

'Be serious, okay? You want a girl, or don't you?'

'I already *got* a girl,' David said.

'So where is she?'

Who the hell knows? David thought.

'Twenty bucks for the agency fee,' the bartender said. 'The rest is between you and the girl.'

'What agency?' David asked.

'Me,' the bartender said.

'You're some agency,' David said.

'White, black, Chinese, Cuban, you name it.'

'Between me and the girl, huh?'

'Strictly.'

'How *much* between me and the girl?'

'It usually runs a hundred an hour.'

'That's almost what *I* charge,' David said.

'That's the going rate.'

'That's the *coming* rate, you mean.'

'What? Oh, yeah,' the bartender said, and grinned. 'So what do you say?'

'I say my father's dying.'

'What?'

'Send three girls to my father's room at St. Mary's. Tell him they're a present from his son.'

'What?'

'Who doesn't love him,' David said.

'What?' the bartender said.

'Never mind,' David said.

128

The bartender shrugged and walked off.

Two o'clock in the morning, David thought. The telephone doesn't ring at two o'clock in the morning unless somebody's dead. He couldn't think of anybody who might be dead. He hoped it was his father.

Hey, wait a minute, he thought.

Hey, shit, I didn't think *that*, did I?

Did I?

Your mother is dead, his father told him.

Flat out.

Your mother is dead.

A heart attack. Sixty-nine years old, perfect health, she dies of a heart attack in the middle of the night; his father calls at 2:00 A.M., your mother is dead, bingo.

David said, 'I'll be right there.'

'It can wait till morning,' his father said.

Well, everything can wait till morning, David thought. Your mother dies, it can wait till morning, right? Probably *wished* she would die, the bastard, so he could –

Well, wait a minute, you don't know if that's true.

Your Honor, I beg the Court's indulgence. Hearsay . . .

Sustained.

It *was* true, David thought.

Shit, it *had* to be true. He left home, didn't he? Well, she kicked him out, he thought.

I don't want to think about it, he thought.

He sipped at his martini. The bartender was watching him. He ambled over to David just as he was finishing the drink.

'You want another one of these? Or you want a girl instead?'

'Neither,' David said.

He added a tip to the check, signed it, and walked out of the bar and up the long curving marble steps that led to the ornate lobby. Hillary Watkins was sitting in one of the brocaded chairs. Elementary, my dear Watkins, he thought.

'Ah, there you are,' she said. 'I've been waiting for you.'

He could not recall having asked her to wait for him. Married men were not supposed to ask young, long-legged English girls alone in a deserted town to wait for them.

'How are you?' she said.

'Fine,' he said.

'Have you had dinner yet?'

'No.'

'Neither have I. Why don't we eat together? I'm ravenously hungry, it's almost nine o'clock.'

'No, thanks, not tonight. Thank you.'

'Tomorrow night then?'

She was watching him closely. Her long legs were crossed. She was wearing a white dress. A sprig of flowers was in her hair. She looked like a bride. A young bride.

'Well, I don't know what tomorrow will be,' he said.

'Tomorrow will be Friday,' she said.

'I suppose it will,' he said. He felt suddenly very weary.

'It might do you good to forget your troubles for a while,' she said.

'It might indeed.' What troubles? he thought. My father is dying is the only trouble I've got.

'Let's make it definite for tomorrow night, shall we?'

He said nothing.

'Or would you rather ring me up when you get back from the hospital? What time do you normally get back from the hospital?'

'Seven-thirty,' he said.

'Ring me,' she said. 'I'm in room seventeen-twelve.' Her green-eyed gaze would not leave his face. 'Will you ring me?'

'I'll see what happens tomorrow,' he said.

'Or later tonight, perhaps. If you find you're hungry.'

He looked at her.

'I have no other plans,' she said. 'I'll be in my room.'

'Well, thanks,' he said.

'How *is* your father?' she asked.

'So-so,' he said.

'I'm awfully sorry.'

'Yes, well,' he said, and shrugged.

'I lied to you,' she said suddenly. 'I'm not twenty-nine. I'm thirty. I was thirty last month. I simply can't bring myself to admit it.'

I lied to you, too, he thought.

He said nothing.

'Well, good night,' she said, and uncrossed her legs and rose. 'I suppose I'll order something from room service. I'm sure they're still serving, wouldn't you think?'

'I would guess so.'

'Yes.' She hesitated. 'You're sure you won't join me?'

'I don't think so, thanks.'

'Well, good night again,' she said. 'If you should want to talk or anything . . .'

'Yes, thank you.'

'It's seventeen-twelve.'

'Seventeen-twelve,' he said.

'Yes.'

'Okay.'

'Good night, David.'

'Good night, Hillary.'

He watched her as she walked to the elevators. He went to the front desk and asked for his key. The clerk asked him if he still planned to check out tomorrow.

'Is that what I told you?' David said.

'Yes, sir, when you registered.'

'Better extend it a few more days. I'm not sure what . . .' He paused. 'My father's very sick, you see. He's in the hospital here.'

'I'm sorry to hear that, sir. Shall we extend your stay till Sunday then?'

'Yes, Sunday, please,' David said.

'We'll do that, sir. Good night, sir.'

'Good night,' David said.

The elevator stopped on the twelfth floor; it always stopped on the twelfth floor. The fifteenth-floor corridor was empty; it was always empty. He wondered when the South American contingent would arrive. Never, he thought. He went to his room and fumbled with the key in the lock and finally got the door open. The room was neither too hot nor too cool, would wonders never? He undressed down to his undershorts and then went into the bathroom to brush his teeth. He looked at himself in the mirror.

'You're a damn fool, Counselor,' he said to the mirror.

He snapped off the bathroom light and went back into the bedroom. He drew the drapes. He took off his undershorts and got into bed and pulled the covers up over him. He lay looking up

131

at the ceiling. He could find faces in the rough plaster surface of the ceiling. He kept staring at the ceiling.

His mother had found the receipt in the back of his father's top dresser drawer, what they used to call his chifferobe. It was in a Phillies cigar box that also contained four cellophane-wrapped cigars. His mother had thought the box was empty; she periodically went through his dresser to clear out the clutter. If the box had been empty, she would have thrown it out. She opened the box and discovered the four cigars and the receipt. There was a jeweler's name on the receipt. Samalson Brothers on Jerome Avenue, where his father had just opened another new business. The address on the receipt was right next door to his father's shop. The receipt listed a pair of diamond earrings at four hundred and twenty-five dollars plus tax. The receipt was marked "Paid In Full." A signature was scrawled at the bottom of the receipt. She thought it read Ezra Samalson, but she couldn't be sure. She looked for a date on the receipt. In the upper right-hand corner, she found the numerals 6/12/53.

What was in June this year? she wondered.

A birthday? An anniversary? Certainly not hers. Her birthday was in April, and her anniversary was in January. So what was in June? Why had her husband bought a pair of diamond earrings for four hundred and twenty-five dollars plus tax on June the twelfth? Was he holding them as a surprise for her? Holding them till *next* January, when they would be celebrating their twenty-fifth wedding anniversary? Holding them till next April, when she would be forty-six years old? That was a long time to be holding a present; this was still only August. But if he *was* planning a surprise, then where were the earrings? The receipt was in the cigar box, but where were the earrings?

She searched through the top dresser drawer, and then through all the drawers in the dresser. She found no earrings. She went into the spare room where he kept all his boxes and cartons full of junk, and she searched through each of them and could find no earrings. She even searched the medicine cabinet where he kept his shaving stuff. She could not find the diamond earrings he had paid so much money for in June. So where were the earrings? Where *should* a pair of diamond earrings be? she thought. On a woman's *ears*, she thought. Morrie has another woman, she thought.

She told David about the receipt when he got home that day. He had been out shopping for new clothes. None of his old clothes fit him; he had gained fifteen pounds in the Army. He was still wearing his Army suntans. She told him the minute he came into the apartment. She showed him the receipt. Four hundred and twenty-five dollars. That's a lot of money, David thought. He did not yet understand why his mother was showing him the receipt.

'So where are they, these earrings?' his mother said. 'Do *I* have them? Then who has them?'

David's grandmother was dead by then; she had died when he was overseas. His widowed Aunt Anna was an old lady, and, besides, his father had never really liked her and certainly would not have spent four hundred and twenty-five dollars on her. His Uncle Max had married a woman named Rachel Simon when David was twelve years old. They lived in New Jersey now, where his Uncle Max owned a successful delicatessen. David's mother described his Aunt Rachel as 'stuck up,' and they hardly ever saw them anymore. Besides, would his father have spent so much money on a sister-in-law? For what reason?

'It's a woman,' his mother said.

'Maybe cousin Rebecca,' David said. 'Or Shirley.'

'Rebecca lives in California, he hasn't seen her in five years. Shirley just got divorced, God knows where *she* is. It's not your cousins,' his mother said, 'it's a *woman*.'

'Well, you don't really know that,' David said. He could not believe this about his father. His father? Buying a pair of diamond earrings for a woman who was not David's mother? No, he could not believe it.

She confronted her husband when he got home from the store that night.

She showed him the receipt, just the way she had shown it to David. She demanded to know what he had done with the earrings he'd bought in June. He kept changing his story.

First he said, 'What earrings? Where'd you get that piece of paper? I never saw it before in my life.'

She told him she'd found it in his cigar box, in his dresser drawer.

He said, 'Somebody must've put it there.'

'Who?' she asked.

'Somebody who wants to cause trouble.'

'Who's in the house but you, me, and David?'

'People come in all the time,' he said. 'Friends, people.'

'Do these people go in your dresser drawer? In your cigar box?'

'Who knows where people go?' he said.

'Morrie,' she said, 'it was *you* who put that receipt in your cigar box.'

'What are you, a fingerprint expert?' he asked, and laughed. 'Sherlock Holmes, we got here,' he said to David.

'Who'd you give those earrings to?' she wanted to know.

He remembered then that he had bought the earrings for a friend of his who used to work for him when he had Weber's Army & Navy Surplus Supply Outlet, right after World War II. A man named David (Listening, David thought it odd that his father had chosen *his* name for his mysterious bygone friend) who knew he could get a break for him at the jewelry store right next door.

'Some break,' his father said. 'I could break his *head* for all the trouble he's causing me.'

He smiled.

David's mother was not smiling. David's mother had her arms folded across her chest. David's mother's eyes were flashing lightning bolts.

'David *who*?' she asked. 'This *friend* of yours.'

'Schwartz.'

'I don't remember anybody named David Schwartz.'

'The one who used to work for me when I had the Army-Navy store.'

'I don't remember him.'

'He called me up, asked me if I could get a break for him on a pair of diamond earrings. He knows I'm in business, he knows I have connections.'

'So you laid out the money for him.'

'Sure, he's an old friend. He used to *work* for me, Esther!'

'You laid out all that money.'

'What was it, a lousy four hundred bucks, something like that?'

'You know what it was,' David's mother said.

'Something like that,' his father said, and shrugged.

'Did he pay you back?'

'Certainly, he paid me back.'

'When?'

'Last month sometime, who remembers? Just before he left for Chicago,' his father added, and David suddenly knew he was lying.

'Oh, he went to Chicago,' his mother said.

'He *moved* to Chicago.'

'So he's not *here*, right? To call and ask about these earrings you bought for him.'

'He's not here, right.'

'Where is he in Chicago?'

'Who knows? I haven't heard from him since he moved.'

'You're a lying bastard,' his mother said. It was the first time in his life David had ever heard her use profanity. 'Get out of my house.'

'What are you talking about?'

'Go live with this woman you give diamond earrings to.'

'*What* woman? Esther, please, you don't really think I bought earrings for some *woman*, do you? Can you really believe that?'

David's mother looked him dead in the eye.

'Yes,' she said.

He left that same night. He hadn't seen his brother Max in maybe three, four years, but he drove to New Jersey and asked him if he could stay with him for a few days. He also cleaned out the joint savings account he shared with David's mother, withdrew $2,400 from it the very next day, leaving a balance of $121.32. He was gone for almost two weeks before David wrote his anonymous letter. The anonymous letter was in David's own hand, but he signed it 'A worried friend.' He addressed the letter to his father at Uncle Max's delicatessen in New Jersey. The letter read:

Dear Morris:
   I haven't seen you around the building or in the neighborhood

*for the past few weeks. I hope nothing is wrong. I hope you know
that your son and your wife love you and miss you very much. I
hope you will come home soon.*

Warmest personal regards,
A Worried Friend

He never knew whether his father received the letter or not; he
certainly never mentioned it to David. But he did come home
several weeks later, the day after David began his first semester at
N.Y.U., in fact. He was driving a new car. A 1954 Chevrolet. He
had traded in the old Chrysler and had added to its resale value
almost all the money he'd withdrawn from the joint savings
account. He was smoking a big cigar when he pulled up and
honked the horn. David went to the window; he somehow knew
the person downstairs honking the horn was his father. And
there he was, smoking a big cigar and opening the door of a
brand-new car, and looking like Rockefeller himself in a new
tropical suit and a new snap-brim Panama hat that entirely hid his
baldness. His mustache looked very trim and very black. David's
mother joined him at the window. His father was standing
outside the new car now, his hand on the shiny black fender. He
looked up at David's mother. 'Hello, kiddo,' he called up to her.
'I'm back.'

Just as if nothing had happened.

David's mother never forgot those earrings, though, or the
mysterious lady who had occasioned their purchase. Her whole
life long, she made little digs about the incident.

'Morrie should open a jewelry store, he's such a diamond
expert.'

Or: 'Morrie has a good friend in Chicago, right, Morrie?'

Or, more pointedly: 'Morrie cheats. But only at poker, of
course.'

David wondered for a long time whether his anonymous letter
was what had caused his father to come home. He sometimes felt
that his father started becoming a pain in the ass right *then*, in
September of 1953, when in his magnanimity he decided to
return to his forlorn family and exact from them the proper
measure of repentance for having falsely accused him. David
wondered about *that* a lot, too – *had* his father been falsely

accused? Or was there indeed a mysterious lady someplace, wearing his father's four-hundred-and-twenty-five-dollar diamond earrings? His lie had seemed such a clumsy one; surely a man as clever as he could have come up with something a bit easier to swallow. ('You don't expect me to swallow that, do you?') On the other hand, would he have lied so blatantly if he really *had* purchased those earrings for another woman? Maybe she hadn't existed at all. Maybe there really was a friend named David Schwartz who had moved to Chicago. Who the hell knew?

Eventually, David stopped thinking about his father's alleged infidelity. He preferred not thinking about it. He thought about it again, years later, when his mother died. He thought about it when his father was choosing a coffin, and again when he sold his mother's fur coats – but that was another story. Now, after four years of *not* thinking about it, he was thinking about it once again. He was thinking about it because of the words he'd read in his mother's letter this morning. *I honestly was giving you a fair chance but I guess you did not want it as you are still lying to me.* The letter was still in his jacket pocket, in the closet across the room. He wondered if he should read the rest of the letter.

No, the hell with it, he thought.

Who the hell cares?

He was suddenly ravenously hungry. He looked at his watch. Almost ten already; my, how the time does fly when you're having a good time. He wondered if room service was still serving. He picked up the phone and dialed twenty-two for the front desk.

'Is room service still serving?' he asked.

'No, sir,' the desk clerk said. 'Seven A.M. to nine-thirty P.M., sir.'

He put the receiver back on the cradle. Miami Beach in the off-season, he thought. He wondered if there were any crumbs left on Hillary Watkins' dinner tray. He was tempted to dial 1712 and ask her if there were any leftovers he might have. Is there anything left on your tray? he would ask. What are you wearing? he would ask. He wondered what young, long-legged, full-breasted English girls wore to bed at night. T-shirt and knickers? Did they still call them knickers? Surely they didn't call bikini panties *knickers*? He was tempted to call her and ask her what she called her panties.

He wished he had another drink.

He lifted the phone received and dialed 1712.

'Hello?' she said.

'Hillary? It's David.'

'Well, hello', she said.

'What are you wearing?' he asked.

'Pardon?'

'What are you . . .?'

'Yes, I thought I heard you. Why do you want to know?'

'Do you still call them knickers?'

'Well, I suppose if I were wearing any, I *might* call them that, yes. Although, actually . . .'

'What *are* you wearing?'

'Nothing at all,' she said. 'And you?'

'Why don't you . . .?'

He cut himself short.

'Yes?' she said. 'Why don't I what?'

'Nothing,' he said. 'Good night, Hillary,' he said.

'Did you want to talk about something?' she asked.

'No, I don't think so.'

'Well, all right then,' she said. 'Good night.'

There was a click on the line.

He went to the drapes and closed them. He went back to the bed. Lied to me about being thirty, he thought. Jesus.

Well, he'd lied to her too. Tiny little white lie. Shy, self-effacing David Weber averting his soulful brown eyes and boyishly muttering, 'Well, I'm not used to this sort of thing. Meeting a young girl . . . and . . . talking this way . . . sharing an afternoon this way . . .'

Bullshit.

A lie.

Tiny white lie.

Not so tiny.

Well, Your Honor, one might reasonably argue that if 80 percent of all married men have experienced at least *one* extramarital relationship, then half a dozen or so over the course of almost twenty-two years of marriage might not be considered excessive. Half a dozen, more or less, relatively innocuous liaisons with women who'd meant nothing at all to the defendant, Your Honor, save for the momentary satisfaction they offered. Women who will offer you their comfort, Your Honor, as a learned bartender associate once remarked, see *Weber v. Martini*, merely accommodating women who were willing to offer comfort and solace and tea and sympathy and perfectly good blow jobs after Molly had retired from that profession, so to speak. Well, who could blame her? We were both under considerable strain afterward, we were both – listen, let's not get on *that* again. But you see, Your Honor, it's sometimes difficult to apportion guilt is all I'm trying to say, especially under circumstances as stressful as those were, the death of an only –

Forget it, he thought.

Pick up the phone, he thought. Call the English girl again. Ask her if she's blond down there, ask her if she owns a quivering, quaking quim, ask her if my father will die tonight, like all the others.

The British once ruled an empire.

Maybe she'll have some answers.

He turned off the bedside lamp and fell into a troubled sleep.

Friday

There were two shopping bags full of mail. They rested on the floor between him and Bessie. He had met her in the Emergency Room waiting room, as they'd arranged yesterday. He had known, even before he was fully awake this morning, that today would be the longest day. The two shopping bags full of mail somehow fortified his surmise.

'This is only the first-class,' Bessie said. 'There's more first-class at the building, but I couldn't carry it all. And the other stuff, too: The packages.'

The clock on the wall read ten-thirty.

A man holding a bloodied handkerchief to his face was sitting on the leatherette couch opposite them. His T-shirt was slashed across the front and drenched with blood as well. David figured the man had been in a knife fight. The man watched with interest as David pulled some envelopes from the first shopping bag of mail. He seemed not to be in any pain. He kept the bloodied handkerchief pressed tightly to his face. No one had yet come to see what was the matter with him.

'A lot of this seems to be bills,' David said.

'Well, he was always sending away for things,' Bessie said. 'Plates and stamps, other things.'

'What I thought we'd do,' David said, suddenly overwhelmed by the mass of envelopes stuffed in the shopping bags, 'is just separate the letters from the rest . . .'

'Yes.'

'. . . and read him the ones he wants us to open.'

'That would be good,' Bessie said.

He began sorting through the mail, separating what were obviously bills or first-class mail offerings from what appeared to be personal letters. A nurse came from behind the counter.

'Mr. McGruder?' she asked.

'Yes?' the man with the bloodied handkerchief said.

'Will you come in now, please? Doctor will see you.' She looked at David and Bessie. 'Are you with him?' she asked.

'No,' David said.

'This isn't the public library,' she said.

'My father's in Intensive Care,' David said.

'That's on the third floor, the nurse said.

'I know that. We thought . . .'

'There's a waiting room up there. This is Emergency,' she said. 'We can't have you sitting here reading your mail.'

'It's my father's mail,' David said idiotically.

'Whoever's,' the nurse said. 'Mr. McGruder? Will you come with me, please?'

David picked up the mail he'd already sorted and placed it on top of the other envelopes in the first shopping bag. He picked up both shopping bags and followed Bessie through the labyrinth of corridors that led to the main lobby. They took the elevator up to the third floor. But instead of going directly to the Intensive Care waiting room, they settled instead on one of the leatherette couches just beyond the elevators and the third-floor nurses' station.

It took him almost twenty minutes to go through the mail. Included among the envelopes he had separated as bills were several from doctors. He opened one of them. It contained a slip of paper and a return envelope. The slip of paper read:

COURTESY NOTICE

This is to remind you that your account is still unpaid.

Your check TODAY will be appreciated.

Thank you.

The doctor's name was Carlos Herrera. Apparently, he had been the anesthesiologist during the first operation. His fee was $1,175.00.

David opened another envelope. The enclosed statement for professional services was from three doctors who called themselves The Pulmonary Medical Group. The statement was a computer printout. It read:

Dear patient:

This is a statement representing your recent hospitalization charge of $615.00.

We do not accept assignment of Medicare claims. Upon

143

receipt of your payment, this office will file your Medicare claim for you in order that you may be reimbursed by Medicare.

We have a signed form and we'll file your claims as soon as your payment is received.

If you would like to discuss payment of your account or filing of your insurance, please contact our bookkeepers or insurance clerk.

Thank you,

Insurance department

Note: An itemized statement of this charge(s) will follow.

'You don't have to pay any doctor bills,' Bessie said. 'They try to get you to pay them direct, because sometimes Medicare takes a long time. Just forget about them. When my husband died, *alav ha-sholom*, I didn't pay nothing. The doctors got their money direct from Medicare.'

She's giving a lawyer advice, David thought, and said nothing. He put the statement back into the envelope and looked at his watch. It was five minutes to eleven.

'We'd better go in now,' he said.

The tube was still taped to his father's mouth. The Cuban nurse had told David it was attached to a respirator, to help his father breathe a bit more easily. The respirator huffed and puffed beside the bed. The tube was still beaded with drops of moisture. His father's eyes looked moist. There was a bewildered expression on his face. Bessie leaned over the bed and kissed his cheek.

'Hello, Morris,' she said, 'how are you feeling today?'

His father lifted his hand and then let it drop onto the sheet. The bewildered expression remained on his face.

'We brought some mail for you,' David said. 'Would you like me to read it to you?'

His father nodded.

'You tell me which ones you want me to open, okay?'

His father's eyes closed and opened in assent, as if nodding were too tiring an effort.

144

David turned over the first of the small sheaf of envelopes in his hand and looked at the return address.

'This is from R. Zimmerman,' he said. 'Do you know anybody by that name? In the Bronx?'

They eyes closed and opened again.

'Shall I read it to you?'

His father blinked permission. David opened the envelope and began reading the letter.

'My dear Morrie, I hope everything is well with you. Myself I feel fine. The weather is good here. I would love to know when you are coming to New York. I am anxious to see you. I miss you very much. Two ladies have called me up to find out if you were at my house. I told them you were supposed to come but I did not know when. I am supposed to go on a trip which is not important so please let me know when you are coming so I would know what to do. Keep well. Take care of yourself. Rose.'

He put the letter back into the envelope.

'Do you know someone named Rose Zimmerman?' he asked. His father nodded.

'Were you planning to go up to New York again?' Another nod.

'Well, you'd better hurry up and get out of here,' David said, smiling, and turned over the second envelope in his hand. The return address was printed on one of those stickers the veterans' organizations sent when soliciting funds. 'This is from Mrs. L. Di Marco,' he said. 'Shall I read it to you?'

His father nodded.

The letter was dated May 16. It was written on lavender stationery with a small printed drawing of a butterfly in the lower right-hand corner.

'Dear Morris,' David read. 'A few lines to let you know I was worried that you did not write to me. You can still write to my niece in Scarsdale, she will mail me your letter until I let you know where to send it. The doctor said I am OK but have a very bad case of arthritis in my hand and I cannot use it yet. The pain is so terrible that I cry sometimes. Let me hear from you. I miss your letters. You are the only one I think about a lot. I am glad that you are OK. I will be by my cousin in Brooklyn for a few more days as my niece in Scarsdale works. I will let you know where I will be when my niece finds an apartment or house when I will go back to Scarsdale. But I will let you know where to send my mail. Love, Lucy.'

His father opened his eyes wide, as though in surprise. He brought his hand to his belly. He opened his mouth. It seemed he would scream out in pain. His mouth and his eyes remained wide open. His belly seemed to ripple under the sheet.

'Are you all right?' David said at once. 'Shall I get a nurse?'

His father shook his head. His hand was resting flat on his belly. His eyes returned to what was now their normal look, moist and somewhat glazed, unfocused, bewildered.

'Are you sure you're all right?' David said.

His father nodded.

David looked at the next envelope.

'This is from Mrs. Di Marco, too,' he said. 'Shall I open it?'

His father nodded.

The same lavender stationery, the same printed butterfly drawing in the lower right-hand corner. The letter was dated May 17, the day after she'd written the one David had just read.

'Dear Morris. Received your letter of Sunday. I sent another letter before this one as I thought that you did not write to me. I feel a little better now, but I still can't pick up anything with my hand. Sorry I never send you any pictures. Maybe someone else will. I'll close with love as I cannot write as my fingers hurt. I am very, very glad that you are OK. Love, Lucy.'

His father sighed.

'Are you all right?' David asked. 'Are you sure you don't want me to get a nurse?'

He nodded.

'This is the last one,' David said, and turned over the envelope. 'From a Mrs. J. Klein in Brooklyn. Shall I open it?'

His father nodded and then lifted his hand. His forefinger moved.

'I don't know what you're trying to say, Pop.'

His father pointed at the letter. His finger made a jabbing motion.

'Do you want me to read it?'

His father nodded. In exasperation, he dropped his hand to the sheet again.

David opened the envelope. There was a Father's Day card inside the envelope. He remembered all at once that Sunday would be Father's Day and suddenly felt guilty for not yet having bought his father a present. He always sent him a box of good cigars on Father's Day. *I'm wise to you, Davey. You send the old man a box of cigars on his birthday, and you think that's enough*. There was a separate handwritten note folded into the card, but David first read the inscription on the card itself, 'Dear Morrie,' and then the printed rhymed sentiment, and then the words 'Love, Josie.'

His father lifted his hand. He jabbed at the air with his finger again.

'What?' David said, puzzled.

His father kept jabbing his finger at the card.

'Oh,' David said. 'Is this the woman you were telling me about the other day? Josie?'

His father nodded slowly, patiently.

'The one whose address you wanted me to have?'

Another patient nod. His son the lawyer had finally understood. Four years of French, David could imagine him thinking, and he *finally* understands what I'm trying to tell him.

'I have her address now,' David said. 'It's on the back of the envelope. There's a note here, too, shall I read the note?'

His father nodded.

'Dearest Morrie,' he read. 'What happened to you? I did not hear from you since your postcard in April. I believe I wrote two letters to you explaining all that had been going on. To top it off, the Post Office lost some of my Hold mail and did I have more headaches and problems. Therefore I don't know how much of my mail went astray. Nothing in this world is right anymore. God help us with all that is going on and no system anymore. You stated in your card that you would be up early in June. Where are you? I made one phone call to the number you gave me in March and I asked the lady who answered the phone if you were there. She said you did not come to New York yet. That's it. Please write to me soon and let me know what's going on. I miss you very much. Love, Josie.'

Bessie, who had been standing silently by the bed until now, cleared her throat and said, 'You'd better hurry up and get well, Morris. All these ladies waiting for you.'

His father simply nodded.

'He *is* going to get well,' David said quickly. 'Aren't you, Pop?'

His father nodded.

The Cuban nurse appeared in the doorway.

'I'm sorry, swee'heart,' she said, 'your visitors ha' to go now.'

David looked up at the clock. It was eleven-fifteen. He went to the bed and kissed his father on the forehead. The same damp, hot flesh. 'I'll be back at two,' he said. 'That's less than three hours from now. Two o'clock, Pop, okay?'

His father nodded.

Bessie kissed him on the cheek.

'I'll come later,' she said. 'I'm not sure two o'clock.'

He looked up into her face. He seemed to want to say something to her. David wished he would not look so bewildered. At last, he simply nodded again.

In the corridor, waiting for the elevator, Bessie said, 'This must have been happening a long time. Longer than we know. Could something like this happen overnight? Still, how long *could* it be? We had a party for him at the hotel, before he went up to see you in March. He was fine. Dancing, walking into doors – you know how he walks into a door and makes believe he broke his nose? He was fine. That was only in March, before his birthday, what could it be, three months ago? So who knows? All at once, he's a very sick man, all at once he's dying.' She sighed deeply. 'The way he looks,' she said. 'Such a change,' she said. 'Such a change.'

Sitting in the delicatessen across the street from the hotel, chewing on a fatty pastrami sandwich on stale rye bread, he thought about what Bessie had said. *Such a change, such a change.* Referring to the way he *looked*, of course, and not to what he had *become*.

He could remember his father's last visit north, in March. He usually timed his semiannual pilgrimages so that one of them fell in September (when it was too hot and muggy to breathe in Miami) and the other just before his birthday in March, the better

148

to remind his 'delinquent' son that he was getting on in years (as he often said with a sigh) and didn't know how many more birthdays he'd be here on earth to enjoy. The trips north, David realized now, were less necessitated by a burning desire to see his son and daughter-in-law than they were by the more urgent need to visit all the Josies, Roses, Lucys, and God knew how many other women in the New York Chapter of his father's harem. 'Would it break your heart to come to Miami once in a while? I have a sofa bed in the living room, you and The Shiksa could sleep on it.' How? David wondered now. Where would your *plates* sleep?

His father's visit in March might have been less difficult if Molly hadn't been away for the weekend in Hempstead, visiting her own parents. He remembered wondering at the time if she hadn't planned it that way. Did Molly find his father as big a pain in the ass as David himself did? Despite the way she could still twist him around her finger? If Molly had been there, things might have been different. Molly knew how to handle him. Whenever his father came up with any of his frequent and preposterous proclamations, Molly brushed them aside as though they'd never been uttered.

'You should never order anything but spaghetti and meatballs in an Italian restaurant,' his father said.

'Then that's what you should order, Dad,' Molly answered gently, meanwhile ordering for herself the *tortellini alla panna* as an appetizer and the *osso buco* for the main course.

'How much veal can there be on a *bone* shank?' his father asked.

But he studied Molly throughout the meal, and maybe – just maybe – considered whether his lifelong habit of ordering spaghetti and meatballs (What does he order in a *Chinese* restaurant? David wondered. Chow mein?) wasn't quite as sophisticated as he'd imagined.

Molly knew how to handle him.

David's mother had handled him in much the same way when she was still alive. Whenever his father said anything stupid (It was odd that David had never recognized his inanities then), his mother would flatten him in a minute with a gentle, 'Oh, be quiet, please, Morrie,' or, on occasion and with the same pleasant smile, 'Don't be such a dope, Morrie.' When he was a boy, David could not possibly conceive of his father as a 'dope.' Each time his mother squelched him, he would feel fiercely protective and would sometimes whisper a discreet, 'Mom, please,' which his mother would wave off with an airy smile.

The first glimpse he'd had of the man his father was to become – or perhaps the man he already was, although as yet unrecognized – was on the very day his mother died, when David went with him to the funeral home to select a casket. His father shopped the rows upon rows of coffins as though he were considering stock for a new store he might open and close in a wink. He finally settled on a simple pine box that cost him only a couple of hundred dollars. He explained away his choice with a solemn, 'In keeping with the Orthodox tradition,' an excuse in direct contradiction to the fact that he hadn't been inside a synagogue – Orthodox, Conservative, *or* Reform – for as long as David could remember. That was the first time David noticed how short he was. He had always thought of his father as a tall man; now, suddenly, he seemed short.

His mother had left all her belongings to her 'beloved husband, Morris,' with the exception of her jewelry, which she directed be divided equally between her two surviving sisters. But the language in the will (even though David himself had drawn it) was somewhat vague about the disposition of two full-length fur coats, a mink and an otter, which David's trust money had enabled her to buy. The language read, and David had thought it perfectly adequate at the time, 'As for any of my other possessions for which my husband, Morris, may have no use, it is my wish that they, too, be shared equally between my sisters Naomi Blatt and Ruth Epstein.' His father had no conceivable use for a pair of fur coats styled respectively in the years 1968 and 1969. He offered them to Molly, but Molly had a mink of her own, as well as a raccoon, and, besides, she told him she would feel funny wearing clothes that had belonged to her mother-in-law. She suggested to David's father that he simply send the coats to the sisters, as directed in the will. David's father said, 'What for? They both live in Florida. What use can they have for fur coats in Florida?'

David advised him that by any reasonable reading of the will, the coats could be considered 'other possessions for which my husband, Morris, may have no use,' but his father remained adamant. 'I'll *find* a use, don't worry,' he said. David's mother's initials were stitched into the lining of each coat. With the dedication of a cat burglar trying to fence stolen goods, his father looked through the telephone directories for all five boroughs, searching for any female with the initials E.W., calling at random to ask the baffled woman on the other end of the line if she might be interested in buying a pair of mint-condition fur coats. David told him he was inviting a midnight visit from a burly intruder who would conk him on his bald head and *steal* the coats from him. His father said, 'So what am I *supposed* to do with them? I have no use for them,' acknowledgment in itself of his wife's codicil, the contradiction completely lost on him. He steadfastly refused to send the coats to his sisters-in-law and at last sold them to a furrier on Canal Street for almost exactly what the funeral had cost him. It was David's later contention that his father had been enormously annoyed by his mother's untimely heart attack and had been determined that she herself (or at least her *coats*) should bear the cost of her burial.

The man who sat opposite him at the restaurant table on that weekend visit in March fussed over everything. He ordered a sirloin steak and then complained to the waitress that it was too well done – 'Is this shoe leather?' – and asked her to take it back and substitute the pork chops instead, big Orthodox Jew that he was. While eating the pork, he told David he shouldn't be eating pork, it gave him heartburn, he could already feel shooting pains in his chest. When David asked him why he *was* eating pork if he *shouldn't* be eating pork, his father said, 'What am I *supposed* to eat? That shoe leather she tried to palm off on me?' David was eating a dozen clams on the half-shell, ordered as a main course, and drinking the remains of his Canadian and soda. His father said, 'You shouldn't mix clams and alcohol. Your Uncle Martin, my brother, *alav ha-sholom*, died of mixing clams and alcohol. They turned to rocks in his stomach.' As far as David knew, his uncle's death had been caused by a fall from a ladder and a subsequent concussion. Mildly, he responded that he'd been mixing clams and alcohol for years now and to his knowledge still had no rocks in his stomach. 'The rocks are in your *head*,' his father said, and then immediately, 'Okay, I'll clam up, but don't say I didn't warn you.'

After he had devoured the pork chops he said he shouldn't have been eating, apparently forgetting his earlier fears of an imminent angina attack, he ordered coffee and dessert, and went off to the bathroom while the waitress, frightened by his imperious air, scurried out to the kitchen. When he came back to the table, he said, 'There are no paper towels in the bathroom. I told them. I ask them what I was supposed to dry my hands on – my shirttails?' Sitting, he suddenly smiled and said, 'Confucius say, "Woman who cook carrots and peas in the same pot unsanitary." What's taking her so long with that coffee?'

The sugar bowl contained little packets of sugar, each one imprinted with a different astrological sign. He looked through the bowl for his own sign, and then read aloud and with obvious delight the character analysis printed below the symbol. 'Pisces is a water sign. You are endowed with charity, sympathy, and sensitivity. Your colors are sea blues or greens. Your stones are aquamarine or coral. Your plants are water lilies or ferns.' Nodding with pleasure, he began searching through the bowl for packets of sugar imprinted with the other eleven astrological signs.

'My friends'll get a kick out of these,' he said, arranging them on the table before him. 'The people I play cards with.' Then, to David's astonishment, he began stuffing the packets of sugar into his jacket pocket.

'Pop!' David said, shocked.

'What is it?' his father said, looking up sharply, surprised by his tone.

'Don't steal the sugar, huh, Pop?' David said, and tried a weak smile.

'*Steal* it?' his father said. '*What?*'

David was glancing nervously past his father's shoulder toward the swinging kitchen doors, fearful that the waitress might reappear just as he was engaged in his act of petty larceny.

'Pop,' he said evenly, 'you're embarrassing me, really. Molly and I come here all the time. Please put the sugar back in the bowl.'

'We're *paying* for this sugar,' his father said. 'It's included in the price of the meal.'

'Not a dozen packets of it.'

'Suppose I want to use a dozen packs in my coffee?'

'You drink your coffee without sugar or milk,' David said. His heart was pounding.

'What difference does *that* make?' his father said. 'For every person who drinks it black, there's another person who uses two, three, four packs of sugar. They figure on such things, David. It's called shrinkage. When I was still in business, I . . .'

'Shrinkage is stealing,' David said.

'Baloney,' his father said, and did not return the packets to the sugar bowl. The waitress appeared a moment later with his coffee and dessert. He took one sip, looked up at her, said, 'This is ice cold, bring me some hot coffee, will you, please? Do you know what the word *hot* means?'

He did not once mention Bessie on that trip in March.

The first David learned of her was when she called to tell him his father was in the hospital.

'I'm a good friend of his,' she said, 'we play cards together, I give him dinner sometimes.'

The 'friends' he described during dinner that night were a group of men and women approximately his own age, with whom he played cards every night. The games they played varied from bridge to penny-ante poker to gin rummy at a nickel a point. They played in various apartments and hotel rooms on the beach – but never in his father's apartment. 'Why should I have card players in?' he asked. 'They spill drinks, they drop ashes on the carpet, who needs them making ashes of themselves?' he said, and smiled. He himself, David thought, scattered ashes as though they were the vestiges of countless cremated bodies. His vest – he almost always wore a vest – was a favorite target, but neither did he neglect his lap, or the tablecloth, or Molly's prized Oriental rugs, or indeed anywhere or anyplace but an ashtray. He lighted a cigar now, blowing out puffs of noxious smoke that obliterated the table and almost suffocated David. 'I'm smoking only good cigars these days,' he said, puffing out smoke. David could not remember what his 'bad' cigars smelled like, but he suspected they must have been poisonous.

His father had become an expert on everything. That his expertise was based on a combination of folklore, pretense, and total ignorance seemed not to trouble him in the slightest. In the car on the way back to the apartment, a radio newscaster was talking about two New York City cops who'd been shot when they stopped a speeding automobile. 'It was their own fault,' his father said. 'They should have approached the car one on either side of it. That way, he wouldn't have been able to shoot *both* of them.' He had no knowledge, of course, about whether the cops had flanked the suspect vehicle, or approached it head on, or indeed crawled into it through an open window. But here was the learned Scotland Yard inspector, holding forth on established police techniques as though he himself had prevented a thousand holdups in his time, oblivious to the didactic sound of his own voice, knowing only that *he* would have handled the situation differently and better.

In similar fashion, the moment they entered the apartment again, he advised David first that he ought to convince The Shiksa to paint the walls in different colors instead of the awful white they were now painted – 'You'll have to get permission from the landlord, you know' – even though David and Molly were perfectly content with the clean, expansive look of the place, and then suggested that they add on another guest room by dividing their large living room in half – 'What would that cost you, another wall? Two, three thousand bucks at the most? I'll let you have the money if you're short.' (How generous you are with my money, David thought, and was immediately contrite afterward.) His father also informed him that the new wallpaper in the powder room was too quiet ('Couldn't you find something a little jazzier?'), asked if he thought Molly would like him to send some coupons that would give her a ten-cent discount the next time she bought instant coffee, and wondered aloud if David ever said the *kaddish* on the anniversary of his mother's death each year ('Do you ever even *go* to temple anymore? It isn't right to

154

become godless, you know' – this forty-five minutes after eating pork chops), his brown eyes misting over as they always did when he spoke of the dear departed wife whose mink and otter he'd refused to dispense with as per her wishes, sprinkling cigar ashes on the newly upholstered couch and stinking up the entire living room with his El Ropo fumes.

Comfortably seated, puffing smoke, his father explained his daily Miami Beach routine. He awakened at eight each morning, prepared himself a breakfast of orange juice, corn flakes with sliced bananas, a cup of coffee drunk black as always, and a toasted English muffin spread with strawberry jam and either cream cheese or butter. He then retired to his bathroom for his morning toilet. He shaved every other day, and he used to shower *every* day until he had to begin stacking his plates in the bathtub because all the closets were full. 'You should see those plates, David, they're beautiful.' He now took a sponge bath each and every day, he told David with some pride, as though he alone in a city of unwashed barbarians observed any sanitary rules at all. After breakfast, he went into the living room, spread out his correspondence on the table there, and methodically answered each and every letter he received from relatives and friends all over the United States. (He had surprised David on his visit last September by scanning the pages of the Bronx telephone directory to 'see if there's any Webers still living up there.') He told David that he never wrote twice to anybody who didn't immediately answer one of his letters. 'Why should I waste time with delinquents?' he said.

At twelve noon, each and every day, his father took the elevator down from his fifth-floor apartment on Collins Avenue and Lincoln Road, bought the *Miami Herald* and the *New York Daily News* at the drugstore on the corner, and read both papers cover to cover while eating his lunch in a deli on Washington. He always ordered the same thing for lunch. A cheese omelet and a bottle of cream soda. 'Too much coffee is no good for you,' he said, and then demonstrated the premise with trembling hands and stuttering, 'It m-m-m-makes you n-n-n-nervous.' He strolled up Collins Avenue after lunch each day – 'It's terrible now, full of Cuban prostitutes, even in broad daylight' – as far as Twenty-first Street, and then walked back to the apartment to take a nap before dinner and his nightly card game. He told David that he usually had dinner with one or another of the widows in his building. 'I reciprocate, don't worry,' he said. 'I help them do their shopping, I buy them an ice cream cone every now and then. Listen, do you know what dinner out would cost me every night? Six or seven dollars a night, am I right? This way I'm ahead of the game.'

Elvira Brufani on the third floor prepared spaghetti and meatballs (his favorite Italian restaurant gourmet dish) every Tuesday and Thursday night. Elvira had been married to a barber who'd passed away last June. 'The man was very wealthy, David, he owned a chain of shops all across Manhattan. She gets dividends on blue-chip stocks every month.' On Mondays and Wednesdays, his dinners were prepared by a woman named Shirley Levinson, whose husband had been 'a wealthy garment manufacturer' and who cooked kreplach, borscht, perogin, boiled beef, knadls, 'and a lot of other delicious stuff like your mother used to make, *aleha ha-shalom*.' On Fridays and Sundays, he ate in the apartment of a woman forbiddingly named Harriet Hammer – 'No relation to the private eye,' he said, his eyes twinkling – who was a meat-and-potatoes, no-nonsense dame, the female equivalent, to hear him tell it, of Morris Weber himself.

In March, listening to his father, still not knowing that Bessie even existed, David suspected that Harriet Hammer was the sole recipient of his lingering sexual urges. 'I spend a little time with her, you know, after dinner. The others, I usually go straight to my card game.' David also suspected, from little hints his father dropped, that Harriet was a black woman, and he could only guess at what down-home fare his father might be enjoying every Friday and Sunday night. In Harriet's soul-food kitchen, did his father order chitlins, hominy grits, ham hocks, black-eyed peas, buttermilk, and a little *shtup* on the side?

Better than this rotten pastrami, for sure, David thought.

Such a change, such a change.

He wondered again when the change had taken place. He hadn't been that way all along, had he? Surely not. Not with David's mother there to restrain him. Then it must have happened after she died. He must have decided then and there to

156

begin living the life he'd really *wanted* to live all along.

Clear out all this junk, and I could make a nice room for my sewing machine.

Esther, it's my hobby!

His hobby, *all* of his hobbies, had overtaken his life.

David suddenly wondered how long he'd known all those women who were panting for his arrival in New York. Was one of them wearing a pair of diamond earrings that had cost four hundred and twenty-five dollars plus tax back in 1953? And how about all the women down *here* who wined and dined him on alternate nights? Was there also an obliging widow who fed him on *Saturday*? Bessie, maybe? Had Bessie known before this morning about the women in New York? Did she know about the women right here in Miami Beach? Jesus, he thought, what can *any* woman possibly find to love or even *like* about that meddling, miserly, opinionated, grasping, ungiving, unshaven, unwashed, unsightly, *short* little son of a – I don't mean that, he thought.

Pop, I don't mean that.

I'm sorry, Pop, I didn't mean it.

Don't die, Pop, he thought.

Please don't die.

The waiting-room family was changing.

Mrs. Daniels and her fat daughter Louise were not there for the two o'clock visit. Neither was Mr. Di Salvo. Mrs. Horowitz was the only familiar face. Flushed and excited, she took a seat beside David and immediately lit a cigarette.

'So how's your father?' she asked.

'All right, I suppose.'

'They did the operation?'

'Yes.'

'What did they find?'

'Nothing.'

'Doctors,' she said, and let out a stream of smoke. 'I'll tell you something, Mr. Weber, I never want to get as old as my mother is. The minute I can't lift my own valise, that's it. I'll take a pill. Thirty seconds, it'll be all over.'

'What kind of pill could you take?' a young woman across the room asked. She was a tall redhead wearing white slacks and a tight black sweater. She was very proud of her breasts. She kept toying with a strand of pearls dangling between her breasts. The woman sitting beside her, a few years older, David guessed, was also redheaded. She was wearing white shorts and a tomato-colored tube top. Her breasts were as spectacular as the other woman's, but she had nothing dangling between them, nothing with which to toy. The Dolly Sisters, David thought. Ike and Mike.

'They have these pills,' Mrs. Horowitz said. 'Like the Nazis had during the war. You bite on them, and it's all over.'

'I wouldn't want to bite on a pill,' one of the Dolly Sisters said.

'It would taste bitter,' the other one said.

'They have pills that aren't bitter,' Mrs. Horowitz said.

'Where do you get these pills?'

'From your doctor. He'll prescribe them. You tell him you can't lift your own valise, he'll prescribe a pill. Thirty seconds and good-bye.'

'I'd rather die in my sleep,' a man sitting near the television set said. He was short and fat and wearing a business suit and tie.

'Or on a tennis court,' one of the Dolly Sisters said.

'After a great serve,' the other one said.

'An ace,' the first one said.

'What's an ace?' Mrs. Horowitz asked.

'When your opponent can't even reach it,' one of the Dolly Sisters explained.

'A heart attack on a tennis court. That's better than a bitter pill,' the other one said.

'*Life* is a bitter pill,' the man in the business suit said philosophically.

The real danger is living, David thought.

'Live to be like my mother in there?' Mrs. Horowitz asked. 'What for? Hitting my own daughter? Telling me not to come to see her anymore? What for?'

'My brother had a heart attack,' the man in the business suit said. 'But not on a tennis court. And it didn't kill him.'

'How old is he?' Mrs. Horowitz said.

'Seventy-eight.'

'Seventy-five is what I want,' Mrs. Horowitz said. 'That's

enough. Who wants people carrying my valises? Twenty more years, that's enough.'

'Wait till you're seventy-five, though,' one of the Dolly Sisters said. 'You won't think it's enough then.'

'You won't think it's *nearly* enough,' the other one said.

'There are very active people at seventy-five,' the man in the business suit said.

'We were on a cruise last year,' one of the Dolly Sisters said, 'there were seventy-five-year-old *sex* fiends on it. Am I right, Helen?'

'Sex fiends,' her sister agreed, nodding.

'There are very active people at seventy-five,' the man in the business suit said again.

'English mostly,' Helen said. 'The sex fiends. Am I right, Jean?'

'English,' her sister agreed, nodding.

'Where was this cruise?' Mrs. Horowitz asked.

'On the Rhine,' Jean said.

'In Germany,' Helen said.

'There were *Englishmen* going to Germany?'

'Tons of them.'

'After what the Nazis did?' Mrs. Horowitz said, shaking her head.

'The world forgets,' the man in the business suit said philosophically. 'The world has a short memory.'

'Who's your patient here?' Mrs. Horowitz asked the Dolly Sisters.

'Our mother,' they answered in unison.

'What's wrong with her?'

'A stroke,' they said in unison.

'Can't we go in now?' the man in the business suit said. 'I'm running the store all alone with my brother sick. It's almost two o'clock. Can't we go in?'

The pink lady tore her attention from the television screen. She looked at the clock. 'Just a few more minutes,' she said.

'A pill,' Mrs. Horowitz said. 'Thirty seconds, and it's all over.'

'How are you feeling, Pop?' he asked. 'Are you feeling a little better?'

159

His father nodded weakly.

'I just had the worst pastrami sandwich I ever had in my life,' David said. 'I thought you had good pastrami down here in Miami.'

His father looked at him blankly.

'Not that you want to hear me beefing about it,' David said.

His father raised his hand.

'Yes, Pop?'

He brought his hand to his mouth.

'*You* want some pastrami? You're better off without it.'

His father shook his head impatiently. He touched his lips again.

'Some water? Something to drink?'

His father shook his head. He dropped his hand wearily.

'I'm sorry, Pop, I don't understand. Shall I get the nurse?'

His father nodded. David went out into the corridor. The Vietnamese nurse was at the nurses' station.

'My father wants something, but I don't know what. Could you come in, please?' David said.

The nurse looked at him blankly. The Dragon Lady, David thought. Inscrutable. Without saying a word, she came from behind the counter and walked into his father's room. David followed her.

'Did you want something, Mr. Weber?' she asked.

His father raised his hand to his lips again.

'He doesn't want water, I already asked him,' David said.

'Some ice, Mr. Weber? Did you want some ice chips?'

His father nodded.

'I'll get you some ice, Mr. Weber,' she said, and walked out.

'Is your mouth a little dry?' David asked.

His father nodded.

'You're looking much better now than you did this morning,' David said. 'Good color, good . . . His voice trailed. 'Plenty of plates you've got there in the apartment,' he said. 'Those small boxes are plates, aren't they?'

His father nodded.

'Plenty of them there. Lots of mail for you to look at, too, when you get out of here. It'll just be a while now, Pop. Nothing to keep you from getting well now. Just a matter of . . .'

160

The Vietnamese nurse was back. He wondered if she had overheard him. He wondered if she knew the exploratory surgery had found nothing. He wondered if she knew he'd been lying to his father. She handed David a paper cup full of ice chips.

'Try to give him the smaller pieces,' she said, and left the room.

He went to the bed.

'Here's your ice, Pop,' he said. 'Do you want it now?'

His father nodded.

He took a small sliver of ice between his thumb and forefinger, placed it between his father's lips.

'Here you go,' he said.

The ice slid between his father's lips and into his mouth. His lips moved. A dribble of water worked its way down his chin. David pulled a Kleenex tissue from the box beside the bed and wiped his father's chin.

'More?' he asked.

His father nodded.

David searched for another small sliver in the paper cup. He found one and held it to his father's lips. The inside of his mouth looked red and raw. The sliver of ice disappeared. His father moved the ice around inside his mouth.

'Does that feel good?' David asked.

His father lowered his eyelids and raised them again.

'Do you want some more?'

His father shook his head.

'I'll put it here on the windowsill, if you want more later,' David said.

A look of pain crossed his father's face. Again, as he had done during this morning's visit, he brought his hand to his belly. His belly rippled under the sheet. He kept his hand flat on the sheet. The wave subsided.

'Little pain?' David asked.

His father did nothing. No nod, no blink of the eyes, nothing. He seemed to be concentrating on his belly, on his hand spread flat on his belly.

'Have they been giving you anything for pain?'

Still, his father remained motionless, his hand on his belly. He lifted his hand from the sheet. The fingers widespread, he waggled his hand from side to side, the way one might signal 'so-so' if you'd asked him how he was feeling.

'What does that mean, Pop?' David asked.

His father kept waggling his hand.

'Shall I get someone?'

His father nodded.

David went out into the corridor. A tall, strapping young man with muscles bulging in his green T-shirt was just passing the door. 'Excuse me,' David said. 'My father needs help.'

The muscular young man walked into his father's room. The weight-lifter, David thought. The one his father had told him about. Allan? Alvin?

'Hello, Morrie,' he said. 'How are you feeling?'

His father stared at him blankly.

'Not so good, huh, Morrie? Don't worry, you'll feel better.'

'His mouth looks very raw,' David said.

'That may be from all the medication,' the young man said. 'Sometimes you get a yeast infection secondary to the use of antibiotics. What can I do for you, Morrie?'

His father lifted his hand and made the same wigwagging motion.

'Do you have to urinate, Morrie?'

His father nodded. There was apparently a sign language all the nurses began to understand after a while. If a man waggled his hand from side to side, it didn't mean he was feeling only so-so, it meant he had to pee. A universal sign language spoken only by the sick and dying and understood by their keepers.

'There's a tube in your penis,' the young man said. 'It may give you an urge to urinate. You don't have to worry about wetting the bed, Morrie. Just urinate whenever you want to, okay?'

His father sighed.

'Was there anything else, Morrie?'

His father shook his head.

'Now you get better, you hear me? We all want you to get better, Morrie.'

He patted the sheet covering his father's legs and left the room. David remembered what his father had said about him. *He used to lift weights. He picks me up like I'm a baby* . . .

'It's a hell of a thing to be eighty-two,' David said, 'and to have to worry about wetting the bed, isn't it, Pop?'

His father nodded wearily. He lifted his hand again. His forefinger trembled. He made the letter M on the air.

'Molly?' David said. 'She's fine, Pop.'

His father's finger snaked on the air. An S.

'Stephen?' David said.

His father nodded.

'He's . . .'

He looked at his father.

'He's fine, Pop,' he said. 'Do you want more ice?'

His father nodded.

He took the paper cup from where he had left it on the sink counter. The cup was cold in his hand. He carried it to the bed. His father opened his mouth in anticipation. He saw the raw, mutilated-looking flesh inside his father's mouth. He reached into the cup for a sliver of ice.

Last summer, they bought the Italian ices, he and Molly, from a roadside stand on the way from the airport to the hotel. Ices in a cup. Lemon ices for Molly. Chocolate ices for himself. The Sardinian sun was very hot, even so late in the afternoon. They sat in the parked Fiat eating the ices. Beyond, the green waters of the Costa Smeralda sparkled. They could hear the gentle murmur of the sea.

The villa near the hotel was magnificent.

Moorish in design, approached by a long dirt road lined with twisted cork trees, it sat in pristine isolated splendor on a point of land overlooking the bay below. A massive entrance archway framed a pair of thick oaken doors that opened onto a tiled living room, its windows shuttered against the fierce Mediterranean sun. A woodburning fireplace was on the far wall, flanked by a pair of arched doors. A clerestory ran around three sides of the living room. When they threw open the shutters, they saw a small garden in the center of which an orange tree was bursting with ripe fruit.

There was a tiled terrace at the back of the house. A flight of wooden steps led from the terrace to a private beach below, where a small blue rowboat bobbed on bluer water. A staff of three – housekeeper, gardener, and cook – stood by beaming and *davening* as Norman Rosen showed them through. Norman

163

explained that they came with the house, and that their days off were Thursday and every other Sunday, just like in America. He hoped that David could be unpacked and ready for a meeting with the wops and himself by five-thirty that afternoon, and that he'd be ready to start work on the contracts first thing tomorrow morning.

'I'll tell you the truth,' he said, 'these Italian lawyers are giving me a pain in the ass. *We're* ready to shoot a movie here, and all of a sudden *they're* finding things wrong with papers they've had for two months already. I hope you work well under pressure, David, I sincerely mean that. Unpack, I'll see you at the hotel in half an hour. You just drive around the cove, you know the way, huh? Molly, as beautiful as you are, I'll have to ask that you busy yourself elsewhere while we're in conference, okay? See you later, David,' he said, and left the house.

For the next three days, locked into a suite at the hotel, David wrangled with the Italian lawyers. None of them spoke English. Their interpreter was a twenty-four-year-old Italian girl named Arabella. She did not know how to translate 'bottom line' into Italian, but she came to work each day dressed in a blouse slashed invitingly low over her naked breasts. Her dark eyes spoke to him. He had difficulty concentrating on the monumental tangle before him. The Italians had made an antipasto of the simple contracts David and his partner had labored over for months. Norman's director and crew were scheduled to arrive at any moment. His stars would be here in a week. The Italians shook their heads vigorously each time Arabella translated David's thoughts to them. Whenever she fumbled for a word, he patted her hand consolingly.

On the fourth day, he retired to the second bedroom of the villa, where he began revamping the contracts at a long table Giovanni the gardener moved in from the hallway. Molly had fallen into the habit of sunning or bathing topless on the small secluded beach below. When he mentioned to her that perhaps she ought to dress more decorously for the beach, she said, 'Don't be silly, this is Italy.' But she did agree to cover up whenever Giovanni was down there raking – much to the old man's annoyance. The revisions were difficult. David kept losing track of what his notes had meant when he'd scribbled them. The

164

director and crew would be arriving that night, but the co-financing Italians refused to part with a single lira until the contracts were altered to their satisfaction. David worked on them all that day while Molly sunbathed and swam below. He kept thinking about the Italian translator magnificent breasts.

Ralph Lonigan, the film's director, was forty-eight years old, almost forty-nine, exactly David's age that summer, but he nonetheless seemed like a mere callow youth, perhaps because he had an unruly crop of flaming red hair on his head and a galaxy of freckles all over his cherubic face. He cornered Molly that night at a table on the candlelit terrace and explained that as a director he was naturally concerned with more than surface appearances, which was why her contradictory Irish looks and Jewish roots were so fascinating to him.

'I could have fallen over dead when Norman told me you were Jewish,' he said. 'But, after all, what *are* appearances, anyway? Is Irish *Irish* if Irish is really *Jewish*? Do you understand what I'm saying, Molly? In my job, I'm constantly forced to delve into personality, hoping to fathom seemingly inexplicable phenomena. When I'm directing a film, I have to be able to plumb the depths of a character so that he or she will become readily accessible to an audience.'

David was sitting within earshot with Norman and an executive from Cinécitta, whose studio facilities Norman would be leasing in Rome. He listened.

'Have you ever done any acting, Molly?' Lonigan asked.

'Me? No.'

'What *do* you do?'

'Well . . . I'm a housewife.' Molly shrugged. 'That's what I do.'

'Surely you're more than that,' Lonigan said.

'I used to be a nurse.'

'Ah,' he said.

'But that was long ago.'

'It must have been a rewarding profession. Nursing,' he said.

'Well, I suppose,' Molly said shyly.

'Helping the sick.'

'Yes.'

'You were probably very good at it.'

165

'Well,' she said.

'But you've never done any acting?'

'No, no.'

'You're so beautiful, I thought perhaps . . .'

'Thank you.'

'Beautiful expressive eyes. Green,' he said. 'And a marvellous mouth. You must photograph wonderfully.'

'I don't know, I guess so,' she said, and laughed huskily.

'How old are you, Molly?'

'You're not supposed to ask a woman her age,' Molly said, and lowered her eyes.

'We're both grown-ups, Molly. I'm forty-eight, does that make you feel any better? I'll be forty-nine in September.'

'Well . . .' Molly said, and raised her eyes to meet his.

'How old are you? Tell me.'

'Forty-four,' she said.

'You're joking! You look ten years younger!'

'I'll be forty-five in September.'

'When in September?'

'The sixth.'

'My birthday is the tenth.'

'How about that?' she said, and laughed.

'We ought to have a party,' Lonigan said.

'We ought to.'

'You look *much* younger,' he said. 'I'm amazed.'

'Oh, sure.'

'So young, so vital. Do you have any children, Molly?'

She hesitated. 'No,' she said.

'That must account for it. Somehow, women who've never had any children seem to hang onto their youthfulness.'

Molly said nothing.

'God, that mouth!' Lonigan said. 'What I could do with that mouth. On film,' he said.

Molly smiled.

'And that smile! God! You're so very beautiful, Molly.'

Rising slowly from where he was sitting, David walked over to where Lonigan was leaning toward Molly to light her cigarette. Very pleasantly, he said, 'Excuse me. Molly, it's getting late. I think we'd better start back.'

'Oh, *must* we?' she said. 'It's such a lovely night.' She blew out a stream of smoke and said, 'Thank you, Ralph.'

'I've got work to do tomorrow,' David said.

'Tomorrow's Sunday.'

'Tell that to Norman.'

'May I just finish this last cigarette?'

'I'd really rather go, Molly. It's almost two o'clock.'

'Is it that late already?' she said, and rose immediately, and immediately snuffed out the cigarette. 'It was nice talking to you,' she said to Lonigan. 'We'll have to continue our conversation sometime.'

'Soon, I hope,' Lonigan said, and rose, and took her hand, and said, 'Good night, Molly, it was a pleasure.'

'Good night,' she said. 'I enjoyed it.'

Their handclasp lingered.

'Well, good night,' Lonigan said at last.

'Good night,' she said again – a trifle breathlessly, David thought. He was suddenly furious.

He led her off the terrace and over the small bridge and into the courtyard and held open the passenger-side door of the Fiat for her, and then slammed it when she was inside the car, and came around to the driver's side, and opened the door there, and climbed in behind the wheel, and slammed *that* door, too.

'My, aren't we noisy tonight,' she said.

'What was that all about?' he asked.

'What was what all about?'

'The tender love scene up there.'

'What tender love scene?'

'Why were you encouraging that jackass?'

'He's not a jackass.'

'Why were you encouraging him?'

'I wasn't.'

'Then what was that big operatic farewell? "We'll have to continue our conversation sometime," ' he mimicked. 'What the hell was *that*?'

'It was saying good night to someone who seemed to take a sincere interest in me.'

David stepped on the accelerator and went screeching out of the gravel driveway to the main road. At the stop sign he turned right without braking and began the drive to the villa, speeding around the curves, scarcely taking his foot off the gas pedal.

'Try not to get us killed, okay?' Molly said.

'I didn't realize until tonight,' David said tightly, 'that you were *quite* so susceptible to flattery.'

'Please watch the road,' she said.

'The man was sitting not three feet from where I could hear every word he was saying . . .'

'You shouldn't have been listening.'

'But that didn't stop him from making the most blatant overtures, which *you* encouraged . . .'

'I did nothing of the kind.'

'. . . when you *must* have known he was trying to get in your pants!'

'Yes, I'm sure everyone in the world is just dying to get in my pants.'

'Molly, he was coming on with you, and you *know* it!'

'I didn't detect it.'

'No? "God, that mouth!" ' he mimicked. ' "What I could do with that mouth." '

'On *film*,' Molly said.

'I'm glad you remember every word he said.'

'I found him interesting.'

'You must have,' David said tightly, and stopped the car. 'Giggling and cooing and batting your lashes and holding hands and generally behaving like a cheap middle-aged *cunt*!'

Molly blinked at him. Wordlessly, she opened the door on her side of the car, stepped out into the road, slammed the door behind her, and began walking back in the direction of the hotel.

'Do you want some more of this, Pop?' he asked.

His father nodded.

'I'll try to find another small piece for you, okay? The smaller pieces are easier for you, aren't they?'

Another nod. The bewildered look. The goddamn persistent bewildered look.

She did not return to the villa until four in the morning. He looked at the bedside clock when he heard the front door opening and closing, and then he rolled over on his side and pretended he was asleep. She did not put on a light. She undressed in the dark and then got into bed. He imagined he smelled the aftermusk of intercourse on her. She fell asleep almost at once. He lay awake for the next hour, and finally fell asleep himself.

He awakened shortly after nine to the persistent purring of a turtledove in the garden. He made his own breakfast – this was Sunday and the help's day off – and lingered over it, hoping Molly would wake up and join him. His anger was gone now. But more than that, he recognized the cause of it. All Jews are guilt-ridden, Molly was fond of saying. This time, she was right. Would he have flared up at her so violently if he hadn't felt guilty over his own flirtation with that goddamn nubile translator in the come-hither blouse? Not to mention – but that was another story.

No, he thought, that's the *same* story. The same old story for the past four years.

He went to the stove, took the kettle from it, and poured himself another cup of coffee. He sat at the table and listened. The house was silent. Molly was still sound asleep. Was it possible she had really gone to bed with Lonigan last night? This innocent middle-aged housewife, Your Honor? *I'll be forty-five in September*. Can any of you possibly imagine this honest, forebearing, loving wife and bereaved mother breaking the sacred vows of a marriage that had endured since 1959? Almost twenty-two *years*, ladies and gentlemen of the jury! Would this admittedly still beautiful woman endanger such a lasting union? Sure, David thought. Why not? And who could blame her? Well, come on, he thought, get off it, will you? What's done is done.

And what had they been, after all, those minor excursions of his? A black court stenographer whose skirt kept riding up recklessly over her knees as she worked her Stenotab machine and flirted wildly with her eyes. Twenty-seven years old. It had lasted for two months. A woman attorney in Philadelphia, where he'd gone to settle a claim made against one of his clients by a daughter who'd moved there from New York. The lawyer had been a redhead. She kept calling him 'Counselor' in bed. Come fuck me again, Counselor. Shades of Molly Regen before the accident. Looking at himself in the bathroom mirror that night in Philadelphia, mildly drunk on the bottle of champagne he had shared with his learned adversary, he had said out loud, 'You're a damn fool, Counselor.' Perhaps he was. The half-dozen other women over the past four years since Stephen's death. Well, perhaps a dozen. Perhaps more. Who the hell was counting? What *really* counted was that he was *still* doing it, never mind what's done is done. If the Italian translator had given him the slightest sign of encouragement, he'd have laid her on the spot while the Italian lawyers protested the favored-nations clause.

Everything used to be so perfect, he thought. Why did it have to change? Why us?

He finished his breakfast and went into the room where his papers were spread out on the long table. Molly did not get up until almost eleven. She went directly into the bathroom, where he heard her showering, and then into the kitchen, where he heard her padding around barefooted. In a little while, she appeared on the beach below the window where he was working. She took off her bikini top and stretched out languidly on a towel, her face turned toward the sun, her arms at her sides, palms upward. A white speedboat came churning in over the water. The pilot cut the engine, threw an anchor over the side, and then stepped over the gunnels into shallow water, his red hair glowing in the sun. Lonigan.

'Molly!' he called, as though surprised to find her there.

She rolled over in response to his voice, propped herself on one elbow, and turned to face him.

'Hello, Ralph,' she said. 'Good morning.'

'It's afternoon already,' he said, and sat on the towel beside her.

Bare-breasted, as casually as if she were the vicar's wife entertaining one of the local gentry who'd dropped in for afternoon tea, she sat in conversation with him, exchanging words David could not hear. He watched them from the window above. In a little while, they both rose from the towel. Molly was still bare-breasted. She made no effort to retrieve her discarded top. Instead, she walked together with him to the boat. He helped her to climb into it, offering his hand. He got in himself and started the engine. He pulled in the anchor. He came back to the wheel. The boat backed away from the beach and then roared forward around the point of land, out of sight.

They did not return until almost two hours later. Lonigan dropped anchor again, and they both waded ashore and stood

170

chatting at the water's edge for another ten minutes. Lonigan took her hand at last, said his farewells, waded back to the boat, pulled in the anchor, and then gunned the engine and backed out of the cove.

David was ready to kill her.

He kept waiting for her to come in to apologize. She did not. At a quarter to five, he packed the pages he'd revised – only three of them, small wonder considering his anger – and went out to the living room. She had put on a hooded caftan she'd bought in one of the Porto Cervo boutiques. She looked cool and sleek in the white cotton; pale horse, pale rider dressed like an Arabian princess, all shrouded and secret after parading naked for a stranger! She was reading. A paperback. He could not make out the title from where he loomed large and menacing in the arched doorway. Her legs were crossed under her, hidden by the voluminous folds of the caftan. Only her bright painted toenails showed at the hemline. The hood was up over her head, partially hiding her face. The ceiling fan rotated idly. There was the sound of buzzing flies in the room. She turned a page.

'Well, well,' David said, 'look who's here.'

Molly looked up. She said nothing.

'How was your boat ride?' he said. 'Have a nice little boat ride?'

'Very nice, thank you,' she said.

'How do you compare getting laid in a boat . . .'

'I didn't get laid in a boat.'

'. . . with getting laid on a roller coaster, for example?'

'I've never tried either.'

'What *did* you try? A little deserted beach someplace?'

'I don't want to talk to you,' Molly said, and went back to the book again.

'If you don't mind . . .'

'I *do* mind.'

'Put down the book, Molly.'

She slammed down the book.

'Where'd you go?' he asked.

'What business is that of yours?' she said.

'Where'd you go with him?'

'I am not in the habit of being called a cheap *cunt*,' she said coldly, 'a cheap middle-*aged* cunt, no less, by anyone in the

171

world, and especially not by someone who's supposed to love me so terribly much he won't let me *breathe*!'

'Where'd he take you in that boat?'

'None of your business,' she said, and rose suddenly and went into the bedroom. He heard her opening and closing drawers in there. He stood in the living room for a moment, and then he followed her. An open suitcase was on the bed. She was throwing underwear and blouses into it haphazardly, packing blindly. Turning to the dresser, she took a hairbrush from its top and then stared at it as if forgetting why she had picked it up.

'You going someplace?' he asked.

'Away from *here*, that's for sure,' she said.

'What the hell are *you* so angry about?' he asked. '*You're* the one who went off naked in a boat . . .'

'Oh, big deal. I had my *top* off. This is Italy! Half the women in the *world* walk around here without . . .'

'That's not the point!'

'Well, what *is* the point, because I seem to be *missing* the point! What was I *supposed* to do when he came driving up in the boat? Jump up like a dumb virgin and reach for my towel and start shrieking? If you want to know something, *that* would've been worse than just sitting there without my top on. You goddamn jackass, don't you think I know the difference between teasing a man and just sitting there in the sunshine? I'll tell you what this gets down to, if you want to know what it gets down to. You're a guilt-ridden Jew who . . .'

'It gets down to you sending out *signals*!' David said.

'I did *not* send out any signals!'

'Then why did he come here today?'

'Because he wanted to *talk* to me, as peculiar as that may sound. He really had an interest in knowing who the person Molly Regen . . .'

'You're not Molly Regen anymore.'

'I wish I was!'

'You're not twenty-two anymore, either. "So *young*, so *vital*!" I'm surprised he didn't jump on you right at the table last night. I'm surprised he waited for . . .'

'Jesus, you're infuriating!' she shouted, and hurled the

172

hairbrush to the tiled floor, shattering its plastic handle. 'Don't you think *I* have anything to say about it? Don't you think it's *my* business who I choose to, who I, who I, you bastard, you've got me stuttering! This is *my* body,' she said, cupping her breasts fiercely, 'and I've got a *mind* up here,' she said, bringing her right hand up and hitting her forehead with her open palm, the slap smacking home the word, 'and if you think that *you* or anyone else . . .'

'Tell it to Betty Friedan,' he said.

'Sure.'

'Or Gloria Steinem.'

'Sure, you prick.'

'Or Erica Jong. Why don't you go tell Erica Jong?'

'Why don't you go fuck yourself?'

'If you goddamn women libbers think being *faithful* to someone is the same as being *owned* . . .'

'I *am* faithful to you,' she said coldly.

'Are you?'

'No,' she said. 'Okay?'

'What?'

'Are *you*?' she said.

'What?'

'You heard me.'

'You *did* go to bed with him, didn't you?'

'No, I didn't.'

'Then what . . .?'

'No more lies,' she said, 'I'm tired of all the lies. You know what *you've* been doing, I know what *I've* been doing, let's stop the lies! For God's sake, let's *stop* them!'

'I haven't been doing anything,' he said.

'Stop it,' she said.

'I haven't.'

'She called from Philadelphia.'

'What? *Who* called from . . .?'

'Your lawyer friend.'

'Molly, I swear to God . . .'

'Jesus, *stop* it! I'm about to walk out of here, can't you please stop lying?'

173

'A dumb call from Philadelphia . . .'

'And others. You've been sleeping around, David, okay? Ever since . . .'

'No, I haven't.'

'Shit,' she said, '*must* you keep lying?'

'I'm telling you I *haven't*.'

'Well, I *have*, okay?'

'No, you haven't, Molly.'

'What did you expect, David?'

They looked at each other.

'All right,' he said.

'All right,' she said.

'Do you want to know why?'

'No.'

'Because after the accident . . .'

'I said *no*!'

'. . . you became a different person, Molly. You stopped . . .'

'I don't want to talk about it.'

'When *will* you want to talk about it?'

'Never,' she said.

'Molly . . .'

'*Never!*'

Drained, they stared at each other.

'So,' he said, 'what now?'

'You tell me.'

'Are you really leaving?'

'Do you want me to leave?'

'Do what you want to do,' he said.

'Fine, then. I'll finish packing . . .'

'Don't forget your diaphragm,' he said, and was immediately sorry.

'Oh, don't worry,' she said. 'My clothes, my diaphragm, my passport . . .'

'Your diaphragm *is* your passport.'

'Thank you, you prick. I'll use it at the airport with the first man I see, or on the ferry, or however I get off this fucking . . .'

He caught her by the wrist.

'Let go of me,' she said.

'Tell me who.'

'Let *go* of me, damn it!'

'*Who?*'

'What difference does it make? Oh Jesus, what difference does it make anymore?' she said, and burst into tears. He let go of her wrist. He watched her helplessly standing there in the white caftan, her shoulders heaving, her hands covering her face. He went to her. He took her in his arms.

'Molly, Molly,' he said, stroking her hair.

'I'm not a cheap cunt,' she said, sobbing.

'I know you're not,' he said gently.

'You said I was.'

'Molly, I'm sorry.'

'I'm a person,' she said.

'I know, darling.'

He stood holding her trembling in his arms. He held her close. He touched her face, he stroked her hair, he wiped the tears from her eyes.

'I love you, Molly,' he said.

'I love you, too,' she said, sobbing.

'I loved you from the minute I met you.'

'You didn't,' she said, sobbing. 'Please don't lie.'

'I did.'

'No.' She shook her head. 'Valentine's Day,' she said.

'I loved you long before then.'

'Then why didn't you *tell* me?' she said, and burst into violent tears again.

They made love that night the way they once had, long ago, when they were very young. In the villa next door, someone was playing a mandolin. A dog barked. There was the sound of a speedboat out on the water. Moonlight glanced through the open arched window. On the beach below, they could hear waves lapping the shore.

They left Italy a week later.

Before a month had gone by, it was as if Italy had never happened. *Hello, kiddo, I'm back*. Not that simple, it was never that simple. Nor did he even know who was to blame this time. Had Molly tirelessly labored over his cock one night, her mouth fruitlessly beseeching while his thoughts were on another blonde, another time, another place? Had *he* reached around *her*

175

one night, his cock hard against her ass, his hand exploring, only to find her tight and dry? He knew only that before the end of August, he called the black stenographer one morning and spent four frantic hours in bed with her that afternoon. It had become habit by then. Nothing had changed, everything had changed. They all were Molly, none of them were Molly. Whatever they had known together had effectively ended on the day Stephen died, and there was no going back.

He brought roses home that afternoon. He arranged them in a vase in the living room. When she came in shortly before the dinner hour, she scarcely glanced at them.

'Did you see the roses?' he asked.

'Nice,' she said.

The clock on the wall of his father's room read two-fifteen.

David carried the paper cup to the sink, kissed his father on the forehead, and left the hospital.

He should not have walked the four blocks from the hospital to the hotel. He had told himself he needed the exercise, but the heat and the humidity were intolerable, and he was soaked with perspiration before he'd walked a block. He showered the moment he got back to his room. It was two-thirty when he ordered the drink from room service. He put on a robe when the waiter knocked on the door. He signed the check and added a tip to it. The moment the waiter was gone, he took off the robe, sat naked in the easy chair facing the blank television screen, picked up the drink and sipped at it.

His mother's letter was still in the pocket of his jacket. He went to the closet and took the letter from his pocket. He looked at the envelope. He sipped at the drink. He walked to the window and looked down at the pool area. The South American party had not yet arrived. The pool looked empty and deserted. He sat down again. He drank a bit more. Then he looked at the envelope again. *To mom, with love, David*. Why had his father put the letter in an envelope that had David's handwriting on it? So that it would immediately catch David's eye? Had he *wanted* him to find the letter? Why had he saved it at all?

He opened the envelope.

His mother's small delicate hand. The pages browning around

176

the edges, the ink fading. He kept staring at the letter in his hand. Then he began reading.

Dear Morrie,

I am writing this because when I talk I get too excited and of course it stands to reason. I honestly was giving you a fair chance but I guess you did not want it as you are still lying to me. Even this week if I did not ask you about how much money the store made Wednesday, you would not have told me you had taken the day off as you said to go to your brother's in New Jersey.

So please this is such a simple request. I am asking you please . . .

He stopped reading exactly where he had stopped yesterday morning, in his father's apartment. Did he really want to know? Was it really important that he know? He picked up the glass, took a long swallow of whiskey. He put down the glass. He looked at the letter again. He began reading again.

So please this is such a simple request. I am asking you please to sit down and ask yourself if you must continue this lying and cheating and if this is really what you want then please go away as I am getting ill and I don't think I deserve that, do you? You said last night that what you do is none of my business. That is really not so and you know it. Husband and wife must tell one another everything if they wish to be happy. Oh please I'm asking you in God's name, if this is what you really want from life then please oh please go away and leave me here to make a happy home for our boy who was away so long. So please again is that what you want? If it really is then good-bye and may God bless you. Please answer this honestly and please don't tell me that what you do is your own business because that is not what I am asking you.

Esther

He thought that was the end of the letter. He had been putting the handwritten pages one behind the other as he'd finished reading them, and her signature seemed to indicate an end. There was yet another page, he realized. It began without a P.S., as though his mother had not quite concluded her thoughts and, despite her closing signature, felt compelled to add to them, to make herself finally and irrevocably clear.

If you want to continue this sort of thing then there is nothing anyone can do but give you your freedom. I know who the woman is Morrie. I know who you bought those diamond earrings for, we both know who she is, and that you can have her and her husband in our house to have dinner and play cards is shameful. I do not know how she can be doing this to my home, I do not understand. I am so embarrassed all the time. You are making me ill Morrie. So please I beg of you please answer this and tell me what it is you want. If you want to stay here with me and our son then it must be without any more of the lying and cheating that is killing me. But if your answer is that you want to go, then there is nothing I can do.

She did not sign the final page. He looked over the letter again. There were three pages in all, each headed with a Roman numeral. I, II, III. He folded the letter. He felt his eyes misting with tears. He put the letter back into the envelope. His mother's constant sniping at his father. She'd known he'd never stopped lying and cheating, and had decided to live with it. No wonder it was a heart attack that finally killed her.

He carried the letter back to the closet and put it in his jacket pocket again. He was starting back toward where he'd left his drink when the telephone rang.

He's dead, he thought.

It always comes on the telephone, he thought.

He picked up the receiver.

'Hello?' he said.

'David? Hi, it's Hillary.'

'Hello,' he said.

'I've been trying to reach you.'

'I was at the hospital.'

'How is he?'

'Well, not so hot.'

'I'm sorry.'

178

He said nothing. There was a long silence on the line.

'You'd had quite a bit to drink last night, hadn't you?' she said.

'A little.'

'I suspected as much.' She paused. 'Do you remember phoning me?'

'Yes.'

'Do you remember what you asked?'

'Vaguely.' He remembered completely.

'Why'd you want to know what I was wearing?'

'I really don't know,' he said.

'Did you want to have sex?' she asked. 'On the phone?'

'I suppose,' he said. 'Maybe. I don't know.'

'Might have been interesting,' she said. She paused again. 'I'm here at the pool,' she said. 'It's like a mausoleum. Why don't you come join me for a drink and some sun?'

'I have to be back at the hospital at four.'

'That gives us at least an hour.'

'Well . . .'

'Do come,' she said, and hung up.

He went to the window. He looked down at the pool. He could see her walking from the telephone to one of the lounge chairs. She was wearing a white string bikini and high-heeled sandals. She had become very tan in the past several days. She took off the sandals, smoothed the towel on the lounge, and stretched out on her belly. He saw her reaching behind her to untie the strap of the bikini top.

He looked at his watch, and then went into the bathroom, where his swimming trunks were draped over the shower-curtain rod. He thought suddenly of the enema bag in his father's apartment. How long had he been struggling alone with what he'd called his 'blockage?' How many secret enemas had he taken in that overflowing apartment? He's a man dying because he couldn't shit, David thought. He filled his apartment with shit, he lived his life wallowing in shit, and now he's dying because he couldn't shit. He looked at his watch again. He did not want to go back to that hospital at four o'clock. He did not want to continue this senseless vigil. Die already, he thought. For Christ's sake, *die!*

179

He looked into the mirror.

'Die,' he said aloud, and then he put on his trunks and went downstairs to join Hillary.

'I lied to you,' she said.

No more lies, he thought. Molly's words last summer. But the lies persisted.

'You told me,' he said. 'You're not really twenty-nine.'

'That, yes,' she said. 'But about being divorced as well.'

They were stretched out on lounges side by side. They were drinking gin-tonics. Gin and quinine, she called them. He was on his back, his eyes squinted against the strong glare of the sun. She was on her belly, the bikini strap untied, her blond hair loose. Her arms were dangling over the end of the lounge. The drink was on the tiles before her. She kept toying with the straw. She smelled of coconut oil.

'Matter of fact,' she said, 'I've never been married.'

A cloud passed over the sun, bringing temporary relief.

'It was easier to lie,' she said.

No more lies, he thought. Please.

The cloud passed, the sun blinked on again. He squinted his eyes against it. In England, he remembered, a person with a 'squint' was cross-eyed. Language barrier, he thought. He waited.

'You see, I've just ended a rather long-term relationship,' she said. 'With a man, of course. These days, one feels compelled to clarify. I'm *not* that way, though on occasion I've been sorely tempted.'

She turned her face to him and smiled. Her eyes were intensely green in the sun. She looked away and began toying with the straw again.

'We were supposed to have gone to Marbella together,' she said. 'Actually, I lied about that, too. My firm didn't *really* have to sack anyone down here, I volunteered to come. So I wouldn't have to go on holiday with him. I'm quite good at lying, I've had a great deal of practice over the years. He's married, you see.'

She reached behind her to tie the bra strap. She rolled over and then sat up cross-legged, Indian fashion. Remembering her drink, she reached behind her for the plastic cup. Her breasts

180

threatened the skimpy string top. She sipped at the drink and then began toying with the straw again.

'He's quite a bit older than I am,' she said. 'Older than you, actually. Twice my own age. Sixty.'

'Uh,huh,' David said. English mostly, one of the Dolly Sisters had said. The sex fiends.

'I met him when I was nineteen. I was still living in London, working for a small lingerie shop in Mayfair. Nineteen years old and still a virgin, can you believe it?'

What's left to believe? David thought. Lies?

'He came in looking for a pair of panties. Knickers, do you prefer? Panties, actually. He bought a rather nice pair, very sexy, pale blue and lace-edged. Cost him six pounds. He asked me if I'd care to model them for him one night. I was utterly shocked! I thought he was a dirty old man, and I told him so. Actually, he was only forty-nine at the time – this was, after all, eleven years ago. Just your age, come to think of it. That's odd, don't you think?'

'So what happened? *Did* you model them for him?'

'Oh, of *course* I did. The very next night, in fact. His wife was away in Sussex, it was one of those dreary November weekends, rainy and gray, we spent the entire time in bed. Well, not the *entire* time. We did pause to eat, and we went to two movies, but mostly we made love. Which is what we've been doing – mostly – for the past eleven years. I suppose. Nineteen when I met him, can you imagine?' She shook her head again. 'Until, finally – three weeks ago, actually – I decided I'd had enough. *Quite* enough, thanks. I plan on seeing a psychiatrist when I get back to Oxford, the university has hordes of them, you know. See if I can't get my head together somehow. Eleven years! When I think of it!'

She sipped at her drink again.

'So,' she said. 'Story of my life. Tedious, isn't it?'

'No,' he said. 'In fact . . .'

'I had to have been out of my mind,' she said. 'Running down to London whenever his wife was away – this was after I'd made the move to Oxford, actually my first attempt at breaking away from him. Six years ago, I was twenty-four. Impossible, of course, I simply *had* to keep seeing him. All those places I've been to on the continent were with him. Idyllic, in a way. Love with the proper stranger and all that. None of the bother of having to *live* together, of having to really *know* a person. Anyway, I've ended it. Or at least I *hope* I have.' She shrugged. 'You've caught me at a good time, David.'

'Have I?'

'Indeed. You have no idea how long it took me to fall asleep after you rang me last night. There *you* were in your narrow bed, contemplating all sorts of kinky sex, and there *I* was alone in mine, staring up at the ceiling in a perfect dither. Should I ring him back, or should I not? Will he think me brazen if I do? Will he think me hopelessly prudish if I don't. I must have visited the loo a dozen times after your call. Eventually, of course, I ended up doing what we should have done *together*. Am I shocking you? Don't tell me,' she said. 'You're happily married, and you wouldn't *dream* of compromising your integrity.' Her eyes met his. 'Are you?' she asked.

He did not answer.

'Forgive me,' she said, 'I know this is a difficult time for you, and I've no desire to make it any more difficult. But I haven't stopped thinking about you since I first saw you sitting alone in that vast crimson room.'

'I don't understand that,' he said.

'Nor do I. But take it for a fact.'

'I'm flattered.'

'You needn't be, you're a quite attractive man.' She paused. 'And you?' she said, arching her brows. 'Have you been thinking of me?'

'If not you, then someone who was once very much like you.'

'Was?'

'A long time ago.'

'Who?'

'Someone.'

'Did you love her?'

'With all my heart.'

'Then love me,' she said.

He sensed the air of tension the moment he stepped into the waiting room. He had lingered too long by the pool with Hillary and had arrived at the hospital at six minutes to four. By the time he'd taken the elevator to the third floor and walked down the corridor to the waiting room, it was close to four o'clock. But there was none of the minutes-before restlessness among the people gathered there. The clock on the wall read two minutes to four. The minute hand lurched visibly as he glanced at the clock. A minute to four. But no one was standing. Something was wrong. He looked around at the faces. The Dolly Sisters. The fat man in the business suit. Another man, a newcomer he had not seen before. Mrs. Horowitz. He saw reflected on all the faces an unnatural calm that shrieked panic.

'There's an emergency inside,' Mrs. Horowitz said. 'They won't let us in.'

'Until it's resolved,' the pink lady said.

She was the same bossy woman who'd been training the new volunteer yesterday. David wondered what 'resolved' meant in her vocabulary. Dead? He took a seat beside Mrs. Horowitz and lit a cigarette. She was already smoking. Her face looked more flushed and excited than he had ever seen it.

'Do they know who it is?' he whispered.

'They won't tell us anything,' she said, loud enough for the bossy pink lady to hear. 'It could be anybody.'

It's my father, David thought. Who else could be dying in there?

'It's my mother,' Mrs. Horowitz said. 'I know it is.'

'You don't know that,' one of the Dolly Sisters said. Helen, was it?

'My brother looked fine this morning,' the fat man said.

'Does this happen a lot here?' the newcomer asked. 'These emergencies?'

'Excuse me, sir,' the pink lady said, 'but do you have a patient here?'

'My father,' he said.

'His name?'

'Arthur Henley.'

'And you say you're his son?'

'If he's my father, I'm his son,' Henley said.

Good for you, David thought.

'What happens if this isn't settled by the time visiting is up?'

Henley said. 'Will they let us in no matter what time it is?'

'That's up to the head nurse,' the pink lady said. 'Right now, they have their hands full.'

'What's happening in there?' Mrs. Horowitz asked. 'Do you know what the emergency is?'

'I have no idea,' the pink lady said.

'Can you find out?'

'The sign on the door says "No Admission," ' the pink lady said. 'That means me, too.'

'Well, can you make a call in there?' the fat man said. 'Find out who's in trouble?'

'They have their hands full,' the pink lady said. 'Excuse me, sir, but do you have a patient here?'

'Yes, I have a patient here. I was here yesterday, nobody asked me did I have a patient here. Why do you think I'm here if I haven't got a patient here? You think I like hospitals?'

'What is your patient's name?' the pink lady asked, unruffled.

'Carmine Bastiglio.'

'Would you spell that, please?' she said, looking at her clipboard.

'It starts with a B, look under your B's. Bastiglio.'

'Oh, yes,' she said, finding the name. 'Are you a relative of the patient, sir?'

'I'm his brother,' Bastiglio said.

'I'm sure this will be resolved in no time at all,' the pink lady said. 'Would anyone like coffee?'

No one answered.

'If no one wants coffee,' she said, 'I'll have to wash out the pot and lock up the coffee maker. I have to leave no later than four-fifteen. I have to take the keys down to Mrs. Thorpe in the Volunteer Section and then catch the hospital jitney to the bus stop. That takes time,' she said. She looked at her watch. 'Last call,' she said cheerfully. 'Anyone for coffee?'

'Without coffee,' Bastiglio said philosophically, 'the entire system would collapse.'

'Would you care for some coffee, Mr. . . . .?' She consulted her clipboard, seemed about to try pronouncing his name, gave it up, and said, 'Sir?'

'No coffee, thank you,' Bastiglio said. 'I never got in the habit.

184

If my brother hadn't got in the habit, he wouldn't be here now with a heart attack.'

'No coffee?' the pink lady said. 'Anyone? Are you sure?'

'No *coffee* already,' Mrs. Horowitz said testily.

'I'll wash out the pot then,' the pink lady said, as though ready to carry out a dire threat.

'My mother's *dying* in there,' Mrs. Horowitz whispered, 'and *she's* hocking us about coffee.'

'You don't know it's your mother,' one of the Dolly Sisters said. The younger one. Jean.

'She looked terrible today,' Mrs. Horowitz said.

'In there, they *all* look terrible,' Bastiglio said philosophically.

'It's no picnic in there,' Helen said.

'Really,' Jean said.

'I haven't even *seen* him yet,' Henley said. 'My father. He was operated on this morning. What if it's him dying, and I don't even get to see him?'

'An emergency doesn't necessarily mean someone is dying,' the pink lady said from the sink, where she was washing out the coffee pot.

'No, it means somebody's dancing up and down the aisles in there,' Mrs. Horowitz said, and everyone laughed.

The laughter broke the tension, but only for a moment.

'I hope I get to see him before he dies,' Henley said.

'How long is this going to *take* in there?' Helen asked.

'As long as it takes to resolve,' the pink lady said, and carried the pot to the cabinet and then locked the entire coffee maker inside it. She looked up at the clock. Everyone looked up at the clock. It was a quarter past four.

'It's taking forever,' Bastiglio said.

'I have to leave now,' the pink lady said.

'*Alevai*,' Mrs. Horowitz said.

'I happen to understand Yiddish,' the pink lady said, and started out of the room. At the door, she turned and said, 'Please don't try to go in until they take the sign down.'

As she turned in the doorway again, the Cuban nurse materialized in the corridor outside. It's my father, David thought. They've sent the Cuban nurse to tell me my father is dead. The pink lady sidled past her quickly, as though she wanted no part of this. The Cuban nurse hesitated in the door frame, her eyes searching the room. They came to rest on Mrs. Horowitz.

'Missis Horiwiss?' she said.

'Oh my God,' Mrs. Horowitz said.

'Could I please speak to you for a moment?'

'Oh my God!' she said. She threw herself into David's arms. 'It's my mother,' she said. 'Oh, Mr. Weber, it's my mother!'

He held her close, patting her shoulder, murmuring words of comfort. In the doorway, the Cuban nurse stood with solemn, sad brown eyes. She nodded confirmation to him. The Emergency had been resolved. Mrs. Horowitz's mother was dead. David kept holding her. She wept against his shoulder. He was surprised to find that he himself was weeping. At last, she drew away from him. She looked into his face, saw the tears in his eyes, and registered a small puzzled look. She nodded her gratitude to him, and patted his hand, and took a tiny lace-edged handkerchief from her handbag. She blew her nose, and dried her eyes, and went out to join the Cuban nurse in the corridor. David sat where he was. He could hear them whispering outside, near the window streaming sunlight. In a moment, the Cuban nurse came back to the waiting-room door.

'You ca' go in now,' she said.

Mrs. Horowitz was still standing by the window streaming sunlight, her head bent, her back to the corridor, weeping softly as David passed her and went into the unit and into his father's room.

His father was sleeping peacefully.

David moved a chair beside the bed and sat. He put his hand on the side railing of the bed, and rested his forehead on it, and closed his eyes. He did not awaken his father. He sat for the next fifteen minutes with his eyes closed, his forehead resting on his hand. When he left the room at last, he was surprised to realize he'd been praying.

The phone was ringing as he unlocked the door to his room. He threw the key on the dresser and picked up the receiver.

'Hello?' he said.

'David, it's me,' Molly said.

'Hi.'

186

'How is he?'

'I just got back from the hospital this minute. He seems okay. He was sleeping when I left him.'

'What does the doctor say?'

'I haven't spoken to him today.'

'Well, why haven't. . . ?'

'I planned to call him in a few minutes. I just got back to the room, Molly.'

She detected the edge to his voice. She was silent for several seconds.

'Have you called Uncle Max?' she asked.

'Not yet. He's on my list, too.'

'Did you enjoy yesterday?' she asked.

'What?'

'Your lunch. Your swim. Your long walk on the beach.'

'Yes,' he said.

'You didn't call this morning.'

'There was nothing to call about.'

'Well . . . let me know what happens, will you?'

'I will.'

There was a long silence.

'How's the weather up there?' he asked.

'Hot,' she said.

'Here, too,' he said.

Another silence.

'When will you be coming home?' she asked.

'I don't know,' he said. 'I'm supposed to check out on Sunday, but I guess . . . I just don't know.'

'Jerry called this morning,' she said.

'I've been expecting that.'

'He said to tell you things are piling up at the office. He's hoping you'll be back by Tuesday.'

'Sooner than that, I hope.'

'I wish you'd talk to the doctor.'

'I will,' he said. 'I'll call him as soon as we're finished here.'

'Get some sort of prognosis,' she said.

'Yes.'

'Well, all right then,' she said. 'Call me.'

'I will.'

She hung up. He pressed the receiver rest button, got a dial tone, and dialed room service. He got the same waiter he'd spoken to on his first day here at the hotel. At least it sounded like the same waiter. He did not want to go through the Canadian club soda routine again.

'This is Mr. Weber in room fifteen twenty-nine,' he said. 'Please send me two scotch whiskeys and water, please.'

'Ri' away, sir,' the waiter said. 'Fi' minutes.'

The drinks did not arrive until fifteen minutes after he had placed the order. Close, he thought, but no guitar. He looked at his watch. It was a little past five o'clock. He would wait another five minutes and then call Kaplan. Sitting on the edge of the bed, sipping at the scotch, he dialed information and got numbers in New Jersey for both his Uncle Max's delicatessen and his home. He had finished the first of the drinks when he called Kaplan. He got the answering service. The woman there told him she would have the doctor call back as soon as possible.

'How soon will that be?' he asked.

'He should be calling in soon, sir,' she said.

'Thank you,' David said.

He debated calling his uncle, decided he would keep the line free until Kaplan returned his call. When the phone rang at five-thirty, he thought it was Kaplan calling back.

'Hello, David?' Bessie said.

'Bessie,' he said, surprised. 'How are you?'

'No use complaining,' she said. 'Did you see your father?'

'Yes, he's all right.'

'What does the doctor say?'

'I haven't spoken to him yet. I'm waiting to hear from him now, in fact.'

'So I'll get off the phone,' Bessie said, but she did not get off the phone. There was a small silence. 'Do you know the ring your father has?' she said. 'The one he wears on his pinky all the time?'

'Yes?' David said.

'I have it here,' she said. 'With the other things he gave me to hold when I went with him to the hospital. His wallet, his eyeglasses, his address book. I don't know what's in the wallet, I didn't look. But I'm worried about the ring. He'll never talk to

188

me again if I lose that ring. I never seen him without that ring on his finger.'

'His mother gave it to him,' David said.

'I know, him and his two brothers, they all got the same rings. So what I'll do – you'll be at the hospital tonight?'

'Yes.'

'I'll bring it tonight. His wallet, too, all the other stuff. His keys you already have. This way, it'll be off my mind. I'm a little worried carrying it on the bus, the crime down here, they'll break your head for a nickel. But I'll make sure I keep my hands on my pocketbook. So I'll see you seven o'clock.'

'Good-bye, Bessie,' he said.

'Good-bye,' she said.

He put down the receiver. The phone rang again almost at once. He picked up the receiver again.

'Hello?' he said.

'Mr. Weber?'

'Yes, Dr. Kaplan, how are you?'

'Fine, thanks,' Kaplan said. 'Have you seen your father today?'

'Just a little while ago. He was asleep.'

'Yes,' Kaplan said.

'Have *you* seen him?'

'I'm at the hospital now.'

'How is he?'

'More lethargic than he was yesterday. Not quite as alert. His temperature's dropped a little . . .'

'To what?'

'Just under a hundred.'

'That's a good sign, isn't it?'

'The change isn't appreciable. His lungs are clear now . . .'

'Good,' David said.

'But I'm frankly worried about his kidneys, Mr. Weber. We can maintain his blood pressure with medication, but if his kidneys continue . . .'

'Why? What's wrong with his blood pressure?' David said.

'It's dropped to fifty.'

'Is that low?'

'Very low. Well below the normal range.'

189

'Well . . . what does that mean? His blood pressure dropping?'

'The blood pressure indicates how well the heart is pumping. We've already begun medication, we've put him on Dopamine to support the blood pressure. But, as I said, if his kidneys continue failing . . .'

'*Are* they failing?'

'I'm afraid they are.'

'Yes, what then?'

'He might need dialysis.'

'What's that?'

'A kidney machine.'

'To do what?'

'To purify his blood.' Kaplan paused. 'Would you be in favor of that?'

'I'm not sure.'

'In any case, I'd like to do a tracheotomy in the morning,' Kaplan said. 'We don't like to leave a respirator tube in the throat longer than forty-eight hours.'

'Is that what a tracheotomy is? Removing the respirator tube?'

'No, no. We'd open his throat surgically and clamp a tube there. In the trachea. It's a very simple procedure, we can do it in his room. It wouldn't take more than ten or fifteen minutes at most. He'd be a lot more comfortable afterward.'

'When does he stop being *himself*?' David asked.

'I'm sorry, what . . .?'

'When does his body become just a . . . a middleman for all those machines?'

'Well, that's what you've got to start thinking about, Mr. Weber.'

'What do you mean?'

'Dialysis. Whether or not you want us to put him on a kidney machine.'

'Can I withhold permission if I choose?'

'You can.'

'What happens then?'

'If his kidneys fail and he has no dialytic support?'

'Yes.'

'He'll die,' Kaplan said.

'When will I have to make this decision?'

'We're watching him very closely,' Kaplan said. 'I assume you have no objections to the tracheotomy.'

'Not if it'll make him more comfortable.'

'It will.'

'Fine then.'

'I'll do it first thing tomorrow morning.'

'If he's still alive,' David said, and sighed.

'Well,' Kaplan said, 'let's hope he is.'

'Yes,' David said.'

'Good night, Mr. Weber.'

'Good night,' David said.

He went to where he'd left his drink, took a long swallow, and then set the glass down again. He went to the bed, picked up the slip of paper on which he'd scribbled his uncle's numbers, and dialed the one at the delicatessen.

'Max's Deli,' a man said.

'Uncle Max?'

'You want Max Weber?' the man said.

'Yes, please.'

'You can get him at home,' the man said. 'You want the number?'

'I've got it,' David said. 'Thank you.'

He hung up, waited for another dial tone, and then dialed the second number on the sheet of paper.

'Hello?' a voice said.

'Hello, Uncle Max,' David said, smiling. 'This is David.'

'*Who?*' the voice said.

'Is this Max Weber?' David said.

'This is Max Weber, who's *this?*'

'David.'

'David who?'

'Your nephew,' David said.

'Ha-ha,' his uncle said.

'Uncle Max, this is David. Your nephew.'

'Ha-ha,' his uncle said again. 'What is this, some kind of joke?'

'Uncle Max, it's me, David. Your nephew.'

'What nephew? Some joke, very comical. Ha-ha.'

'Is Aunt Rachel there?' David said.

'No, she's *not* here. Who's this?'

'Uncle Max, can I please speak to Aunt Rachel?'

'I told you she's not here. What are you, a comedian?'

'Uncle Max, your brother is dying,' David said. 'Morris is . . .'

'What brother? Ha-ha, very comical,' his uncle said.

'Uncle Max . . . please . . .'

'What do you want, funnyman? You like telling jokes? Very comical. Ha-ha.'

'Okay, Uncle Max,' David said, and hung up.

He sat with his hand on the telephone receiver for a very long time. He's senile, he thought. Jesus Christ! Dashing Uncle Max with his flashy Studebaker and his dark-haired, dark-eyed beauties. Uncle Max with his little silver mustache comb. Oh my God, he's *senile!* Tears rushed to his eyes. He hit the dial of the phone with his bunched fist, and then stood up abruptly and went to where he'd left his drink. He drained the glass. The phone rang.

Here it is, he thought.

The phone kept ringing.

I don't want to answer it, he thought.

He went to the phone. He lifted the receiver.

'Hello?' he said, and took a deep breath.

'David?'

He let out his breath.

'Hello, Hillary,' he said.

'I've been trying to reach you, your line's been engaged.'

'Yes, I'm sorry. How are you?' he said.

'Fine. Are we still on for tonight?'

'Tonight?'

'Dinner,' she said. 'Or have I frightened you off?'

'I'm not sure about tonight,' he said. 'My father's . . . I'm just not sure about him.'

'Oh, David, I'm *so* sorry.'

'I think I may just stay here in the room. In case anyone tries to reach me.'

'You *do* have to eat, David.'

'I can always get something from room service.'

'Of course, whatever you say.' She paused. 'Will you be going to the hospital again?'

'At seven o'clock.'

'Would you care to join me for a drink before then?'

He looked at his watch.

'I don't think so,' he said. 'I've had two already, and I.
may have some decisions to make later on.'

'What sort of decisions?' she asked.

He did not know if he felt like discussing this with her.

'Well,' he said, 'really, it . . .'

'Please tell me, David.'

'Whether or not to keep him alive,' he said.

'Oh, David,' she said, 'How *awful* for you. Will you call me
when you get back from the hospital? I'll be here. However late it
is. Please promise you'll call.'

'I promise.'

'I hope everything goes well for him.'

'I hope so, too,' he said.

There was an air of gaiety in the waiting room tonight.

The Dolly Sisters were dressed to the nines. Helen, the older
one, was wearing a shimmering green silk dress with matching
heels. The shoes had ankle straps. When David was a boy, he and
his friends used to call them 'whore shoes.' They pronounced it
'hoo-er shoes.' The dress was very low-cut. Her breasts swelled
in the scoop top. She fiddled with a string of green beads nestling
in her cleavage. Her sister Jean was wearing a silver dress with
silver shoes. They looked like Christmas, the Dolly Sisters.

'We're going to a wedding reception,' Helen said.

'Our cousin got married this afternoon,' Jean said.

'Our mother's doing much better,' Helen said.

'She looked terrific this afternoon.'

'Maybe I'll come with you,' Bastiglio said. He was wearing the
same suit he'd had on during the four o'clock visit.

'Sure, come along,' Helen said.

'More the merrier,' Jean said.

Bastiglio was very happy. He told everyone in the waiting
room that they'd be transferring his brother to a private room in
the morning. The pink lady was a plump, jovial black woman
who offered coffee to everyone in the waiting room. She made it
seem as if she were pouring champagne. Arthur Henley, the

newcomer who'd been worried that he wouldn't get to see his father before he died, smacked his lips when he tasted the coffee.

'This is very good coffee,' he said to the black pink lady.

'My husband says I should open a restaurant,' she answered, grinning.

Henley smacked his lips again. 'You should, you should,' he said.

David thought the coffee was very good, too. He asked Bessie if she was sure she didn't want a cup. Bessie shook her head. Of everyone in the waiting room, only Bessie looked glum. She sat with her head bent, her hands in her lap, in the same attitude of prayer as this morning.

'It looks as if the old man's going to make it,' Henley said. 'I talked to his doctor, he told me he's going to be fine. Few more days in Intensive Care, they'll be moving him to his own room.'

'I'll drink to that,' Bastiglio said, and lifted his coffee cup as though in a toast.

'How's *your* patient doing?' Helen asked David.

'His condition is stable,' David said. It was odd how quickly you picked up the hospital jargon. Stable. His mother used to call the room in which his father kept all his junk a stable. His father's apartment this morning had looked like a stable.

'They sometimes rally very quickly,' Jean said.

'I've seen miracles happen here,' the pink lady said solemnly.

'That's what it's going to take, David thought. A miracle.

His father looked wonderful.

The bewildered look was no longer on his face. His eyes had lost their unfocused, glazed appearance. They darted brightly in his head.

'How are you doing?' David asked.

His father nodded. Even the nod seemed more vigorous.

'You look good, Morris,' Bessie said. 'Did you rest this afternoon?'

His father nodded again.

'I brought your ring and your wallet,' Bessie said, 'all your other stuff, too. To give to David. So I wouldn't have to worry about them, okay?'

His father nodded again.

'Do you remember those summers out on the Island?' David asked. 'When Grandma used to yell not to go in the water with your rings on? You, and Uncle Martin, and Uncle Max?'

His father's eyes smiled. The respirator tube was still in his throat, but Kaplan would remove that in the morning. He'd be more comfortable. He was going to beat this damn thing, after all. He smiled around the respirator tube. He was going to be all right.

'Well, it looks like there's been some mail for you,' David said. 'I picked it up at the nurses' station. Do you think they're happy with their station in life?' he asked, and again his father smiled around the tube. David reached into his jacket pocket. He had bought his father a Father's Day card in the hotel gift shop. He had written his father's name and address on the envelope. In the upper right-hand corner, he had drawn a stamp and then had inked what he hoped would look like cancellation marks across it. He flashed the envelope briefly and then ripped open the flap.

'Well, well,' he said, 'I wonder who *this* is from.'

His father already knew. His eyes were twinkling in anticipation.

'To Dad,' David read from the card. 'Shall I read the poem?'

His father nodded. His eyes and his mouth were still smiling.

'There are many fathers in this world of ours,' David read from the card, 'and most of them are fine. But there's only one who's best of all, and that's the one who's mine.' He paused. 'Guess who signed it?' David said.

His father nodded, smiling.

'David and Molly,' David said.

His father nodded again.

'That's nice, Morris,' Bessie said.

'And you'll have a big box of cigars waiting for you when you get out of here,' David said.

His father's hand came up from the sheet. He extended his forefinger. On the air, he made the letter 'S'. He was asking about Stephen again. He was wondering whether Stephen had sent a card as well.

'Stephen?' David said.

His father nodded.

David hesitated a moment. The only other thing he had in his jacket pocket was the envelope containing his mother's letter. He took the envelope containing his mother's letter. He took the envelope from his pocket.

'Stephen's written you a letter,' he said.

His father nodded.

David opened the envelope. He took his mother's letter from it. He looked at the letter. He drew in a short, sharp breath.

'Dear Grandpa,' he said, and hesitated again. The words in his mother's handwriting read *Dear Morrie, I am writing this because when I talk I get too excited and of course it stands to reason. I honestly was giving you a fair chance but I guess you did not want it as you are still lying to me.* 'Dear Grandpa,' he said again. 'What are you doing in the hospital? Mom and Dad tell me you weren't feeling so good, but that you're feeling much better now.'

His father nodded.

Bessie was watching David.

'I want you to get better real fast, Grandpa,' David said, glancing up from the letter. 'I want you to be the way you were, Grandpa. I want you to come visit us as soon as possible. I want to light your cigar for you, Grandpa. I want you to put a cigar band on my finger. I want to hear you say, "And now for the lighter side of the news." '

His father smiled around the tube.

'I miss you very much, Grandpa,' David said. His voice broke. 'I love you very much, Grandpa.'

He folded the letter. He put it back in the envelope.

'You see, Morris?' Bessie said. 'Everyone misses you and loves you.'

His father raised his hand again. He looked across at the wall. His forefinger traced a circle on the air.

'No, don't worry about those shelves,' David said.

'Don't worry about nothing but getting better,' Bessie said.

His father nodded.

'I can't get over the way you look, Pop,' David said.

'He looks wonderful,' Bessie said. 'Next time I come, I'll bring the scissors, I'll trim your nails.'

'Many man swallow, but fu man chew,' David said, and again his father smiled.

The Vietnamese nurse appeared in the doorway.

'Time's up,' she said.

Bessie went to the bed. She kissed his father on the cheek.

'I'll be here tomorrow morning,' she said. 'Sleep well, Morris.'

He touched her arm. Gently.

'Yes, Morris?'

His eyes met hers.

'Yes, honey,' she said. 'You're going to be fine.'

She moved away from the bed. David took his father's hand in his own. He leaned over the bed.

'I'll see you in the morning,' he said.

His father nodded.

He kissed his father on the forehead.

He hesitated.

'I love you, Pop,' he said, and wondered if he meant it this time.

In the corridor outside, he said, 'He really looked good, didn't he?'

'He looked terrific!' Bessie said. 'I didn't see him look so good since he first came in here, I mean it.'

'I think he's going to make it,' David said.

'I think so, too.'

'I'm not kidding myself, am I?' David said. 'I mean, he really *did* look good, didn't he?'

'Marvelous,' Bessie said.

'He's going to fool us all,' David said.

'God willing.'

'I think he will, I really do.'

'I think so, too.'

'*Boy*, he looked good.'

'His eyes so bright!'

'And the smiles? Did you see him smiling?'

'Of *course* I seen him!'

'Boy' David said.

'Listen, let me give you his things,' Bessie said, 'before I forget.'

'She unclasped her handbag. She took out a small paper bag. 'I was so nervous on the bus, you got no idea.'

197

He accepted the bag.

'I wrapped his ring in a little tissue,' Bessie said.

'Thank you,' he said. 'I'll take good care of it.'

'For when he gets out of here.'

'Soon, I hope,' David said.

'*Alevai*,' Bessie said.

He called Hillary the moment he got back to the room.

'David!' she said. 'How's your father?'

'Much better. Do you know a good Italian restaurant down here?'

'Are we on for dinner then?'

'If you're still available.'

'I'm available,' she said.

'Quarter to eight?' he said. 'In the lobby.'

'Super,' she said, and hung up.

He was whistling when he went into the shower.

Well, he thought, he's really going to pull through, the old bastard. He really is. Surprise us all. Still a few tricks in the old bastard's bag. Jesus, he really looked *good*! I'll have to call Molly, tell her to stop worrying, he'll be okay. He started singing in the shower. Gene Kelly. He soaped himself and sang 'Singin' in the Rain.' He let the water pour down on him. He stayed under the water for a long time. He turned the water to icy cold just before he got out of the shower. The water beat down on his shoulders and head. He was shivering when he got out of the shower, but he felt better than he had in a long time.

He was toweling himself when the phone rang.

Molly, he thought.

Good. Get that over with.

He picked up the receiver.

'Hello?' he said.

'Mr. Weber?'

'Yes, Dr. Kaplan?' he said.

'How are you?'

'Fine, thanks,' David said. 'I just got back from the hospital, my father looked terrific.'

'Well,' Kaplan said, and the single word struck an ominous note. David waited. 'His condition is still grave,' Kaplan said. It was the first time he had ever used the word 'grave.'

'He didn't look that way to me,' David said. 'There seemed to be a big difference between when I saw him at four o'clock . . .'

'It's really too early to expect any appreciable change,' Kaplan said. 'I don't think it's possible to expect any change just yet.'

'But his eyes were . . .'

'It would be a good week at least before we could see any real change for the better,' Kaplan said.

Why the hell did he sound so *down*?

'Each day he maintains his status is encouraging, of course,' Kaplan said.

Then why do you sound so down? David wondered.

'But . . . Mr. Weber,' Kaplan said, 'I must be frank with you.'

'Please,' David said.

'I'm very concerned about his condition. We're *all* concerned. His condition is grave. Very grave. We're supporting his blood pressure with medication . . .'

'Yes, but that was this *afternoon*,' David said. Why are we going over all the same shit you gave me this afternoon? he thought. I just came back from seeing him, he looked fine. 'I just saw him,' he said aloud. 'He looked fine, really. If you're going back to the hospital again, why don't you take a long look for your . . .?'

'I won't be going back to the hospital tonight,' Kaplan said.

'Well, in the morning then. When you go there in the morning, you'll see . . .'

'Mr. Weber,' Kaplan said, 'if he makes it through the night, I'll be very much surprised.'

'What?' David said.

'I'm sorry,' Kaplan said again.

Well, don't be so sorry, David thought. Go over to the hospital and see for yourself. You're the doctor, go take a *look* at him.

'Mr. Weber,' Kaplan said, 'how do you feel about autopsy?'

'He's not dead yet,' David said sharply.

'In the event,' Kaplan said.

'I don't know *how* I'd feel about autopsy. I don't want to talk about autopsy. I just got back from the hospital, my father looked *fine*. If you went over there and took a look at him, you wouldn't be asking me about autopsy.'

'I'm in constant touch with the physicians on duty,' Kaplan said.

'I didn't mean to imply . . .'

'I know this is a difficult time for you.'

Yes, it's a difficult time for me, David thought. I'm being jerked from pillar to post, yes, it's a very difficult time. So don't ask me about *autopsy*, damn it!

'I don't want to discuss autopsy,' he said aloud.

'I can understand that. But a postmortem diagnosis . . .'

'If you can't find what's wrong while . . .'

'. . . might allow us to . . .'

'. . . he's still *alive* . . .'

They both fell silent.

'I'm sorry,' David said.

'This inability to heal,' Kaplan said.

One more time, David thought. Just tell me one more time how *baffling* it all is.

Kaplan said nothing.

'Well, let's see what happens in the morning,' David said.

'It's in God's hands,' Kaplan said, and hung up.

Terrific, David thought. Leave it to God. Dumb sons of bitches can't find what's wrong, so leave it to God, right, let *God* take care of it. Call in the Supreme Surgeon, let *Him* diagnose the case. *I'm in constant touch with the physicians on duty*. Good, you stay in touch. Run around with your finger up your ass and stay in touch with all the other busy little assholes who don't know any more than you do. Carve him up afterward. Take out his liver and his spleen, weigh his lungs and his heart, and then shake your goddamn head and tell me it's all very baffling.

The phone rang.

He lifted the receiver.

'Hello!' he said sharply.

'David?' Molly said. 'What's the matter?'

'Nothing,' he said.

'You sound . . .'

'I just had a long talk with Kaplan. I saw my father a half-hour ago, he looked terrific. So that stupid bastard starts asking me about autopsy.'

'I've been wondering when you'd get angry.'

'I'm not angry, I just wish they'd make up their *minds*.'

'Who, David?'

'*All*, of them! The doctors, my father . . .'

His voice trailed.

'David?'

'If he's going to die, I wish he'd hurry up and do it.'

Molly said nothing.

'Or get better,' David said. 'Either way.'

Still, she said nothing.

'I was going to call you,' he said.

'I thought you might have gone out to dinner.'

'No, I haven't eaten yet. I just got out of the shower.'

'*Will* you be going out?' she said.

'Yes.' He paused. 'How about you?'

'I've already eaten. I may go to a movie.'

'Well, I'll call you in the morning then.'

'Yes, all right,' she said.

'Good night,' he said.

'Good night,' she said.

How very accommodating we've both become, he thought. How very adept we are at understanding each other's shorthand. We will not speak to each other until tomorrow morning because neither of us wants any surprises tonight. *What* surprises? he wondered. There *are* no more surprises. Our marriage is as predictable as death.

But my father may yet survive the night, he thought.

'Sorry I took so long,' the waiter said. 'Slight emergency in the kitchen.'

'Oh? What sort?' Hillary asked. 'Not a fire or anything, I hope.'

'The Cubans are arguing,' the waiter said.

'The Cubans?' David said.

'The chef and his assistant.'

'They're *Cubans*?' David said.

'Yes, but they know how to cook Italian.'

'I'm sure,' Hillary said, and arched her eyebrows.

'Anyway, here's the wine, sir,' the waiter said. He showed the label to David. 'Would you like me to open it now, sir?'

'Please,' David said.

The waiter pulled the cork. He poured a little of the wine into David's glass. David sniffed at the wine and then tasted it. 'Yes, that's fine,' he said.

The waiter filled Hillary's glass, and then David's.

'Enjoy it,' he said.

Hillary lifted her glass. They clinked glasses and drank.

'It's quite open-nosed, don't you think?' David said, playing the game he used to play with Molly.

'Yes, very much so,' Hillary said, picking up on it at once.

'Woodsy,' he said.

'Bad beginning, though,' she said.

'Good middle, however.'

'Explosive end,' she said. 'But don't you find it the tiniest bit acidic?'

'Metallic, I might have said.'

'Quite. Altogether a very nervous wine.'

'Virtually neurotic,' he said, and they both laughed.

She was wearing white again. Her tan was magnificent against it. Jade earrings dangled from her ears, echoing the color of her eyes. Her lipstick was very red. She smelled of mimosa.

'Do you think the Cubans will know how to make a piccata?' she asked.

'A *piñata* might be more their style,' David said.

'I suppose we can always find a *Cuban* restaurant with an *Italian* chef.'

The food was surprisingly good. They both kept marveling over it. It was only nine o'clock when they finished the meal. There was a little more wine left in the bottle. They finished that as well and decided they would skip coffee.

It was still very hot in the street outside.

'Shall we walk back?' he asked.

'Yes, of course. Exercise away some of the weight I'm *sure* I gained in there. That really *was* remarkably good, wasn't it?'

'Considering.'

'Is what I meant. *Cuban* chefs. God, it's *hot*!'

'We can take a taxi if you . . .'

'No, don't be silly.'

They walked in silence for a while.

202

'I'm glad you didn't lie to me,' she said. He turned to her, puzzled. 'About being married, I mean.'

'Oh.'

'Besides, you *are* wearing a wedding band, you realize.'

'Am I? I hardly notice it anymore.'

'You *will* take it off, won't you?' she said. 'Later?'

'If you like.'

'Yes, I would.'

They continued walking.

Her stride matched his.

Long legs. High-heeled sandals clicking on the deserted sidewalk.

'What's your wife's name?' she asked.

'Why do you want to know?'

'Forgive me, I'm far too curious.'

'It's Molly,' he said.

'Good Irish name,' she said. 'Is she Irish?'

'Jewish,' David said.

'And you? Are you Jewish as well?'

'Yes.'

'I thought you might be. The name,' she said.

'And the nose,' he said.

'Is there something wrong with your nose?'

'I've never particularly liked it.'

'Looks fine to me,' she said, and took his hand.

She was still holding his hand when they walked into the hotel. He went to the front desk for his key. 'Fifteen twenty-nine,' he said to the clerk. The clerk looked at Hillary.

'Yes, sir,' he said, and handed David the key.

The clerk watched them as they walked to the elevator. The elevator stopped on the twelfth floor, as it always did. The doors closed. She kissed him on the mouth. They clung together. The doors opened again on the fifteenth floor. They stepped into the corridor and kissed again. Wordlessly, they walked to his room. He had difficulty unlocking the door. At last, he turned the key, and swung the door wide and snapped on the light. She stepped into the room.

'Nice,' she said. 'Much nicer than mine. And *I'm* a travel rep.'

He closed and locked the door. He remembered the Do Not

Disturb sign. He unlocked the door and opened it again. He hung the sign on the knob.

'How clever you are,' she said, and went into his arms the moment he had closed and locked the door again. He pulled her close to him. She pressed against him. They kissed fiercely. His hands found her ass. She ground against him. His hands tightened on her.

'Would you like to fuck me now?' she asked.

'Yes,' he said.

'Mmm, yes,' she said.

They broke away from each other. She glanced down at him.

'My, my,' she said, smiling, and rolled her eyes. 'Is this the loo? I shan't be a moment.'

He watched her as she went into the bathroom. She turned to smile at him and then gently closed the door behind her. He heard the sink tap running. He turned off the lights, and went to the bed and sat on the edge of it. Behind him, the window cast a reflected glow into the room. He could hear the sound of the sea. He took off his shoes and socks. In the bathroom, the water stopped running. There was a long silence. The bathroom door opened a crack. She peeked around the edge of the door. He saw her naked shoulder.

'Should I leave anything on?' she asked.

'Whatever you like,' he said.

'Whatever *you* like,' she said. 'I'm down to panties and heels.'

'Fine,' he said.

She opened the door wide and stepped into the room. The bathroom light was on behind her. She stepped out of sunlight. Long blond hair. Dangling green earrings. Breasts spattered with freckles. Gossamer white bikini panties. High-heeled white sandals. She paused in the wedge of light spilling from the bathroom.

'Do I suit you?' she asked.

'Very much,' he said.

She came to the bed and sat beside him.

'But you're still dressed,' she whispered.

She unbuttoned his shirt and ran her hand over his chest.

'Take off your wedding band,' she whispered.

He took off the ring and placed it gently on the phone table.

'Was she Molly, this woman you loved to death?'

'Yes,' he said.

Her hand found him.

'And are you going to love *me* to death?'

'Yes,' he said.

Her hand tightened. 'Fuck me to death?'

'Yes.'

'Yes, my pussy, my mouth . . .'

'Yes.'

'Everywhere, yes,' she whispered.

He undressed in the glow of the light from the window. She took off one earring, tilted her head, took off the other. She placed both earrings on the phone table. She lay back on the bed then, watching him. They're all Molly, he thought. None of them are Molly, he thought. Never quite Molly. She cupped her breasts with her hands. She squeezed the nipples. 'My nipples are so hard,' she whispered. She dropped one hand to her crotch. She began stroking herself. 'Pussy's so wet,' she whispered. He draped his clothes over the chair near the window. He could still hear the sound of the sea. 'Look at that prick,' she whispered.

He went to the bed.

Her hand found him again.

'Will you fuck me now?' she whispered.

'Yes,' he said.

'Mmm, yes,' she said.

The telephone rang.

He flinched from its sound as though someone had struck him in the face with a clenched fist.

'Let it ring,' she whispered.

He looked at the telephone.

'Don't answer it,' she whispered.

The phone kept ringing.

'Come fuck me,' she whispered.

He picked up the receiver.

'Hello?' he said.

'Mr. Weber?' Kaplan said.

So here I am, he thought. Alone at last. Son dead, mother dead, father dead, marriage dead. Little Orphan Annie. Do orphanages take fifty-year-old men? Forty-*nine*, excuse me. Can they find a good home for a forty-nine-year-old orphan going on fifty?

He had ordered two martinis the moment Hillary left the room. The martinis were gone now. He debated ordering a third one. All gone, see? His mother spooning bread and milk into his mouth when he was still in his high chair. All gone, David, see? All gone, he thought. It is amazing how quickly a long-legged English girl in bikini knickers and heels can get dressed when the telephone rings and a doctor tells you your father is dead. Call me later, David. Scrambling into her clothes. I'll be in my room, please call me. Breasts jiggling into her bra, blond hair disappearing into the folds of the white dress, head reappearing, dress sliding down over white lace bra and white lace panties, call me later. Amazing how fast a cock can shrivel when someone tells you your father is dead. The tube in my father's penis.

I have to call Bessie, he thought. Molly first, then Bessie.

He dialed the New York apartment. Molly's voice came on the line. *I'm sorry, we can't come to the phone just now. Will you leave a message when you hear the beep?* Well, she'd said she was going to a movie. Second movie this week. Big movie-goer, my Molly. Had it really been a movie? Or was the 'movie' tall and blond and blue-eyed? Younger than Molly perhaps. Did the 'movie' leave on his undershorts and shoes? Black shoes and black socks? Where did she go to fuck this 'movie' of hers? His place? Your place or mine? he thought. I *have* no place, he thought. I guess I'll call Bessie. I'd call Uncle Max, but he'd only think it's funny that my father died, Ha-ha, very comical. Will Uncle Max even come to the funeral? What arrangements will I have to make *this* time? Ship his body up north, how do you do that? Is there a service that ships bodies? Come on, Molly, he thought, get finished with your goddamn *movie*! My *father* is dead!

He picked up the phone and dialed room service. There was no answer. He looked at his watch. Twenty after ten. Room service closed at nine-thirty. All gone, he thought, everyone gone. He suddenly felt like talking to the Cuban nurse. He wanted to ask the Cuban nurse how it had been at the very last. Kaplan had told him on the phone that his father had died quietly at ten minutes past eight. That would have been just about when he and Hillary had been pretending to be wine mavens. *Bad beginning, though.*

206

Good middle, however. Explosive end. Not at all explosive, David thought; nothing spectacular, no fireworks. Kaplan said he'd died a quiet death. But what the hell did Kaplan know? It was all very baffling to Kaplan. Maybe the Cuban nurse could amplify. *I'd ask for amplification, Davey, you know what I mean?* He supposed he would have to call Sidney, too. Tell him his services as a chauffeur were no longer required. Tell him his son's debt had been canceled by death. How do you like that one, Pop? Debt? Death? *You* call Sidney, he was *your* pal. Call him from the great beyond, wherever that might be, far from the sea someplace, give him a ring, Pop. Tell him, Hi, this is your cousin Morrie, I died tonight at ten minutes past eight, quietly, my heart just began beating slower and slower and slower, and then it stopped. Check it out with Dr. Kaplan, he'll tell you.

I'll bet the Cuban nurse could tell me more, though, David thought. She was probably there when it happened, whispering reassuring 'swee'hearts' in my father's ear. I don't even know her name, he thought. I have to call Bessie. He pulled the telephone directory from under the phone table. What had Bessie told the bossy nurse that day? Wednesday? Thursday? Who remembered? All the days were the same. *I'm his sister*. Goldblum, was it? He opened the telephone book and began searching under the G's. He had trouble reading the small print. Get to be fifty, he thought, you can't even read the phone book. He found a listing for a Goldblum, B. on Fourth Street. Long trip to the hospital every day, he thought. All the way from Fourth Street. By bus, no less. He wrote the number on the hotel pad near the phone. She's probably asleep, he thought, it can wait till morning. His father's words when he'd called to tell him his mother was dead. *It can wait till morning*. Well, no, he thought, it *can't* wait till morning. Too damn *many* things have been waiting till morning. Morning never comes, don't you know that? Morning is like those South Americans who never arrive. Where the hell are all those South Americans? Call her, he thought. Get it over with.

He dialed the number.

'Hello?' she said. She *had* been asleep.

'Bessie,' he said, 'this is David.'

'Oh,' she said. She already knew. The tone of his voice had already told her.

'Bessie,' he said, 'I'm sorry to have to . . .'

'Oh,' she said again.

'My father died tonight,' he said.

'Oh.' The pain in that single word.

'I thought you might want to know.'

'Thank you,' she said.

'He died quietly,' David said.

'Thank you,' she said.

'I'm sorry,' he said.

She was silent for a very long time. He wondered if she was crying on the other end of the line. Then she said, 'He was my best friend I ever had.'

Another silence.

'Well, good night,' David said.

'Good night,' she said. 'Thank you.'

He put the receiver back on the cradle. The little paper bag with his father's belongings in it was on the dresser across the room, where he'd left it. He went to the dresser and opened the bag. His father's wallet, his eyeglass case, his address book, his ring wrapped in a Kleenex. He unwrapped the tissue. He held the ring between his thumb and forefinger. The initials M.W. twined into the heavy gold. The small diamond chip. *Boys! Yoo-hoo! Don't go in the water with your rings! All that gold, the diamonds, the diamonds!* His grandmother's heavily accented voice ringing out over the sea where her three sons were swimming. His father wanted The Shiksa to have his ring. *I want Molly to have it, do you hear me?* Come on, Molly, he thought, finish with your damn movie already, will you? Don't you want to know about the ring? Don't you want to know my father left you his ring?

He went back to the telephone.

He dialed New York again.

The answering machine again.

I'm sorry, we can't come to the phone just now. Will you leave a message when you hear the beep?

So go to hell, he thought, and slammed down the receiver. The phone rang almost at once. He picked up the receiver again.

'Hello?' he said.

'David, it's me. Hillary. Are you all right?'

208

'So-so,' he said, and thought of his father waggling his hand at the male nurse.

'I'm worried about you,' she said.

'No, don't be.'

'I just wanted you to know I'll be here if you need me.'

'Thank you,' he said.

'I'll be here,' she said, and hung up.

He put the receiver back on the cradle. It was nice to know that Hillary would be there if he needed her. Poor honest mixed-up Hillary with her married lover in Marbella, poor Hillary on the rebound and trying to find, in an alien land in an off-season, between the sheets with a total stranger, whatever it was she thought she'd lost. Poor Hillary, he thought, poor *all* of us. I'm drunk, he thought, and I'd like to get even drunker. I'd like to go downstairs to the bar, and pick up two martinis and carry them up to room 1712 to share with Hillary Watkins, who has offered comfort. Women who will offer you their comfort, he thought. *Weber v. Martini.* I've been accepting the comfort of all the Hillarys in the world for the past five years, so what difference will it make tonight?

Molly, where are you? he thought. *You're* the one I need!

He picked up the receiver. He dialed New York again.

'Hello?'

Thank God, he thought.

'Molly,' he said, 'it's David. I've been trying to reach you.'

'I just got in this minute. What is it?'

'He's dead.'

Silence.

Will all you men whose mothers are still living . . .

'Molly?'

'Yes, I'm here.'

'He died at a little past eight. Ten past eight.'

'I'm sorry,' she said.

'We'll have to make arrangements,' he said.

'Yes.'

'I'll have to find out how to ship the body up. He has a funeral plot in the Bronx. Next to my mother's.'

'Yes.'

'I suppose there are people who do that sort of thing.'

'Yes.'

'We'll have to call all the relatives, too.'

'Yes.'

'Arrange for a service, a funeral home, all of it. Will we have to sit *shiva*? I suppose he would have wanted that.'

'Yes.'

'Molly, are you just going to keep saying "yes"?'

'I'm sorry.'

'Can't we please *talk* about this?'

She said nothing.

'Molly,' he said, 'my father just died. Can't you please *say* something?'

'I'm not good at this,' she said.

'I know that. But Molly . . .'

'I'm not good at it.'

'Molly . . .'

'I loved him, too,' she said. 'I have to hang up now. I can't talk anymore, I really can't. I have to go now.'

There was a click on the line. She was gone.

Well, he thought, she's been gone for a long time now, so how is this night different from all other nights? He thought of Hillary in room 1712. *I'll be here*. He went to the dresser where he had left his father's ring. He picked up the ring. He tried it on his pinky. It slipped onto his finger easily. It fit perfectly. Like father, like son, he thought. Ike and Mike, we look alike. He spread his fingers wide and admired the ring. He turned his hand this way and that. The gold gleamed, the diamond glistened. Like father, like son, he thought again. He went to the telephone. I would like to accept whatever comfort you have to offer, he would say. The way his father had been accepting the comfort of strangers for the better part of his life.

He picked up the receiver.

I am asking you please to sit down and ask yourself if you must continue this lying and cheating . . .

He reached for the dial.

You said last night that what you do is none of my business . . .

He dialed the numeral one.

Oh please I'm asking you in God's name, if this is what you really want from life . . .

210

He dialed the numeral seven.

So please I beg of you please . . .

He dialed another one, and then a two.

Answer this and tell me what it is you want . . .

'Hello?' Hillary said.

He said nothing.

'Hello?'

He still said nothing. The receiver was trembling in his hand.

'Is that you, David?'

He put the receiver back on the cradle.

Yes, he thought, it's *me*. David.

I'm not him.

I never *was* him.

And suddenly he burst into tears.

He stood in the empty bedroom, facing the window with its outside glow, and listened to the sound of the sea and remembered all those stained-glass summers, floating in the circle of his father's arms, the smooth shining sea. All so simple then. All that gold, the diamonds, the diamonds. The gentle swell of the ocean. All so smooth and soft and simple. It doesn't stay simple, he thought. It gets complicated, he thought. The real danger is living. His father had stopped facing that danger a long, long time ago. David's mother had been right; his entire life had been a hobby.

He looked at the ring again.

He took if off his finger. It came off as easily as it had gone on.

'Good-bye, Pop,' he said aloud, and burst into fresh tears.

He wept bitterly for a long time, and then he dried his eyes and sighed heavily and went to the telephone. He let the phone ring at least a dozen times. At last, she picked up on the other end.

'Hello?' she said. Her voice sounded mechanical, like her own answering machine.

'Molly,' he said, 'please don't hang up. We have to talk.'

'What about, David?'

'Everything, Molly.'

'Haven't we said everything a hundred times? A thousand times?'

'No, we haven't.'

'What's left to . . ?'

211

'Stephen,' he said.

'No,' she said.

'We have to.'

'We *don't* have to.'

'Molly, if we're going to survive . . .'

'We're surviving.'

'We're not. Molly, listen to me. Please listen.'

'I'm listening.'

'After the accident . . .'

'I don't want to hear about the accident.'

'We changed, Molly. I'm not blaming you, Molly, we both . . .'

'My *son* died!' she said fiercely.

'My son died, too,' he said quietly.

'I'm going to hang up,' she said.

'No, don't! Please don't, Molly!'

There was a long silence.

'I can't talk about this,' she said. 'You know I can't.'

'Try, Molly. Please, for the love of God . . .'

'I still hurt too much,' she said. It was the first time she had ever uttered these words to him.

'I hurt, too,' he said.

'I miss him too much,' she said.

'I miss him with all my heart.'

'Then don't . . . please let's not talk about . . .' She could not say the name. 'I can't talk about it,' she said. 'Please let me go, David. Let me get off the phone.'

'Not yet. Molly, please. Please listen to me. If we don't . . . if we can't even *talk* about it . . .'

'What difference will it make?' she said. 'Don't you know what we've become?'

'I know what we've become.'

'So what difference will it make?'

'We can go back to what . . .'

'How?' she said. 'Oh God, *how?*' And suddenly she burst into tears.

He listened helplessly to her sobs. He gripped the telephone receiver tightly. He wanted to reach out across the miles that separated them, the years that separated them, hold her close, tell her . . .

'I hate him,' she said, sobbing.

Her words did not register for a moment.

'I *hate* the little bastard.'

He caught his breath.

'I hate what he *did* to us! Why did he have to die?' she said, sobbing. 'He didn't even have a *license*, why did he . . . Oh God, forgive me,' she said.

'Molly . . .'

'I hate him,' she said. 'God forgive me, I hate him.'

She cried for a long time. Her sobs were deep and racking; he thought she would never stop crying. He thought of that day in her First Avenue apartment, when she was moving, her tears then. He thought of the way he had filled her new apartment with roses. He thought of filling her life with roses if only she would stop crying. At last the sobs subsided. He heard her blowing her nose.

'I'm sorry,' she said, and began crying again.

He waited. She seemed to want nothing more from him now than the assurance that he was still there, on the other end of the line. He did not cry with her. He had wept all his tears. She cried for both of them. She cried for his father. She cried for their son. She cried for what had been and for what might lie ahead. And at last the sobs ended, and when she said again, 'I'm sorry,' her voice was steady, and he knew that it was over.

'Molly,' he said, and hesitated. There were so many things to say, so many things to ask. 'Do you love me?' he said.

'What . . .'

Her voice caught. He thought she might begin crying again. He waited.

'What business is that of yours?' she asked.

He smiled.

'Molly,' he said, 'I love you.'

'I love you, too,' she said.

He realized there was nothing more either of them *could* say for now. It would, after all, have to wait till morning.

'Please come home soon,' she said.

213

'I will,' he said.

'I want you to,' she said, and hung up.

He replaced the receiver gently on the cradle. He went to the window and looked out at the ocean for a very long while and listened to the waves rushing against the shore.

Before closing the drapes, he opened the window a little, so that he could hear the gentle sound of the sea while he slept.

THEY'LL GIVE THEIR ALL FOR
A PIECE OF
PARADISE...

California Dreamers

Norman Bogner

Rodeo Drive is Los Angeles' priciest square mile, where the
well-heeled hedonists of fantasy city spend their millions. To this
Mecca of merchandising are drawn the beautiful, the bizarre, the
all-consumingly ambitious:

BOBBY the idealistic architect who longed to build churches – and
instead created citadels for the worship of wealth...

CLAIRE the jilted small-town beauty who followed him West – to
success in a business where only the most ruthless survive...

HILLARY too young, too voluptuous, too rich – she snatched any
thrills she could get, and paid the price...

GIOVANNI ex-movie actor and society restaurant owner – who had
laid-back LA at his feet until he found he cared for someone...

Where money talks – and walks, and makes love – they'll sell
body and soul to buy a dream of paradise...

GENERAL FICTION   0 7221 17604   £1.75

A selection of bestsellers from SPHERE

FICTION

THE VEGAS LEGACY	Ovid Demaris	£2.50 ☐
BODIES AND SOULS	Nancy Thayer	£1.95 ☐
THURSTON HOUSE	Danielle Steel	£1.95 ☐
MAIDEN VOYAGE	Graham Masterton	£2.50 ☐
THE FURTHER ADVENTURES OF HUCKLEBERRY FINN	Greg Matthews	£2.95 ☐

FILM & TV TIE-INS

SUPERGIRL	Norma Fox Mazer	£1.75 ☐
INDIANA JONES AND THE TEMPLE OF DOOM	James Kahn	£1.75 ☐
THE RADISH DAY JUBILEE	Sheilah B. Bruce	£1.50 ☐
THEY CALL ME BOOBER FRAGGLE	Michaela Muntean	£1.50 ☐
RED AND THE PUMPKINS	Jocelyn Stevenson	£1.50 ☐
THE KILLING OF KAREN SILKWOOD	Richard Rashke	£1.95 ☐

NON-FICTION

THE LAST LION	William Manchester	£5.95 ☐
THE ROLLING STONES	Robert Palmer	£7.95 ☐
THE OFFICIAL MARTIAL ARTS HANDBOOK	David Mitchell	£3.95 ☐
GRENADA : REVOLUTION, INVASION AND AFTERMATH	Hugh O'Shaughnessy	£2.95 ☐
DIETING MAKES YOU FAT	Geoffrey Cannon & Hetty Einzig	£1.95 ☐

All Sphere books are available at your local bookshop or newsagent, or can be ordered direct from the publisher. Just tick the titles you want and fill in the form below.

Name _____

Address _____

_____

Write to Sphere Books, Cash Sales Department, P.O. Box 11, Falmouth, Cornwall TR10 9EN

Please enclose a cheque or postal order to the value of the cover price plus:

UK: 45p for the first book, 20p for the second book and 14p for each additional book ordered to a maximum charge of £1.63.

OVERSEAS: 75p for the first book plus 21p per copy for each additional book.

BFPO & EIRE: 45p for the first book, 20p for the second book plus 14p per copy for the next 7 books, thereafter 8p per book.

Sphere Books reserve the right to show new retail prices on covers which may differ from those previously advertised in the text or elsewhere, and to increase postal rates in accordance with the PO.